VENUS
SHINING

Trinity Forest Book 3

JENNIFER ALSEVER

First published by Sawatch Publishing in 2017

For Mom, a beacon of love and friendship— and not at all like the mothers in this book.

1

EMBER

Mom and I used to sit by the campfire when the sky turned black, watching the flames slowly shrink over time, inch by inch. The way the gray ash crept across the glowing embers like a dark shadow, eating the color like a monster. Still and dark as death. But with one poke, one turn of the log, one long breath from puffed-up cheeks, it could all start again. Fire reborn.

"The embers still have potential," she told me one night, hovering over a dying fire, prodding the coals and ash with a long stick. "Before you know it, you've got a forest fire."

My heart pounds with the memory. That's me. After so long in the cold, black air, my ember is lit. I'm not just a flame. I'm a raging blaze. Alive and ready to live, ready to rip Tre from Xintra's grip for good.

But first, I need to find my wallet. I claw inside the desk drawer, rummaging through pencils, markers, cords, a ruler, lip gloss, a Daffy Duck Christmas ornament, a physics test from junior year. No wallet. I can't get on the plane without it. I groan. "Where is it?"

Maddie lies on her stomach on my bed, half paying attention to my desperate hunt. "Your computer is so slow," she says. Her bent elbow digs into the worn lacy bedspread, her hand pressing against her cheek. She taps the keyboard with her other hand.

"I can't get on the plane without an ID," I say. "What did Jared do with it?"

She looks up at me and frowns. "It was like three years ago when you left. How would he remember? You're lucky he didn't throw all your shit out."

I shove the drawer back into the desk so hard it bangs against the wall. A stuffed toucan falls off the shelf and onto my head. I throw the plush bird on the floor and move to the closet. It may have been three years, but it looks like time stood still since I left. Rows of black T-shirts—my favorite color senior year—hang next to tops in various shades of green. My jeans still sit balled up in the corner, beside the blue laundry basket still filled with shoes. This whole room is like a time capsule. I toss a pair of sneakers and some flip-flops on top of the clothes in a duffel bag, then nestle them next to Mom's pink journal we found in the attic.

I squat down and pick up the envelopes addressed to Mom from Lodima. The return address is in Crestone, not too far from here. It's so weird that Mom was friends with Lodima and that she actually *knew* Xintra, the red witch from Trinity Forest. The taker of lives.

The envelopes are worn on the edges, the letters inside yellowed, the handwriting neat.

"What're you doing?" Maddie asks, flipping her head to see me through her dark hair.

"Looking at those letters from Lodima again. Here's one I hadn't read before."

"Read it to me," she says.

I read out loud.

November 12, 1990

Dear Dezi,

I do wonder how you are doing since you left with Xintra, and I found you in Snag. You are always in my thoughts, as I worry how everything has affected you. My Neptune friend, I hope you're finally ready to share what happened and what Xintra has planned. As I mentioned, I will be doing my work around the country for the next several months, and I plan to move through Colorado in January. I would like to stop in to say hello. Please talk to me. Together, we can have an intervention.

Please call if you would like to talk.

Your Venus Friday friend,

Lodima

"She talks like she's an old lady," Maddie says. "Who in our parents' generation even writes letters like that?"

"That's how she talked to me when I met her. I feel like she's an old soul," I say.

"Old soul? I'd say weird soul."

I toss the letter aside and open another.

April 14, 1994

Dear Dezi,

Thank you for finally telling me what happened inside Trinity and for the latest drawing. I will put it on my dresser and wait to see something. Hopefully I can arrange my travel schedule around an intervention. I am still researching to find a way inside Trinity without a proper invite and a magnetic coin. The dreams tell me that it may be years away.

Please call.

Your Venus Friday friend,

Lodima

Letter after letter, they all say the same thing. Mom sent drawings, Lodima wanted more information from Mom. In one note, Lodima wrote that she'd stopped by and knocked on the door of our trailer but no one was home. Another time, she wrote that a curly-haired little girl answered the door but said her mother was asleep. That was me, I'm sure. For a long time, Mom blew off Lodima, and I have no idea why. Later, they planned some sort of "intervention" to stop Xintra—whatever that meant—but it's not clear how they were going to do this.

I tuck the notes into the bag along with the journal. I also tuck away the fact that I'm avoiding Mom's story. I just want to find Tre and move on, live life like a raging forest fire, barreling ahead, unstoppable.

Our last kiss on top of the roof at the party in Los Angeles felt so soft, so give-you-goosebumps amazing. I loved how he tilted his head just the way he always did. But the memory is always interrupted by what happened next: the way Xintra's dark spirits colored his face, jostling for control of his body and transforming him back into Damien. I shiver, remembering how his eyes so eerily shifted into dark thunderclouds. I touch my throat, where his hands clasped me tight, and swallow. Who will show up when I meet him again—Damien? Or Tre?

"Yes!" Maddie shouts. She sits up and raises her arms in the air like she's scored a touchdown. "I didn't think it would ever go through, but three plane tickets to Los Angeles are now purchased."

"Really?" My chest inflates and I race to the bed to look at the computer screen. United flight UA420 to Los Angeles, departing at 8:30 p.m. on Wednesday. I hug her tight. "Thanks, Mads. I'll pay you back."

"Nothing like a little vacation with my best friend and boyfriend—when the rest of the world is dying from a wicked virus." She closes the computer but doesn't look me in the eye.

I bite my cheek and guilt simmers inside me.

"Hey, I'm sorry. You really don't have to go. You just got back from California, and I know your roommate just died and—"

"I want to go. Tickets are purchased." She stands, puts her hands on her hips, and scans the room. "Let's find this wallet."

It could be anywhere. Boxes cover nearly every inch of the carpet, stacked so high you can smell the cardboard from the top of the stairs. We rip open a couple, finding pillows and tapestries from early high school—markers of my pre-Trinity life.

I'm lying on the floor, looking for the wallet under the bed, when a plastic grocery bag drops beside me. Inside is a box of permanent dark brown hair dye. I grin. I can't wait to get rid of this blonde hair and get back to looking like me.

"Thanks," I say, craning my neck to look at my brother standing behind me.

"Someday, you'll have to get rid of the creepy tattoo, too."

I touch my back with my fingers, where the skin is still tender. I half forgot about the giant pyramid with the eye that takes up most of my back, the Trinity Forest symbol I put there out of solidarity for "the cause" when I was living out in the world as the pop star Oshun.

I walked around for so long without control of my body. Xintra's puppet. She remade me into something so far from me, something bubblegum pretty on the outside but black and simmering and evil on the inside. A brainwashed doll to do her bidding. The memory makes me feel dirty, like I need to take a shower.

"Yeah," I say softly. "I will."

Jared smiles. He wears a green T-shirt featuring a pickle with a cartoon face, hands, and legs. It says, *I'm kind of a big dill.*

"We going to LA again or what?" He claps his hands together.

"I got us three tickets," Mads says. "But we can't find her wallet."

"Oh, I got that," Jared says, raising a finger. I sit on the floor while he leaves the room and, a couple of seconds later, tosses my wallet – the one decorated with embroidered black skulls– into my lap. "The police needed it during the search for you. It's been in my dresser since."

"Nice of you to tell me. I've been tearing apart this room."

He leans in and kisses Maddie from behind, wrapping his arms around her waist. I look away. So much has happened since I left—Maddie's a junior in college now... and dating my brother. It's as if Trinity was more than a time vortex; it twisted reality on the outside world, too.

"You two seriously gotta cut that out," I say.

"Deal with it," Jared says. His voice is clipped. Just like it used to be. Just like home. He's rude instead of soft and hesitant and I love it. I missed that so much.

I stand up, hitching up my running shorts with one hand. My clothes from senior year hang on me like I'm a pole. Even my knees look like hockey pucks on sticks. Some girls would die to be this skinny, but I think I look like I'm made of bones.

"Guys, I have a huge favor to ask," I say.

"What's that?" Maddie asks.

"We need to stop by Crestone on our way to Denver." I wave my hand, trying to act casual. "Just real quick."

Jared looks at me and frowns. "What?"

"Where's that?" Maddie asks.

"It's about two hours southeast of Leadville. It's where Lodima lived when she wrote to Mom."

Jared rolls his eyes. "Come on, Emb. She lived there twenty years ago. She could be anywhere."

It's true, but I'm not going to tell him I looked her up on Facebook, those find-your-friend sites, and Googled her name in every way imaginable and found nothing. How can a person just be invisible online?

Maddie holds his hands, still wrapped around her

waist "Yeah, last time we saw her she was in LA. Maybe we look for her when we get there?"

"I feel like she's really in Crestone. I just do. Please?"

Jared scratches his nose and twists his mouth, ready to shoot down the idea.

So I pour out my plea quickly to Maddie with hands pressed together in a prayer. "Pleeeease? Think of it as a road trip. We *have* to drive to Crestone. I just feel it."

Maddie claps her hands together. "You had me at road trip." She turns to face Jared. "We're already going east. What's a little bit south on the way? I've never been to Crestone. It'll be cool."

"Great!" I say, standing up. Decision made.

Jared shakes his head and shrugs. "Whatever."

Maddie grins and rubs her nose on his. Nauseating. It's a lot like when I'd see my parents kiss. I'd be happy for them because they were cute and all, but grossed out just the same. The two of them start kissing, and my brother's arm goes limp by his side. I take his phone out of his hand and turn away, searching the Internet for the weather.

Sure enough, meteorologists expect the hurricane brewing in the Atlantic to be the most catastrophic and most destructive in history. Winds could reach two hundred miles per hour. Three more hurricanes brew on the coasts of Ireland and the Gulf of Mexico.

I feel like there's bubble wrap in my chest, crinkling and tightening. Stress. Anxiety. It's all twisting together inside me.

Xintra is causing these storms. Three end-of-the-world hurricanes, followed by the tsunami, earthquakes and fires. If I remember correctly from my loopy time as Oshun, the Dark Day is only a few days away. The time when all of the storms will collide for one giant state of emergency—and the perfect setting for a coup.

Am I making a colossal mistake taking Jared and Maddie to the coast when everything is supposed to blow up? When we get to the airport, I decide, I'll insist they stay here.

As I gaze at Jared's phone, my skin feels like it just shrunk a size. The tsunami won't *really* happen. Will it?

Xintra managed to put people inside the government. Inside the labs that made the virus that shut down your lungs, make you feel like you're drowning or maybe being buried alive. She did that. How do you even stop it? Her? Any of it?

I push Jared's phone back into his hand, shove the hair dye into my duffel bag. Then I stand, slinging the bag over my shoulder, and move for the stairs. "Come on! Let's go."

They separate their lips. Maddie giggles and the two of them follow me down the stairs, holding hands. They have no idea how the world is about to come apart.

2

ZOE

Blu tugs hard on the hairbrush, pulling it through her thin blue hair. She grits her teeth, and I watch her from the doorway, my presence light like a ghost's. She rarely sees me or feels me until the last moment. Eventually her eyes catch me in the mirror and she gasps.

"I didn't see you there."

I smile faintly. Normally, I enjoy watching the rebirther candidates when they don't notice me—their struggle and powerlessness. Or at times, their cluelessness. But I also enjoy watching the fog over their heads, running like a film, opening a secret door to their hearts. I feed on it, taking in their heartache and then molding and shaping it to our favor.

But today, watching Blu pull the brush too hard through her hair, knowing she wants to feel the pain in her scalp, I feel different. The fog swirls above her head; in it, scenes play of her as a young girl with ratted, mousy brown hair and a dirty T-shirt. She pushed her slack-jawed mother in a wheelchair, over a lumpy hillside. She tried to be cheerful, telling her mom it would all be okay after the stroke, but fear colored Blu's face. Worry swirled through her veins.

Now, as that film plays above her head, I feel surprisingly sad. I scratch my head and squint at her. *She shouldn't be here.* The thought is confusing to me, but somehow I know it's the truth.

"You seem different, Zoe," Blu says finally.

She must see the gears grinding inside my mind. Until recently, I never thought about myself—not since I got to Trinity. I never asked questions: When did I arrive in Trinity? How long have I done this job? It feels like forever. Like I was grown here from a seed, watered by Xintra and her father.

"Different? How's that?" I ask.

"You talk different. Sometimes, you stand different. Your skin—not to be rude or anything—but it's less... I don't know. It's like you're wearing less makeup, maybe?"

"Hmm..." I say with a small smile and then turn away from her.

I know this has to do with Ember. The fact that she even woke up from rebirth—that was remarkable. Unheard of. But when Caius put Ember on the stone table to be sacrificed, I noticed the necklace she wore: the small crystals and the gold-colored nugget in the center. When my fingers happened to brush the necklace during the burning, I felt the conflicted emotions crashing inside my chest. Traces of a previous life streamed past me in a blur of color.

I couldn't put my finger on what it was until later, when I stood in the bottom of the cave from which Ember escaped. I picked up the crystals off the floor of the cave, held the largest stone in my palm, and the sky flooded into my mind; something broke loose. Something crawled out of me in steady, loud drips.

I tucked the gold-colored stone and a few of the crystals into my pocket and never told Xintra about them.

"You okay?" Blu calls from the bedroom.

"Yeah," I say from the hallway, where I stalled, lost in thought. "I'm cool."

I shake off the confusing thoughts and attend to my purpose here in Trinity. Yes, I have a task. I have a job. I should stop questioning and return to the mission: the Dark Day.

"Blu," I call.

"Yeah?"

"Let's go down to the Bath House in twenty minutes. Promise you'll love it."

Xintra has a deadline.

3

EMBER

Gram, clad in a flannel shirt and black helmet, stands in the garage, her shoulders slumping and her back to us. In front of her, a blue flame. The rushing sound of a blow-torch fills the air. She's welding a pipe. A do-it-yourself, jack-of-all-trades grandma.

"Yo, Gram," Jared yells over the hissing of the torch. Maddie stands behind me, as if I offer some protection from Gram and her flaming blue weapon.

Gram turns off the torch and with one swipe of a gloved hand, flips up the goggle lid to her welder helmet. Her gray eyes are like stone.

"We're leaving for Los Angeles," he says. "Wanted to tell you so you don't worry."

An incredibly long, painful moment passes where she stares at us, her expression unchanging. She sighs heavily, her shoulders falling with the air. "Ah, hell."

We stand silent, ready to move, to see if there's more to her thought.

She takes off the helmet and sets it on the workbench. "Ember. I need to talk to you first."

We follow her into the kitchen, where she shuffles around, lighting the stove for a pot of tea. It's like I'm standing on hot coals. I need to leave. My words are clipped. "So what'd you want to talk about?"

She nods to the table, lights a cigarette. "Sit."

Gram moves around the kitchen, and I try to be patient, perching on the edge of a chair at the kitchen table, the duffel bag strap still digging into my shoulder.

Maddie walks by and pushes the strap with a finger so the bag drops to the ground, a signal to me that I should get comfortable. "We'll be out at the car," she says, before tugging on Jared's shirt to bring him outside, giving me and Gram privacy.

A small TV plays on the kitchen counter, airing a live broadcast of a news conference. A young guy with dark hair, a goatee, black jeans and black T-shirt paces on a stage. His face is unmistakable. It's Tre, but it's *not* Tre. He's Damien, CEO of MeToo. My heart tears open, and my nerves detonate.

I focus intently on the TV, and everything in the room —the yellowing linoleum kitchen counter, the smoke billowing around my face, Gram's watery eyes, the smell of moldy dishrags—all of it disappears.

"Ten years ago," Damien bellows from the TV, "if you traveled back in time and told your friends we'd be holding phones and looking at them two hundred and sixty times a day, they would have thought you were crazy. But that future is real. It happened fast. It's just the way of life today."

He continues to pace onstage. "But today marks the

start of the future. Starting now, you won't be staring at a phone, you'll be *part* of that phone, hearing it and seeing it in an entirely new way. The proof is standing right next to me. Ralph Whittaker, ladies and gentlemen—the man who will usher in change, who will embrace new ideas and transformation, the future president of the United States."

My stomach sours.

I remember when we stood on the rooftop in Los Angeles, just after I took control of my body again and awakened from my rebirthed life as Oshun. The electricity between me and Damien could have powered the entire building. He held my arm with two hands, moved in close to me so his breath tickled my face. Slowly, sensually, he traced a finger up the soft side of the skin on my arm, from my wrist to my elbow, up to my shoulder, my neck, my jaw, before gently landing on my temple. The movement was juicy and sexy, and my knees felt weak. My stomach curdles, knowing that I let such an evil side of him affect me.

He told me that night that the device MeToo had developed was injected into the skin to deliver wireless information automatically to your brain. The ultimate wearable device. But its real intent, the hidden agenda, is for Xintra to be able to track and control the survivors of the genocide.

On TV, Damien's voice sounds blood red, with arrogant steel dots. God, I miss Tre's chocolate voice. He turns onstage and points to a middle-aged guy in a suit with graying hair at the temples. He stands a few feet away from Damien and turns on a George-Clooney-style squint and head tilt.

Damien walks over and places his arm around his

shoulder. "Ladies and gentlemen, Mr. Ralph Whittaker!"
On a giant screen behind him, a campaign slogan appears.
Whittaker: Starting over with a New World.

I cringe, distantly remembering my time as Oshun and
the mantra we rebirthers recited about the promise of a
new world. On-screen, Ralph bobs his head and holds up a
single hand as a greeting to the flash of cameras. I spot the
vague outline of an ash-colored fog above his head. I can't
see the rebirthers quite as well as I could when I was
Oshun. It's fading, that bizarre-o gift, as I stretch more into
my own skin. But the ability to see is still there.

Gram says something, but I don't hear. Her voice is a
light purple hum on the other side of a wall in my mind.
I'm focused on the post-Trinity world of Xintra terror.

"He's looking pretty good for just getting an implant,
right?" Damien says, flashing a grin. A false grin.

"What on earth are you so interested in, Emby?"
Gram's voice. The gray and periwinkle color of it finally
breaks through, sharp and jagged. I glance at her quickly,
catching her frown, the corners of her lips pulled down to
the floor by invisible thread. Her hand is characteristically
placed on her right hip.

"Tre," I say, turning back to the TV, wanting her to
hush. "My boyfriend. That's him."

"Boyfriend."

"Yeah." I lean in and turn up the volume.

"What's your boyfriend doing now?"

"He isn't himself. But he runs a tech company, and he's
putting implants into people. So he can watch the
survivors after the Dark Day."

I wouldn't expect her to understand. I can't expect her
to understand. But I don't want to try to explain and miss

what he's doing right now. Still, her presence looms next to me like a heavy velvet curtain.

"Normally we don't have preferences for candidates," boasts Damien, "but MeToo sees something special in Mr. Whittaker. He's a guy who can lead you into the future. A better future. A new world. One where you're not tethered to a phone. One without limits. We are going from the screen we hold to the screen we wear. It will change how we communicate with one another and it will end the traditional phone call as we know it. Mr. Whittaker is a forward-thinker, pushing boundaries into new territories."

On-screen, Damien continues to pace onstage again, gesturing to Ralph, who stands at ease with one hand in his front pocket. Then, Damien falters. Something in his gaze shifts. His eyes look lighter somehow, and he appears confused. The rest of the world might simply think he's momentarily lost his train of thought. But I see Tre, peeking out from beneath Damien's shell of control. I see Tre's soul—his sweet soul—seeping through the cracks. Hope ignites inside me. He's in there!

But in a flash, Damien resumes control. "You see, Mr. Whittaker just inserted a tiny chip in his wrist and another in his temple."

I shake my head over and over. "No, no, no, no," I whine and then cover my mouth with my hand.

Whittaker pulls his cell phone out of his pocket and ceremoniously lets it drop into a small wire wastebasket, held up by Damien.

"No need for that thing," Damien says. "He's always connected to the Internet. Phone calls? Games? Movies? The weather? It's all right there. Wearable. Always on. This, my friends, is revolutionary. This. Is. The. Future."

"Ember!" Gram's voice is shattered glass.

"What?" I snap, glancing at her.

"This is crazy," she says.

I shake my head and shrug, turning my attention back to the TV. "Gram, it's real."

On-screen, a couple of reporters shout questions at Ralph, unable to see the black rebirther fog that hangs low over his head. "Are you really seeing a screen in your vision now? Can you read us a Twitter message?"

Ralph holds up a thumb tucked behind two fingers to point at them. Classic politician. "Sure thing, Ben," he says. He holds up a hand, saunters on the stage next to Damien. "In fact, I'm getting a tweet right now from Lisa from Fort Wayne, Indiana. She asks, 'How are you feeling?' Well, Lisa, I couldn't be happier, and I urge everyone to get a free injectable now. Just another few days left of freebies. Best thing I ever did."

Gram turns off the TV and stands in front of it, her flannel shirt blocking the entire screen. "Ember. You can't go to Los Angeles. I won't allow it. And Maddie and Jared —well, they're just irresponsible for even entertaining this idea."

I glare at her. Nothing has changed. She hated me then; she hates me now.

Her thin lips wrap around her cigarette and her cheeks suck in the hit of nicotine. The smoke flows from her nostrils, making her look like a dragon.

I shrug. "Is that what you wanted to talk to me about?"

"I thought you should get some help." She nods and sits down next to me, slowly sliding a pile of papers across the veneer tabletop. A phone number and the name Detective Howard Moffitt are scrawled on a pink sticky note attached to several brochures. One is titled, *How to Recall Traumatic Events*. I catch the words on another: *Identifying Split Personality Disorder and Delusions*.

My anger is a loaded gun, and it goes off. I push away the papers like they're made of poison.

My voice is bitter and loud. "Gram, you've got to trust me. The only help I need is getting on a plane and waking up Tre." I pick up my duffel and slide it over my shoulder. "Jared and Maddie are on board. Don't worry. I'll call you."

I rise to stand.

"We need to call the police. Tell them you're back." She gazes at the table.

"Not yet." I can't deal with the idea of having to explain to anyone outside of this house what's been happening.

I walk to the front door, put my hand on the knob, and stop and look at her again. "Why did you even want me to go up to the attic to look at Mom's things if you didn't believe me? You have to believe *some* of what I'm telling you. She told you she went to Trinity Forest too."

Gram exhales loudly and leans back in the plastic kitchen chair, tossing her head up to look at the ceiling. "She did *say* she went to Trinity way back when." She swats the air with her cigarette in hand. "I don't know why I told you to go up there. Maybe tie up loose ends in your head. See that this runs in the family, that you aren't alone."

"Did she tell you what happened in Trinity?"

She gazes at me with a blank face before taking a long drag on her cigarette. I turn back to the front door, and swing it open wide.

"She just went off with her boozing friends one night, end of her junior year."

I stop and listen.

"She was spending the night at um, Zinferey something or other's house. Well, she didn't come home for a year or so."

That's because she was locked in a time warp, like me.

"Her friend Lody-mima something or other gets a call and picks her up in some godforsaken place up north. Then your mom starts talking about some magical forest."

"Don't you see the parallels, Gram? Why didn't you tell me this about her?"

She raises her eyebrows and shrugs. "She ran away. Didn't like the wood chopping, the chores and such." She swirls her hand in the air.

"Did you even *care* that she was gone?" I need to know there is something soft underneath that stone shell. I need to know that she loved Mom.

"Hell yes!" she says, her face scrunching together. "Your daughter goes missing, you do everything in the world to get her back. Well, I got her back, and then I lost her again in that car wreck. It just about killed me, losing her. First your grandpa dies. Then your uncle. Then your mom. All of them, dead."

I was so wrapped up in my own grief about my parents that I had never even considered how Gram felt, losing her own daughter in the car accident. Maybe the fact that they were estranged made it even worse. I should have been there to console Gram—and console Jared for that matter. But I was so far down my own dark well that I could see nothing else.

"When Dezi finally came home after going missing, well, I was glad to have her back. But she just couldn't stop talking about the dangers of Trinity Forest."

My body quivers hearing this. Gram slowly sucks in another drag on her cigarette, then exhales it out with her lips in a tight O. The wall clock, shaped like an owl, ticks in the otherwise silent kitchen.

"So. I kicked her out."

The words land with a thud on my chest. Mom must have felt like me, so alone, when no one believed her about Trinity.

My thoughts must be written all over my face because Gram gets defensive. "Oh, don't give me that. She blew off school wandering around and then didn't want to admit that she'd screwed up. I just wasn't going to have that in my house."

I sigh, heaving my shoulders. My bag makes me feel off balance, and my shorts keep slipping down. I feel again like I'm standing on those hot coals. I need to get out of here.

"Well, then she decides to marry your dad, a long-haired hippy from high school. A boy with no plan. Nothin' but a guitar. No money. No job. She wants to stay in this godforsaken nothin' town with him, with no high school diploma. That was just plain dumb."

"Oh." That's all I can manage. Gram didn't even know Dad. She didn't know how awesome he was, how he scraped the windshield in the mornings for Mom, how he'd make us stay quiet so she could sleep on the weekends, how he'd write songs for her. How they just totally lit each other up with one look. They were poor, but they didn't care. They loved each other—and us. Gram's judgment digs into my soul; I am part of them. Both of them.

Gram softens and shakes her head. "You know me and her. Our relationship. She had problems." She stabs her cigarette into the ashtray, blows the last bit of smoke into the air, and walks over to stand directly across from me. She looks so much older now, her collarbones visible, her cheekbones protruding, the corners of her eyes sagging.

"I didn't do nothing to help your mom. Nothing. I'm not going to let that happen this time with you." Gram purses her lips. "I can't lose you again." Her lips flicker like she's trying to find a smile, but emotion pulls the edges of her mouth into that wavering frown.

She reaches out a calloused hand, marked by the dark spots of age, and then squeezes my own. Her touch fills me with love I've never known from her.

Emotion makes its way up my throat and into my eyes, and I hug Gram, wrapping my arms around her wiry shoulders. "You won't. You won't lose me," I whisper.

She pats me a couple times on the back. "Let's go tell the police and get you help."

I hesitate, unsure what to do next. But in my gut, I know what I need to do. I've known since I clawed my way back to myself.

I nod.

"Let me get my purse." She disappears down the dark hallway.

Without a sound, I open the front door, slip out, and race to Maddie's car. "Let's go," I say.

4

ZOE

Damien reads the incantation from *The Book of the Dead*. "We open the gates to a distant other world," he says, his voice echoing off the walls of the stone room. "We call on the ancient Egyptian deities—the great power of Tehuty, who stands by the head of Ra."

He sprinkles clean sand onto the ground and holds up a bronze cup filled with water, oil, and cow's blood. He kneels beside a bowl with five stones inside it, then pours the liquid from the cup into the bowl and stirs it with an apotropaic wand made of hippo tusks and decorated with animal drawings. The smell of incense, burnt myrrh, frankincense, and turpentine fills the room.

I feel numb, maybe even a little nauseous. Usually these ceremonies fill me with a pleasant buzz, a sort of euphoria. Damien moves to the center of our circle in the dark chamber, facing south, and the wind kicks up on the dirt floor. The tiny vortexes spin at our feet and the electricity tickles the hair on my arms, vibrates my spine, and pulls on my scalp. I want to scrape the feeling off my skin. Reflexively, I rub my arms with my palms.

Damien waves his arms, his robe rustling, as he mumbles the incantation. The room hums a low, tuneless sound in unison, a swishing breath of air. Normally, I'm one of the loudest, the rumbling from my chest always rising above the others. But today, I don't want to sing. I want to get the hell out of here.

The others might be experiencing the same thing. Every once in awhile, I think maybe I see a flicker of an eyebrow or maybe a twitch of the lip that might mean somebody else is feeling a similar hesitation. After all, the humming is less pronounced than normal.

Xintra steps forward, and her voice rises above the din. "Atum, god of elements, Weret Hekau! I am Heka! I am Tehuty! Bring ye storms, bring ye rain, bring ye wind the tumult of storm. Bring ye darkness to the earth so the Annunaki will see rebirth."

She raises her hands high in the air. *Bam!* An electric bolt of lightning rises from the floor to the ceiling, making me jump. Xintra's eyes dart to me. We both know it shouldn't surprise me.

The lightning crawls along the stone ceiling of the Trinity House, out to the vortex tunnel, where it will churn the weather across the world. Dread. That's what I feel this time. Goddamn dread.

Afterward, we close the circle, and one by one, fellow members remove their robes, tucking them into bags and briefcases, and file into the tunnel in utter silence. Xintra smiles at me in the dim light, dragging with her a sweet, perfumed scent—the spells she uses to make the rest of the world feel anesthetized. For years, I have been her ally, I have seen beauty and power in her. I have always felt her Annunaki seduction, the desire to plunge into her green eyes.

It's different now.

Inside my pocket, my fingers trace the edges of the amber crystal. Ever since I picked it up, feelings sneak up on me. A pinch of compassion. A dribble of doubt. A wave of sadness. Momentary confusion.

Memories drape over me; the visions poke through much more often. While eating dinner the other night, I thought I heard Momma singing like she did when she shelled fresh peas in the kitchen. *Who is Momma?*

Later, when I passed the piano in the Trinity mansion, it brought back the sting of nerves. I remembered faintly an audition at a music conservatory and a judge with curly red hair peering down her nose at me over her glasses. My instructor—I recall his name clearly, Mr. Rudowski—off to the side, silently tapping his hands like a metronome.

Standing in the basement of the Trinity House, another vision hits me now, a scene that plays out as if through white gauze. I'm standing in the rain, a young man with chocolate eyes and dark skin reaches his hand out to me, laughing. "Let's get you some of that Momma's famous pie," he said. *A friend? Boyfriend? Who is he?* He was rich, I remember. Powerful. Enticing.

Felix.

Damien strides toward his sister, kissing her cheek. "Can't stay long. I need to get to a board meeting and then I'm off to Leadville."

"Leadville?" I shrug off my robe and drape the heavy garment carefully over my forearm.

"Ember. She's still a threat," Xintra explains before pointing a finger at her brother. "But I don't want *you* to go. It's too risky."

"Risky? Why?" Damien asks. "It's a no-brainer for me."

"I'll send Caius to kill her instead." Xintra lights a cigarette.

"I'll do it," I say suddenly, taking a step forward. I need to get out of this place. Something tells me I need an excuse to go home... to find... Momma?

I see her clearly now in my mind's eye. Caramel eyes, strong hands, a pillar of beauty and strength. She had that fortitude that helped me get the scholarship at the conservatory and the silky charisma that convinced Mrs. Madrid to let me come play her piano every day. But working two jobs etched dark circles under her eyes.

The memory disappears and Xintra and Damien's conversation returns, the static of my mind gone, like I'm tuning the station on the radio.

"I can just send a sab in with a sniper rifle and Ember's gone," Damien says. The three of us file upstairs to the living room, which remains separate and hidden from the main house where the rebirthing candidates live.

Xintra takes another drag on her cigarette and, striding up the stairs alongside me, I swear she eyes me, suspicious. "Yeah, why do *you* want to do it, Zoe?"

"Caius didn't get the job done last time," I say. "I want to see her suffer."

"I *wanted* her maimed," she says. "I wanted to set an example by sacrificing her—a warning to anyone who considered trying to slip out of the chakras and out of their rebirthed lives."

The warning makes me shudder involuntarily. She slips off her robe, and Damien hangs it, almost tenderly, with his in the coat closet.

He pulls his phone from his pocket. "Caius it is. I'll get the hit scheduled. Otherwise, Ember could ruin everything."

My mind drifts again. Momma, outside that store with two paper grocery bags in her arms. "*How can you quit? This is your future, baby,*" she said.

Why *did* I quit the conservatory? Yes, my fingers cramped and my back ached from hours of practice. That constant headache and quivery feeling in my throat from the never-ending competitions. But mostly it was the other girls, with their fancy maxi dresses and their lily-white skin, huddled at their cafeteria table, whispering about me. I was different. Different color. Different neighborhood. And they didn't want to see the sameness. They looked at me like a weed in their garden, ugly and unwanted.

It started with whispering, the ignoring, the giggling. Then it became cruel. The Vaseline they spread on the piano seat and keys before my recital. The laxative in my chocolate milk. The paint they poured onto my new leather coat. After enough years of it, I felt like I was dying from a thousand cuts.

And I did quit, but...quitting didn't help. I didn't know the kids in my neighborhood anymore.

The radio in my mind tunes into Xintra's voice again. "How does it look so far, after the spell downstairs?"

"The patterns are forming in Belize now," Damien says. "A tropical storm, but it's getting stronger."

"Perfect." She takes off her black high heels and rubs her foot. "What's the status with the federal group that's trying to develop a legitimate vaccine?"

We sit down on the black leather furniture, and Xintra pours us each a glass of wine. The color of the drink reminds me of the cow's blood used downstairs in the ceremony, and my stomach turns. I leave my wine on the coffee table.

"They got an effective version out in small batches and they're in the process of eliminating the sham vaccine we created," he says. "But don't worry. We've got sabs inside who will stop their production and destroy the people who are the biggest threats."

"Zoe will help you find them," she says.

Damien doesn't even cast a glance at me. He points at Xintra. "Oh, and I've offered free MeToo injections to all government employees so we can track them and remotely release the snapdragon poison if they veer off course."

I gaze at large painting on the wall, a modern piece with orange splatters and a burnt red background. It brings back the distant memory of tasting Orange Crush. I was sipping the soda the day Felix met me outside the grocery store. Stocky with long sideburns, he was way too old for a girl just fifteen. He smelled like Aqua Velva and wore gold aviator sunglasses. He had money and power, unusual around my neighborhood. I remember he put his hand on the brick wall and told me dirty jokes, and I laughed so hard I spit the orange soda out my nose.

The static of my mind fades and the radio comes back to Xintra. She offers her brother a small condescending smile. "You know when you did that incantation downstairs, you looked exactly like this boy I knew in kindergarten."

Damien's face scrambles, as if he's not sure how to take the backhanded remark. It is their usual interaction that I've always enjoyed. Until now. Today.

"Get me my scepter, will you?" she asks.

He nods, races out of the room, and disappears through the dark stone hallway. When he's out of earshot, she snickers and pats my leg. "I do love seeing him grovel." She smiles. "He thinks he's in control, but I pull the strings."

Xintra leans in closer to me, just a few inches away. "I *am* the one in control. Right?" She touches a fingertip to my collarbone, eliciting an electrical vibration that makes my heart flutter.

She turns around to face the window again. "I need you to hurry and get the new recruits rebirthed. I have Ash, Absinthe, Noire, and Belladonna working on it in the other vortexes, but we've brought in a surge of candidates who need to be put through quickly."

I nod.

Damien returns with the thin staff with the looping top and hands it to her with arms outstretched and eyes cast to the ground. She takes it and tilts her head, waiting for him to look at her.

"Damien, by the way, what happened onstage with Ralph? For a moment you looked... lost." She scowls.

The color fades from his face, and he gazes wide-eyed at the floor. "I don't... know. I had strange memories. Like I was seeing my pre-rebirthed life." Intense devotion is written across his face. "It's nothing."

She turns her attention to me. "And you. What's the deal with the wild hair?"

I pat my head, loving the feel of my hair, like a cotton ball of soft, puffy curls. I shrug with one shoulder.

"You don't look like my Zoe. Or feel like her for that matter," Xintra says. "You've changed since Ember escaped. Tell me, Zoe, why is that?"

"I didn't change," I say, gazing directly into her eyes. "But I think she did something to this place. Disrupted something. That's all."

Damien nods. "She might be right. Maybe we should regroup, slow it all down, rework the ferromagnetism so we all stay focused."

"No," Xintra says. "I want to win. It has to be done now."

"You can win, but maybe we give it more time?" Damien says.

"Pick a safer constellation?" I suggest.

"No," she snaps. "The Egyptians *and* the Dresden Codex of the Mayans both talk about the sunspot cycle."

"What's the significance of the sunspot cycle?" Damien asks.

"You should pay better attention, baby brother," she says. "It lines up with our objectives. When the sun's magnetism reaches its crucial point, a colossal catastrophe will occur, ushered by *yours truly*. The magnetism will follow the movement of the Orion and then Venus will make a reverse movement right above the constellation. That's our opening."

"But doesn't that happen every five years?" I ask, realizing I'm poking at her. "Plus, if you create pandemonium with storms and viruses, you'll be destroying the very system that allows you to live in luxury. The planes won't have fuel. The food won't be grown. The people won't be able to serve you. Your father said to wait—"

"There will always be plenty for the Annunaki," Xintra says. "A fresh start." An electricity purrs between us, a familiar and dangerous whirring that brushes my skin like the heat of a flame.

I am no fool. I know her temper. After all, I watched Xintra kill her father, James, in cold blood.

I had already been rebirthed by James by then, so the memory of his death is detached from feeling—as if I'm remembering scenes from a movie. Still, it's clear. An electric buzz hummed. I followed the sound and found Xintra standing over something in the woods, pointing her finger. A glowing blue thread flowed from her fingertips. Electricity. She pointed to her father, lying on his back in a dark suit. The air smelled of burnt flesh. Thin streaks of smoke rose from his body. A black hole gaped in his chest, where his heart should have been. "*He thought he was the chosen one,*" she said. "*He was wrong.*"

5

EMBER

I stand at the driver's side door to Maddie's car. "Is it cool if I drive? I need to feel in control of my life." I open the car door and pause. "Plus, I think I can get us there faster."

"Uh, that doesn't give me much confidence letting you behind the wheel of my car." Maddie puts her hands on her hips and raises her eyebrows.

"Promise no wrecks. If I do, I'll buy you a new car." I sit down in the driver's seat and look up at her with big puppy dog eyes.

"With what? Your millions of dollars locked up in bank accounts with a dead person's identity?"

"Yeah." I shut the door, and Maddie sighs and slides into the back seat.

She puts on her seat belt. "What are you going to do about that anyway? My mom knows a lawyer who could try to get your money, and maybe we can charge Xintra with like, kidnapping or something?"

"Uh, I don't know if they have case law for what happened to me," I say.

Jared goes around to the front passenger side and Maddie sings to him through the open car door. "Want to sit in the back with me?" Her voice is syrupy.

I catch him smiling at her with scrunched-up eyes and a tiny crooked smile—it reminds me of the way Dad looked at Mom.

Maddie leans forward and gives me a stern look with a raised finger. "But seriously, don't go all Mario Andretti on me."

"Safety third," I say, smiling, holding up two fingers, which I am guessing is some sort of Boy Scout salute.

She rolls her eyes. Sitting low in the driver's seat, I miss my truck—which disappeared when I went to Trinity. I have a faint memory of driving a Porsche in Los Angeles. The soft leather, the glowing dash, the way the car accelerated so smoothly. I can't help but miss being rich in a weird, screwed up way.

I buckle up, and Jared snuggles up close to Maddie. Glancing in the rearview mirror, I watch them put their heads together. I still can't get used to it.

I put the car into drive. "Slowly... slowly," Maddie says, bracing herself—a lot like Mom used to do when I first learned to drive.

I grin and then hit the gas; our heads jerk back against the headrests for a brief moment. "Ember!" Maddie yells in a high-pitched voice before letting out a laughing yelp.

I actually do drive safely. We turn on the stereo and a

green-and-white song fills the car. Maddie leans forward on the console and the chaos in the world disappears as we shout the lyrics together, taken back in time by the music. The next song is bright cranberry and yellow. We sing loud, and it feels like it always did between me and Maddie and Jared. It's like that awful senior year between us was this strange blip. Trinity, too. My time as Oshun. Everything, a scratch on the vinyl record of life.

I play "London Calling" by the Clash and the sound of oil black and grasshopper green pops in my vision. Tre would have loved this music. When we were together, he told me this was one of his favorites. I remember how the two of us swung on the rope over the lake, our bodies entwined. It makes me feel woozy again.

"What's with the swoon face?" Jared asks.

"Let me guess. Tre?" Maddie asks.

I nod. "Yeah, he loved this kind of music. I had to hear it for myself."

The memories of us remain crystal clear in my mind, despite all that's happened. The way my heart felt like it expanded inside my chest once I opened up to him and reconnected with another person again. It was like I'd been frozen, stuck in a freezer in some vacant garage for two years, lost in my own thoughts and trying desperately to ignore my pain. All alone. Then came Tre with his dimpled smile and stupid jokes. His chivalry and fight-the-power credo. He *got* me. He *saw* me. He cannot be lost to Xintra because I, in a moment of weakness, succumbed to rebirthing. He just can't.

We drive southwest through small towns and open flat-land, past rocky canyons and past snow-capped peaks.

Crestone isn't far. I can't believe that Lodima was so close to me this entire time.

With an arm around Maddie, Jared looks up information on his phone with his free hand. He reads it out loud. "Okay, let's learn a little about Crestone...." He taps on his phone. "It's apparently called a spiritual mecca."

"What else?" I ask. "I feel like a freaking chauffeur up here by the way."

"You wanted to drive," Maddie sings.

"Okay, listen to this," Jared says. "Crestone has extreme weather. Surrounded by mountains. It has two dozen ashrams, monasteries, temples, stupas, labyrinths and other sacred landmarks. There's even something called a ziggurat, which is modeled on the temples of ancient Babylon."

"Cool," Maddie says. "Who lives there?"

"A bunch of artists, healers, and spiritual people, I guess," he says.

"That figures," Maddie says. "Lodima was a nut. Wasn't she a nut?"

"I think she's wise," I say.

"Dude, get this," Jared says, looking at his phone. "Did you know the area is known for UFO sightings?" He chuckles and doesn't wait for our answer before continuing. "Heh, there's even a UFO watchtower and something called a vortex garden, which psychics say leads to portals to other universes."

Something I never would have believed before Trinity. But I do now.

We drive through the little mountain town of Buena Vista.

"Remember when we hiked Mount Harvard?" Maddie

asks, pointing out the window at the third-highest peak in Colorado. It took six hours to get to the summit and I'd never seen such breathtaking views of blue mountains. It feels like a lifetime ago, back when we had no cares in the world. "We *must* do that again."

"Yeah." I glance at myself in the rearview mirror and see my platinum-blonde hair, a reminder that life is not normal. What's normal when the world is ending soon and there's a huge knot that needs to be untangled to find Tre?

Nerves bang around inside me, and I eat Maddie's bag of Cheetos like they're going out of stock.

"Dude, you are so getting cheese shit all over my steering wheel," Maddie says.

"Would you prefer I lick my fingers and then touch the wheel?"

"How about just stop eating like you're some kind of castaway."

"I'm thirsty," I say.

Jared thrusts the last of his soda up by my shoulder, and I take a huge gulp. "This is crazy, showing up and hunting down Lodima in Crestone," I say.

"It's a little like déjà vu," Jared says.

"Yeah, we're totally good with dipping into stalker territory," Mads says. "Been there, done that."

Jared smiles. "In fact, by law, I'm not supposed to come within thirty feet of you. But then again, you're dead, right?"

I look at both of them in the rearview mirror. I am so grateful they pulled me out of my Oshun world. Now here they are, driving to freaking Crestone and the airport. But they are *not* coming to Los Angeles. I shake my head in disbelief. I am so lucky.

"What?" Maddie asks, catching me staring at them in the rearview mirror.

"Just glad you guys are here for me all the time, and that you're up for anything."

"Always," Maddie says. "But only if you keep your cheese shit off my car."

6

ZOE

My chiffon dress drags along the bright green ferns, mosses, and orchids. Xintra stands in the opening in the rainforest, craning her neck to gaze at the starry sky. She slowly drops to her knees and leans over to scribble something on a piece of paper, and her body disappears in the warm mist and dense greenery.

Closer to her now, I can see she's huddled over the pages of an old book the size of an open newspaper. The book contains drawings of dots with connected lines, which I assume depict various constellations.

The high-pitched stutter of the apapane bird and the rushing waterfall really do make the Hawaiian vortex a Shangri-La to visitors. The raging heat and sweltering magnetism of the Hamakulia Volcano make it Xintra's favorite vortex entrance.

The rebirthing candidates are inside the palatial bamboo house her father built—and as she requested, they're spending time in the Bath House.

It's just the two of us in the rainforest.

She looks up at the sky again and points to a bright dot. "That's Venus," she says, flipping her hair out of her eyes. "And it's almost in line with Mars." She points to a reddish dot, nearly as bright. "It's the Venus Friday constellation. I know it is."

"Didn't your father say he was going to rely on a different constellation? One that wouldn't show for another twenty years?"

She ignores the question, wiping sweat off her upper lip and drying her hand on her black tank top. Out in the open of the jungle, she knows to dress normal to avoid suspicion. Shorts and a tank top. Flip-flops and hooped earrings.

"Why Venus Friday?" I repeat.

"Because." She leans over the book again, dragging her finger along a dot and glancing back up at the sky. She stops and looks at me, and her voice falters for a moment. She looks at the sky once more. "Because I am the sun. I *have* to be the sun."

She slams the book shut and climbs up to stand. "Just a couple more days. We have work to do." She looks at me and points a long finger. Her eyes narrow. "I want you to go to Grand Rapids, Michigan."

Michigan—that's near Chicago. *Felix.* Is he still there?

Momma hated Felix. But by the time I met him, she and I were fighting about everything. What did I mean I never wanted to touch a piano again? Why did I go with those friends? Did I really want to end up working two jobs like she did, cleaning dishes and scrubbing floors? Did I really think I would go out dressed like that?

So I escaped. And I fell in with Felix. That was my

mistake. I can see it now, that defining decision, like a fork in the road going nowhere but taking me away at the same time. Away from Momma. Away from myself. Ultimately, toward Xintra.

"Why am I going to Grand Rapids?" *I thought we have all the rebirthing candidates we need—or at least have time for.*

"I'll show you." Xintra sets the book down and sprinkles snowberry onto the ground. I can smell it immediately. A little bit cinnamon. A little bit mint. She opens a leather pouch on her waist and removes bore's tusk, ground to a fine powder, then places a pinch of it in the palm of her hand. She murmurs a spell I don't recognize. Even standing several feet away, I feel her voice like a wind gust swirling around my head, tickling my arms.

She blows the dust from her hand and a fog hangs in the air before us. Puffing and bending on the edges, the fog has always provided a looking glass for our next recruits. We saw Ember, Tre, and the rest of them moving through the world this way. When she shows me who's in Chicago, I have to admit, I crinkle my nose. "What? Her? She's so old."

In the fog, a woman shuffles along, pushing a shopping cart in a market. Her hair is silver, and she wears a horrid yellow jacket. She looks to be in her seventies. "I want you to get her and bring her to Trinity."

"Why?" I say, looking into the fog. We always target youth, but...the woman looks familiar. The striking blue eyes. The shape of the jaw. She looks an awful lot like Damien. I squint. "Wait—is that your mom?"

Xintra takes a moment to respond. "Yes," she says finally. "I want to witness her death. Do it myself."

"Kill her?"

She nods, wipes away the fog with a swat of the hand, and picks up her book. She begins walking across the jungle to the bamboo house.

I follow her.

"Why?" I ask.

"You ask too many questions lately, Zoe." She doesn't look at me, and her temples twitch as if she's gritting her teeth. "Just bring her to me. Use the north vortex entrance." She stops, swivels around to face me, and that electric energy—her temper—flares. I feel it vibrate along my arms, making the hair on them stand tall. She tilts her head. "Just do it."

I nod before briskly walking away from her to the vortex exit. It takes everything inside me to fake it. She is a psychic knower, and I can't allow her to see my heart that's piercing the cracks of her Zoe. My real heart. Myself. *Nisha*.

Later, in the dark basement hallway at the Trinity House, I sneak into the dim room where Xintra regularly calls on the dead to control her rebirthers. The door squeaks. My heart thumps loudly. If Xintra finds me, I will see the blue electricity shoot from her fingers, feel the wrenching pain before death.

I trot over to the stone carving of the ancient deity Weret Hekau, squat down beside it and dig a hole in the hard, dusty dirt floor with my fingertips. Once I've dug two inches deep, I tuck the gold-colored nugget from Ember's necklace into the ground.

I press it down hard with shaky hands, before covering it with dirt. I stomp on the floor to hide the hole. Soon, Xintra will call on the ancient Egyptian gods and dead souls and use the energy of the vortex to connect with the rebirthers all over the world. But something in this stone will disrupt that connection. I *feel* it in my gut.

Before I leave, I take a bottle of the snapdragon poison from the vault and then close the door quietly behind me. When I step into the hallway, Xintra's perfumed scent alerts me that she's just around the corner. My heart skips a beat. I didn't expect her to return so soon.

"Are you sure of the coordinates for Mum?" she snaps.

I straighten my back. "Yeah," I murmur, keeping my eyes averted, attempting to walk past her without further conversation.

She reaches out with both hands and grabs my shoulders, facing me. Fear strikes me cold.

"You know we're finally going to do it," she says. I turn my eyes up to meet her face, and she's grinning. A bit deliriously. "The storms are at play. This thing is unstoppable. We did it."

"Yes," I say. "We did." I smile but it's a flash, and I resume my regal disposition of Zoe. How can I be two people at once?

I turn away, take a couple of steps down the basement labyrinth corridor. This place is so familiar, it's like these paths are imprinted in my brain.

"Zoe." The acidity of her voice makes me stop flat-footed.

"Yes?" I ask, turning slowly to see her dim silhouette in the hallway.

"I'd be careful if I were you."

I remain silent, and the cool air of the basement clogs my nostrils. My heart thumps. I work hard to hold tight to my psychic shield, a bubble that prevents her from knowing what I've done and what I'm going to do.

"Do I need to be concerned?" she asks.

"No," I say with my back to her. "I want to hurry to ensure I meet your timelines. I must get the others in the Bath House and then I will leave."

Swiftly, I stride up the stairs, careful to stay erect and graceful, holding onto my Zoe disguise. Upstairs, I glide to sit on the cool leather sofa, my posture erect. The house smells like acrid cleaners and death.

Across the room, Bo plays chess with Blu. They're here, stuck. I think of Lilly, of Tre, of Ember, Pete, Chris. Dozens of them. Taken.

I breathe heavily as thoughts race across my mind. I am no longer Zoe. I am no longer Nisha. I am nobody. Only a vessel of regret floating aimlessly through an ocean of time.

After a long exhale, my shoulders collapse, and I gaze at the small vial of liquid in my hands. The snapdragon poison. Damien inserted the serum into the injectable devices, creating an easy way to punish the transgressions of those who might go against Xintra's agenda once the storms hit. And the storms *will* hit. Xintra will have enough people in power now to take control when chaos hits.

The plan is in action, and I have been an integral part of it. Xintra and her father planned it, and Zoe executed it, facilitating every single step. Thousands of murders in the world. Hundreds of rebirths. An Ember. A Tre. A Jeff. A Lilly.

A feeling seeps inside my chest and along my forehead. It's so foreign that it takes a long while before I recognize what it is. Heavy. Smothering. Nauseating. Like acid in my eyes.

Guilt.

I look at the snapdragon vial in my hand. With two drops, a single life is gone.

7

EMBER

The ground is wet in the secluded little town of Crestone, and the gray clouds hang low in the sky. The scent of fresh sage and rain sweeps through the car windows. With its worn Victorian buildings and wide-open streets, the town reminds me a lot of Leadville. A small abandoned hardware store with flaking white paint sits flanked by tall grass. A ladder leans against the outside of the building, and a pile of white deer antlers sits on the small wooden awning over the door. It looks like the set for a western.

"Aren't we near the Great Sand Dunes?" Maddie asks.

"Yeah," Jared says, looking at his phone. "People say the Sand Dunes have some special vibe. They say the whole Southwest is a gate. A vortex."

Vortex. My stomach flips. A memory flashes in my mind and the road ahead of me disappears.

I remember how I sat up on the stone table in the basement of Trinity, and Zoe gazed at me from the foot of the table. The light of the flames flickered on her face.

My breath chokes off in my throat.

"Where do we even go?" Mads asks through an enormous yawn.

"Post office," I say. "Tell me how to get to the post office." I know it's a long shot. But it's the only clue I have to go on right now.

The young girl behind the counter at the post office listens to me, blinking slowly. "We were hoping to find an old relative who once had a box at this address," I say. "Back in 1994."

Blink. Blink. She takes a pencil and taps it on the counter. Again, she blinks. Blink. Tap. Blink. Tap. Tap. I thought this town was made up of happy hippies who spread love and joy. This girl is obviously not one of them.

"What do I look like?" the clerk says. "A detective agency? I can't tell you the whereabouts of people who had post boxes here two decades ago." Her voice is pale pink. "Next!" She looks past us at a woman with arms loaded with boxes, holding the hand of a small child.

The box mom nudges us out of the way, before heaving her loot onto the counter. "I need to mail these. All of 'em."

My skin heats up, and a thumping echoes in my forehead. We're so close. I don't leave the counter; instead, I try to catch the clerk's eye. "Seriously, you don't know a Lodima? This is a small town. You're sure you can't help?"

Maddie tugs on my arm. "We'll figure it out, Emb."

The clerk blows a stringy strand of hair out of her eyes and returns her attention to the box mom. "Where you want these mailed?"

"Seriously. Please. We drove all the way here." I feel like I'm eking out the last bit of soda from a straw.

Maddie leads me out of the post office by my arm, whispering through gritted teeth. "Chill."

I want to jump over the counter and rip out that girl's mousy brown hair and eyelashes, but Mads pulls me out into the parking lot. The sky is gray, the air damp with drizzle.

"So, that's it?" I ask. My hands are balled into fists. "She's going to be the person who determines if I can find Lodima? Her? *That* lady." I jab my finger at the building.

"We just have to think of another plan," she says.

The parking lot has a surprising amount of traffic for a small town. A guy with dreadlocks and wearing pajama pants climbs out of a Volkswagen bus, and another woman pulls up next to us in a dingy coughing car. I walk back to the window of the building, peer inside to glimpse the clerk. She glances up at me, holds my stare, and then rings up the woman with the boxes.

"What's up?" Jared asks, getting out of the car.

"Blinking Bitch Vader in there—"

"Blinking Bitch Vader?" he asks.

"The post office girl blinks a lot," Mads explains. "And yeah, she's rude."

"We drove all the way down here. We have to find Lodima," I say, probably too loudly.

Someone taps my shoulder. I turn around to find a short dark-haired woman with brown skin. "You looking for Lodima?"

Startled, I freeze. "Yeah," I say slowly. "Do you know her?"

"Sure, I know Lodima." Her expression is hard and her

skin is weathered from the sun. "Don't everybody know her?"

"Oh man, what are the chances?" I exhale and grab her green tie-dye T-shirt a bit too forcefully. You would think I just won the lottery.

"I guess if you go to a small town and stand in the parking lot and shout someone's unusual name maybe you'll find someone who knows her," Maddie says.

"I didn't shout," I say, casting a glance at Mads. I turn to this woman again. "Can you tell me where she lives? Or maybe give me her number?"

"I'll show you," the woman says, nodding to the beater humming next to us. "Get in my car."

I glance at Maddie and Jared. "We have a car. We can just follow you."

"If I'm gonna bring you to someone like Lodima, I gotta know you're okay. So just get in my car."

"Or what?"

"Or nothing."

This is strange, but I feel desperate. "Really? Why can't you just give me her information or give her a message?"

The woman shrugs and walks to her car.

"Wait." I take a step toward her. "Sure. I'll go with you." I turn to my brother. "Just follow us?"

"They ain't following me," she says. "Like I say, I want to know you're okay to meet with Lodima."

"How do I know you really know Lodima?" I ask, hesitant. "What does she look like?"

"She gots gray hair, braids, round cupcake face." The woman's expression doesn't change. "I got to get goin'. You coming or not? You can call your friends later."

She wears a necklace around her throat, and it looks so

similar to the ankh cross necklace Lodima gave me in Trinity that I decide to trust her.

"Okay," I say suddenly.

Jared steps up. "Naw, Emby, we could figure something else out, or maybe—"

I wave him off. "Jared."

Maddie looks wary, shaking her head. I disappeared once for three years, and they're not ready for it to happen again—I get that. But this is my chance. My one-in-a-million chance.

"Give me your phone?" I hold my hand out to my brother. He pulls it out of his pocket and hands it to me hesitantly. I hug them both, whispering in Jared's ear. "You can track the phone. I'll be fine."

8

NISHA

She sits in the shade on a bench in Riverside Park, reading a book. Xintra's mother. Tre's mother.

Lina.

Her posture is erect and she wears a 49ers baseball hat. For being in her seventies, she looks surprisingly young. Outside of a few small wrinkles around her eyes and fore-head, her skin looks smooth and her eyes alert. Yet her grief is on full display in the fog rippling over her head.

In it, I can literally see the reverence she had for Xintra's father in her youth. James rarely smiled in Trinity, but in the fog above Lina's head, he flashed a toothy grin and placed a hand on her cheek. A light-haired beauty, Lina gazed up at him with young, bright blue eyes, smiling, drowning in adoration. She held a red-haired baby girl with snow-white skin. And the love she had for that child was so deep, so real, I feel it fill my chest, gushing from my pores. I feel it all the way over here, a hundred yards away.

I watch a youthful Lina dressing a little redheaded

Xintra, tying a ribbon in her hair and kissing her cheek. She smiled with her eyes and watched Xintra run down the steps to play on a rope swing.

More pieces of her life, and the emotions contained in them are so strong, I sink down onto my knees on the ground, watching them in the fog, feeling what Lina felt in those moments. A shudder of fear. A clenched fist of rage. The limpness of desperation.

There's a flash of an older Lina, wrenching away from James's fierce grasp. He gripped her wrist and she tore away from him, shouting, angry. She refused to help him start Trinity, and her resistance to him was a brick wall. Then, in another flash, I see her racing through a lavish home, opening doors, frantically calling for Xintra. She dropped to her knees, placing her forehead on the marble floor, sobbing, before a boy's voice called to her.

"Mommy!"

Quickly, she rose, wiping her tears and forcing a smile as she picked up a small boy. He was her mirror image but with dark hair that framed the crystal blue eyes. Tre.

Another quick flare: a man, Tre's father, paced nervously in the spacious foyer as she pleaded with police officers to find James and her little girl.

Then, Tre, looking like he does today, hugging her inside an airport terminal. The airport was crowded, and a girl with a stonewashed jean jacket and big curly hair passed, pulling a suitcase. Tre boarded the plane to San Francisco, and Lina wiped tears from her cheek and pressed her fingers to her lips. I feel her anxiety from that moment—her tight throat and shallow breath.

Then the final one that feels like a punch in the gut: Lina sank down onto a sofa with the phone to her ear, as the man on the other end explained that Tre disappeared with a child actress. Lina's face turned white, the life falling out of her body, like someone falling through a trap door.

Her agony is so visceral, I feel like a bat struck me from behind. Of all the people I've lured to Trinity over the years, all the times I made them disappear, I never witnessed the pain on the other side of the equation. The loved ones left behind.

I blink, shaking off the feelings as best I can, and approach Lina on the bench.

When I get close enough, her eyes fall on me and she offers a small smile, scooting over in case I want to sit, too. I do, slowly, and then turn to her and extend a hand.

"I'm....Z—I'm Nisha," I say.

She smiles, but her eyes still hold sadness, and she shakes my hand. "Well, hi there. I'm Lina."

"I know where Tre is," I say.

She freezes and then inches backward, wary. "Oh. Is that so."

She doesn't believe me. I sigh and hand her a piece of paper with a Skype name on it and an estimated time to call. "Contact this person for a video call and you'll see."

I stand up.

"I may look like an easy target for scammers, but I'm no dummy." Her expression is firm, but I can see the hope trickle into the fog above. It glows like a little candle.

"Tre loved punk rock. He lived in Germany. He went to California to live with your jerk of an ex-husband because he stumbled upon an Annunaki ceremony on the way home from sneaking out to a club. You wore an ankh cross. You knew about Trinity Forest."

Her lips part and her eyebrows squeeze together. She doesn't respond.

"And I know where Xintra is too. She followed James to build Trinity Forest. And she's going to destroy the world."

I don't wait for her reaction. Xintra will know soon enough that I'm not bringing Lina to her, and I have another stop I need to make before getting back to the vortex.

9

EMBER

"So, what's your name?" I ask, searching blindly for the seat belt in this pit of a car. I can't find anything but gum wrappers and grime. The car smells faintly of spoiled milk, and the seat feels sticky beneath my legs.

"Seat belt's broke." The woman glances over her shoulder and then jams the gas to merge onto the road. The car hums loudly as we drive. She slams on the gas at the green lights and brakes hard on the reds.

"Why do you want Lodima?" she asks, glancing between me and the road.

"I think she can help me find my friend and tell me more about my mom."

"She's retired from all that seeing business. She don't do that. And if you're one of those people who keep harassing her, well, let me tell you there are people here who will *know*."

"Oh, no, I'm not going to harass her. I think she'll want

to see me. I met her a long time ago, and she was friends with my mom."

We pass a white house with green trim that's now a thrift store and then to an adobe home half-buried in a hillside—one side of it is covered by solar panels. Everything takes on a gloomy sheen as dark clouds gather in the sky. The drizzle turns to rain, and the windshield wipers beat the drops away.

She runs a stop sign and drives down a dirt road that looks to be going out of town, along high desert prairie and blue mountain peaks. My heart rate ticks up, and suddenly, I'm thinking this was pretty much a terrible idea. Again, I feel out of control.

Inexplicably, my old Oshun persona gets triggered. "Are you planning on telling me where we're going? This is pretty stupid that you can't just give me an address."

She doesn't answer me for a few beats. Beads of sweat form on my forehead. Green shrubs and grass, cordoned off by barbed wire, whiz past us on the edge of the roadway. I glance again in the side-view mirror and see another car several lengths behind us. It's white. A Mercedes. Male driver.

I suck in a breath when I get a closer look—he looks like the same guy who hit me with the car in the alleyway back in LA, when I was Oshun. In the side-view mirror again, I see that same face, his lips turned down into a frown, his large body scrunched into the car. Skin like mashed potatoes.

This must be a trap. This woman is leading me back to Zoe and Xintra. And this time, they'll waste no time killing me. Oh my God. Not again. My body twitches uncomfortably in my seat. Maybe I should just throw myself out the door... or maybe I'll push this woman out of the way and take over the steering wheel.

"Stop the car. I changed my mind."

She doesn't take her eyes off the road. Instead, she turns left onto a dirt road, leading out to a wide-open prairie. The car bumps along, windshield wipers now flapping faster against the rain. I glance again in the side-view mirror. The white Mercedes follows us from a distance.

"Why do you care so much about Lodima?" the woman asks.

"Like I said, she knew my mom," I snap, glancing back at the mirror again. The white car is gone.

"And?"

"And she gave me a necklace."

"And?"

"And I'm not going to hurt her, okay? Just let me out. I changed my mind."

"I like your spunk," she says, opening a pack of gum and sticking a piece in her mouth. "Want some?"

I shake my head.

"My name is Bea. Lodima and I go way back."

"I'm Ember."

With that, her entire body lights up. It's as if an entirely new person entered her skin. "Well, Jesus. *You're* Ember! Well, why didn't you say so? It's just up here on the right." She chuckles and chews her gum vigorously, popping it with her tongue.

I let out a breath and sink farther into the seat, grateful.

"So whaddya think of Crestone so far?"

"I don't know much about it, but my brother said it's um... spiritual," I say.

"Sure, the spiritual energy here is pretty big because so

many people pray and meditate here," she says. "Plus, there's wind, altitude, and a huge aquifer that sits beneath what's been called the highest desert outside of Tibet."

"Huh," I say.

"Lodi moved here from Leadville because it was just too dangerous there and we can form, I don't know, a protective bubble around her."

I flip my head to look at her, urgency uncoiling inside me. "You know about Trinity Forest, then?"

"Trinity what?" She hands me a glass bottle with a milky liquid inside it. "Want some? It's Ormus. Tastes like seawater. It can balance the left and right hemispheres of your brain."

I grimace. "No. I'm good."

In the distance sits a white dome with a gold spire, surrounded by colorful prayer flags, a wall of stones, bushes, and sage. Bea notices me squinting at it. "That's the Stupa of Enlightenment. People go there from all over. Stupas are supposed to represent earth, water, fire, and air."

Whatever.

I exhale when Bea stops the car in front of a small adobe house. We run through the downpour to the porch, and I rap twice on the bright turquoise door. After a moment, it opens and there she is: Lodima. The woman from the forest. Mom's friend. Her two long braids hang down past her shoulders over a red Native American poncho.

A white-toothed grin eats up her face, and her eyes sparkle in the cloudy light. "Took you long enough," she says.

10

NISHA

The high-rise apartment building watches me, breathing, bustling, full of life. A modern monument to a living city, planted on the grave of my family's clapboard home. It's been thirty-eight years since I followed James into the Snag vortex. I'm not sure what I was thinking. I guess I hoped that Momma would be there, that I'd find home again, that I could yank off Xintra's blanket of death. Stupid.

Here in the city, some things haven't changed. It's faint, but the scent of burnt chocolate still wafts through the air from a nearby chocolate factory, just like it used to when I was little. Exhaust fumes mix with the scent of barbecue and something like the shadowy smell of Play-Doh. The sky is the same low-hanging gray, and Momma would say being outside today was like being inside a puffy, cozy tent.

But reminders of time and change overshadow all that's familiar. The rush of people feels thicker. The horns honk louder. The people drive faster. Everyone walks with their heads down, looking at their cell phones. And this building. The damn building, all angular and modern—with its brick and glass and red squared features, jutting out in architectural hoity-toityness. It stands where our house used to be.

My shoulders collapse. Time and progress has wiped away my old life like a rag clearing a dirty table.

I climb the concrete steps to the brick row house where Felix once lived. I'm sure he doesn't live here anymore, after all these years. Maybe he died. Maybe he went to jail.

The lines and cracks that once crisscrossed the stoop are gone, glossed over with fresh concrete. Even the door is new—the wooden screen exchanged for an army green metal one with a clear glass pane. A lump climbs up to my tonsils, and with a shaky hand, I knock.

I stood right here, in this very place, my hair neatly coiled behind my ear, dressed to the nines in mink and gold. Felix was late. I had my hand on my hip, irritated that I was missing out on all the dancing at the Patio. That was the first of so many times he would let me down and, later, beat me up.

The door opens and an old man around sixty or seventy squints at me. The blood drains from my face, and I feel like I want to vomit. He looks like Felix but he's all puffed up and wrinkled. Age spots dot his forehead below a head of gray hair.

"What the hell..." he whispers. His eyes look watery, but his mouth has the same full lips that could slip into a vicious, terrifying scowl. "You look just like Nisha."

I don't say anything. My voice box is locked, and I don't have a key.

He looks so *old*. The older guy who was once so alluring, so sexy, is now a plumped-up old man, and an angry one at that, with tangled white eyebrows. I remember him handing me the needle that first time, whispering in my ear, *"It's like you're fucking God himself, and chasing that dragon is a magical thing, girl."*

Of course, it was his business. The heroin.

I gaze at him. Lines run from his nose to his lips, like deep parenthesis.

"You don't speak? What you want?" he asks.

"You're Felix," I say finally. My voice sounds more like Nisha's, punctuated with the head nod and the Chicago accent.

"Yeah, so?"

"You're old."

"Yeah, so? Who are *you*?"

"I'm..." I start to answer, but I don't know who I am anymore. My eyes sting, and I turn away from him. I gaze for a moment at the newly planted trees. Same spot I once stood the day that coin landed on the concrete in front of me. I was filled with nausea and cold flashes from withdrawal, and a craving for smack so intense it was worse than thirsting for water for days in a desert.

When I picked up the coin, all of those ugly feelings disappeared, and the warm rush I got from it was better than anything I had ever felt. I knew I needed to go to Snag. When I found James, Xintra's father, he became my gardener; he grew me into Zoe in my new numb and peaceful home.

"Well?" Felix scowls.

"Do you know where Nisha's momma is?" I ask.

"She's dead." My stomach churns. *Momma is dead.*

An older woman calls to Felix from the other room. Her voice shrieks. "Felix! Who's that at the door?"

"That's what I'm about to find out," he says over his shoulder. He nods at me. "You look just like Nisha."

I nod. "What happened to Nisha's sister, Tracy?"

"Dead." He tosses his head and grimaces. "Who the hell—"

"I'm Nisha." My voice is calm. Quiet, but firm.

He recoils, like my words knocked him back a step, and shakes his head. "She's dead too. Why you coming 'round here asking? Who the hell are you?"

"I told you, I'm Nisha." I fold my arms, jut out a hip.

There it is. Fear. He's seeing a ghost from the past, standing right before him, warm breath on his face, unchanged from 1978. The whites of his eyes grow, and he slams the door.

All my family gone. My home gone. This monster who was once so foxy now old and angry and unrecognizable. All that was Nisha Robinson is gone.

My leaden feet fall heavy on the steps as I make my way down to the sidewalk and I raise a hand to hail a yellow taxicab approaching from down the street.

The car pulls up and I open the door, slide onto the hot black seat. Then it hits me. What if I could have gotten clean on my own? I could have turned things around. I could have gone to Tracy, to Momma, marched back into that conservatory head held high.

I didn't *lose* everything because of Trinity. They *took* it from me. Xintra and her father. They did this. They stole from me. Life slipped by as I spent my years in Trinity, wooing generations of rebirthers to live out in the world again under Xintra's command.

Rage, so new and so unfamiliar, washes over me like a violent flood.

She did this. Xintra.

11

EMBER

I perch on the edge of a worn chaise lounge inside the dark, cluttered house. Thunder bangs outside, and the storm darkens the room. The spicy scents of curry and incense intermingle in the small space. A lampshade with little dangly fur balls sits near my shoulder.

"So, Ember, you found yourself again," Lodima says, taking a seat in a wicker rocker across from me.

"Why'd you ever let me go into Trinity?" My words come out like a pile of rocks and my body trembles with anger. "Look at me!" I point to my nose, my lips, my super huge boob job. The bruise on my shoulder and my neck. "I nearly got killed! Multiple times. And you knew! You *knew* about Trinity. You *knew* about Mom. You *knew* about Xintra!"

She nods, and the serene look stays on her face.

"Why didn't you tell me? Stop me?" It wasn't what I planned to open with, but she abandoned me, not once, but twice in the forest. Like my parents. Like the rest of the world. She knew what Trinity was about, and she just left me in the forest that first morning. Without any warning.

She lets out a knowing sigh. "It had to be your choice to decide whether you wanted to go beyond the gate. I've made the mistake of telling people not to go, telling them what Trinity has in store, and it caused great destruction to the world. Your path was set, and it was to go to Trinity." A gray cat with half an ear jumps onto her lap. "You didn't lose yourself entirely, did you?"

I *found me*, I think. And it's true; I did find me. But Tre is still lost. Tre still needs to be found. "I need help waking up a friend. Will you please tell me what you did to wake me up?"

Lodima sighs deeply and rocks back and forth in the chair. She stares ahead at the stained concrete floor, lost in thought for a moment too long.

"Your mom and I were friends." She slowly runs her hand across the cat's silky coat and inhales with a long breath. She exhales with a longer breath. She rocks slowly. It's excruciating.

"I *assumed* that. Nice of you to look out for your dead friend's daughter."

Sometimes my inner Oshun surprises me.

"You read her journal, then?" she asks.

"No," I say. I still don't know *why* I haven't read it. Mom's Crazy Woman Notebook was the key to getting out of Trinity in the end, but... I suppose I'm afraid of what I'll find, of who Mom really was. I'd rather hang onto my memories of her as an adult; I made peace with that version of her.

Lodima's cat jumps onto my lap, surprising me. I put my hands in the air, ready for him to leave. He mews, and the sound is sage green like Lodima's voice, with flecks of muddied amber—like Mom's.

"He likes you," she says. "He can sense good mojo. Axel can spot the good strangers from the bad. His name means man of peace."

I pet Axel's fluffy fur tentatively at first. The vibrating purr calms me with its waves of soft gray green.

"Cats have secret healing power. They are known to absorb negative energy," Lodima says. She sounds like Mom.

I change the subject, just like I used to all the time with Mom. "Thank you for whatever you did for me, but can you help me wake up Tre or not?"

She stands up slowly and holds out one finger. "Stay right there."

She disappears into a back room. I stand up and examine the bookshelves lined with stacks of old newspapers, books, candles, rocks and Egyptian statues and chachkes. Rooster jello molds line the walls near the kitchen.

A few moments later, Lodima returns carrying a cardboard box the size of a microwave. She hefts it onto the wooden coffee table.

"You can have these. They're letters your mom wrote me about her time in Trinity."

I walk over to the box, open the lid, and peer inside. I remove a handful of opened envelopes addressed to Lodima with Mom's familiar handwriting. Maybe these can help me. I greedily tuck them into the waistband of my shorts before rummaging through the rest of the contents in the box—mostly piles of paper with drawings. Faces.

Charcoal faces. Women, men, young, old, every race, every shape. People. Hundreds of them.

I look up to Lodima. "Who are they?"

"The lost." She moves so smoothly it's like she's floating behind the counter in the small kitchen. She removes a bowl from the cupboard and lifts the lid from a pot on the stove. A puff of steam releases the spicy scent of curry.

"People who went missing?"

"Your mom had visions. She would paint or draw the faces she saw to try and remember them."

Slowly, I flip through more drawings until I come to a familiar one that sucks the breath out of me. A tingle rushes across my skin.It's Tre. She saw Tre before I was even born.

The drawing shows the same fierce expression he wore when I first met him. A couple of dark strands of hair fall over his brow. Even in black and white, his eyes are striking. I run my fingers across the sketch, and my heart physically aches. I need to get him back. I touch my fingers to my throat, remembering how he—no, I correct myself, *Damien*—tried to kill me. The memory sucks a bit of my breath away.

But I stare at his face a little longer, longing to see him, touch him, despite the fear that still dances along my spine.

I flip to another picture. This one has no face. It's jumbled, a confusing image of a car marked with jagged red lines and spinning black and white and spinning lines. I stare at it for a minute, turning it around in my fingers, and then I see clearly: it's a car wreck. *Our* car wreck.

My eyes widen. "Mom saw the car accident? She knew we'd get in an accident? That she and my dad would die?"

The words stick in my throat. I clutch the picture tightly, crunching the edges. I want to tear up the drawing, wad it up into a tiny ball, stamp it out of existence.

Lodima stops stirring her curry and gazes directly at me with a soft look. "She didn't know that it was her own car accident, but she saw it. She thought I could save the people in it before it happened, but I was blocked. Perhaps because it was your mom, I couldn't see. Until it was too late."

She walks to me slowly, holding her arms out to me as if we know each other well. And for some reason, I feel like Mom is right here in this room with us. That Lodima's arms are Mom's arms, and I fall into them. I never would have imagined that I'd find that kind of warmth in the arms of a stranger.

"I am so sorry, Ember," she whispers. "It was her path, I suppose. And yours. But it does not make it okay. It does not make it okay."

The ticking of the clock. Her gravelly voice. It all conjures up a concoction of pink and now mustard brown in my Color Crayon Brain, which transforms into a... the only word I can think to describe it is a *vision*. In my mind, I see a bookshelf—and purple crayon dots hover over the third shelf from the top. I shake my head, unable to understand what I'm seeing.

Jared's phone chimes in my pocket, and I pull it out and look at the screen.

It's a text from Maddie.

Maddie: *You alive?*

Me: *Yes*

Maddie: *Where r you?*

Me: *Lodima's house*

Maddie: *Where's that?*

Me: *? Track my phone.*

Maddie: *Coming*

Lodima watches me silently, waiting, blinking slowly.

"Sorry. Maddie just texted me. They're worried."

"As they should be."

Lodima strides to the bookcase and turns on the stereo to play classical music—Bach's sweet melody of Concerto for Two Violins in D minor. I recall the enchanting lavender song playing endlessly in my English teacher's classroom. Lilac dots and murky cotton-candy pink smudges.

Lodima sits down at her kitchen table, tucked into a bay window, and places her bowl of curry in front of her. The scents of ginger, garlic, and turmeric waft in the air. "Want some?"

I shake my head.

"Ember, I have been searching for answers to Trinity for years. Xintra is dangerous. Deadly. But I have to tell you, Ember, you're the only one who can stop this." She takes a bite of curry.

A gurgling laugh croaks out of my throat, and I smile and shake my head. "No. Not me. I just need to find Tre."

I want normal. I want pizza on Friday nights and college textbooks and strumming my guitar on a grassy lawn. I want to stand on the Brooklyn Bridge with Tre holding my hand and then fold myself into the crevasses of his body and fall asleep to the sound of his peaceful breath. I don't want to be in the middle of some stupid, paranormal take-over-the-world scheme.

"Your necklace did something to me as Oshun," I

continue, ignoring her. "Do you have some crystals I can use when I get to LA?"

"I have so many rocks. The magnetic ones there are the ones you need." She points to the corner of the room before turning back to me. "I know you don't believe me, but it's *you*, Ember. *You're* the one. You're an empath. You have the bloodline to stop Xintra from taking over the world."

La la la. Can't hear her. "Thanks for the stuff. I gotta go."

A bright light shines on Lodima's face through the dining room window. She looks like a ghost. The brown sound of an engine signals that a car is arriving.

"That must be Maddie," I say. Lodima stays seated at the table while I rush to the front door and step outside. Get me out of this place.

Just then, the engine revs and the car juts forward, screaming right through the window and into Lodima's dining room. Glass shatters. Wood and metal crunch.

"Lodima! No!" I fling open the front door and run back into the house.

The blood drains from my face, and the world tilts. High-pitched buzzing surrounds me, a ringing that cancels out every other noise, ebbing and flowing, slowing down my reaction time, my movement, the scene around me. Lodima lies on the floor beneath a heap of glass and broken furniture and wood. Blood drips from her mouth. Her red and green poncho is scrunched up around her neck.

Rain blows into the house from outside. The engine revs again and the car lurches backwards, pulling away from what's left of the window.

I kneel down in the broken glass, feel for Lodima's pulse, searching for her life. Her blood. Her heart. But I feel nothing, and I cry out, shaking her shoulders. The pastel colors of Bach's violins dance, grotesquely juxtaposed with the scene of destruction and death before me.

The car's headlights shrink and I run to the adjacent garage to get a better look at it; this was no accident. And, of course, it isn't Maddie's car. It's a white Mercedes.

The porchlight's glare falls on the driver's face for an instant: the man who was following me earlier, the one who tried to kill me in LA. Fear electrifies my skin and I dart back into the house.

My Color Crayon Brain goes berserk and purple dots twirl with the music—just like in my vision a few minutes ago. They hover on the third shelf of the bookcase.

Lodima's words echo in my mind: *You're an empath.*

I follow the colors and reach for the bookshelf where the sparkling, floating color hovers.

My fingers graze a book and I pull it out, knowing that this might be the death of me, taking time to follow this weird vision map. I look at the heavy black book in my hand. *The Book of the Dead.*

Lodima's words echo in my mind again. *You're the one.*

No, I am not. I can't be.

Rocks. Lodima pointed to the corner of the room, saying I needed magnetic ones. I run in that direction and scan the area. A pile of neatly stacked newspapers. A litter box. A couple of plastic containers stacked against the wall on a woven Indian rug. I open the lid of one and see a pile of dark colored stones and some small crystals. I grab the two green plastic containers and the book and dart for the garage. I've got to get out of here.

12

NISHA

The revolving door spins like a glass prism before spitting me out into the lobby of the office tower of MeToo. It's a modern, sprawling glass building purchased with Xintra's blood money. Inside the sparse lobby, I stand at the elevator.

Clumps of people clad in flip-flops and hoodies pass by. I pull out a keycard, a piece of paper with a password on it; and a list of names, email addresses and pages of lists and instructions. Then, holding the snapdragon serum in my right hand, I get into the elevator and punch the button for the seventh floor.

Upstairs, the MeToo office is your prototypical tech workplace, with restaurant-style booths, a communal workspace with standing desks and stools, brick walls, a ton of plants and lots of light. Across the room, people hunch over laptops and huddle on angular orange sofas set around a fireplace. I pass a man asleep in a hammock in a room labeled *Nap Zone*.

I spot a young girl working on a laptop at a high-top wooden table near an exposed-brick wall. "Do you know where I can find an intern?" I ask.

She looks up, like she was just caught stealing, with wide eyes, and then scowls. "I don't know. There was one here yesterday who sat by the orange dice."

"Orange dice?"

"Yeah." She points to two giant fuzzy stuffed dice hanging by wire from the wooden ceiling. Below the dice sits a blonde at a sparse desk. She's typing on a computer.

I stride over to her. "I need about one hundred fifty emails sent out in the next eight hours. It involves a ton of research, and it might require more than one person."

Xintra's greatest weakness has been greedily rushing the process. It's what allowed for Ember to wake up early and, ultimately, me. The stone Ember wore on her necklace must disrupt Xintra's magical connection with the rebirthers—if I can trigger other rebirthers' memories of their past lives then maybe they, too, can wake up and be freed from Xintra's claim.

Except I don't know how long it will take for Xintra to know we've gone AWOL. As soon as she finds out we're awake, she'll come after us—just like she sent Caius to kill Ember in Los Angeles. *I've got to find a way to shield them from her psychic clairvoyance back in Trinity.*

The intern pushes her round glasses up on her nose. "Who are you?"

"I'm Zoe," I say, even though the name tastes sour in my mouth, "and this is coming from the top. I need information about these missing people"—I wave a list of names in front of her face—"sent to these people ASAP." I point to another list, of the same people's rebirthed names.

"If you do it in a timely manner, you will have a bonus waiting in your bank account that will make it so you don't have to work another day this year." I brace myself for her to call out to her superior, question my authority.

She touches her cheek. "I was asked to pull lists of water treatment facilities around the world. Am I no longer on this assignment?"

"Nope. You're doing this instead." I hand her the stack of papers. "You need to find their email addresses and do deep research. Can you get help?"

"Yeah." She nods, eager. "Um, what kind of bonus are we talking?"

"One hundred thousand dollars."

Her eyes light up and her mouth drops open, but she doesn't speak.

I can't help but feel a twist in my gut—I hate to make a promise like this, get her hopes up just to disappoint her. I've had enough of ruining people for a lifetime. But this is the only way. If she helps, she'll be saving people's lives.

"You can't tell anyone," I say. "This is life or death. Urgent."

She nods eagerly.

"Write your name and bank info on this." I hand her a piece of paper. "I'll get you set up. Then get as far away from this place as possible."

At the end of the hall, behind a large walnut door, I slip into an office and wait for Damien. Wait—just like I used to do with people in Trinity. I'd appear to them mysteriously without them noticing. I suppose I've hung onto that slinking ability.

He opens the door to the office wearing a black T-shirt and jeans, and stops when he sees me lounging on the sofa. He grimaces.

"I'm done with the Annunaki, Tre." I emphasize his real name, and he gazes at me, sputtering without words. He's clearly oscillating between identities like I did for so long, a tightrope walker afraid to lose control, afraid of what happens when your toe slips and you fall into the abyss.

It turns out the abyss is freaking scary, but it's just you. Your old life. As fucked up as it used to be. But way better because at least you're in the driver's seat again.

He walks to his desk and places his briefcase on the floor. "What in the world are you talking about? And why are you here?"

Okay then. Pretend you didn't just hear what I said to you. "Yeah, that's what I want to ask *you*. Why are *you* here, Tre?"

"What?" He sits down at his desk, plugs in his cell phone, and opens his laptop. It's what I did, too: pretended that nothing was being shaken up like a bottle ready to burst. "What's going on with you, Zoe?"

"Nisha. My name is Nisha, *Tre.*"

He looks up from the laptop and stands up slowly reaching his full height before putting his hands on the glass-top desk. He leans over it and growls, "What the fuck is wrong with you? Quit calling me Tre. Does Xintra know you're here, that you're going rogue?" He glares at me with dark steel blue eyes. "Because I would be happy to do Xintra a favor and get rid of this Nisha myself."

Damien's no different than Felix or any of those fools I dealt with back home. They put me in the gutter, but I am not letting anybody do that to me again. Certainly not this punk-ass kid.

I stand up, placing my hands on the desk, too, just inches from his. I lean in with my face so close to his, I can smell the nicotine on his breath. "Did you check your email?"

"What? No."

"Check it." I toss my head toward him and stand up straight again, crossing my arms. A full glass of water sits on the corner of his desk. You can't see the two drops of snapdragon poison inside it.

His expression shifts as he taps on his laptop a couple times. The computer rings like a phone. Skype.

He glares at me before frowning at the screen. I reach over to accept the call, tapping the keyboard just once.

Then, a woman's voice. "Tre. Is that you?"

He falls back into his chair. A train wreck plays out on his face: The pinched brows. The gaping mouth. Then a flash of softening eyes and cheeks.

"Trevor, oh my God. It's you! But you haven't...changed?"

I sit down opposite him, watching Tre's reaction.

"I'm not..." How can he explain any of this to his mother? Is he awake?

I lean forward on the table and shout so she can hear me on the computer. "It is your son! He got caught up in Trinity Forest, Miss Lina. He got caught up in Xintra's bull-shit." I lean back in the leather chair.

He frowns at me before returning his attention to the screen.

"It worked," she whispers. "His plan. The witchcraft. The tunnels. I didn't think he would really do it." She pauses. "You're alive! Oh my Lord, my baby is alive!" Her voice is loud and chock full of power. Then suddenly she grows silent for a moment, before I hear her laughing and then sobbing.

Tre watches the screen, his eyes lightening. "I'm so sorry," he says.

He stops and then casts his eyes down to the glass desk for a moment. When he looks up again, his irises look dark gray. He clicks off Skype, shakes his head.

"No." He picks up his jacket and stands up, pushing his chair back so hard it hits the wall with a loud bang. "Xintra will burn you. She'll destroy you." His nostrils flare.

Glancing at the water glass on the table, I reach across his desk, grab the laptop and open the email we sent him. I hold up the computer so it faces him. "Look!" I scream, stumbling after him, shoving it in his face. "Look!"

I'm surprised, but he actually does stop at the doorway and he does look at the screen. I scroll down the email to show him the attachments. "See?"

His arm falls, dropping the jacket on the floor. His eyebrows climb a centimeter. I click on the newspaper photo of him. *Missing California Boy, Trevor Hudson.* Surprise flashes on his face.

He takes the computer from me, sinks down onto the black leather sofa nearby, and scrolls down. Photos of the Berlin Wall, pictures of his high school in California, a newspaper picture of his dad closing a deal to acquire another company. Ember's missing person poster. I can hear the hitch in his breath. Photos of her smiling with friends on Instagram and in the high school yearbook. His face softens. Maybe it's love. Or just pain. Then, Lilly's photos from the *Beehive Diaries* TV show. Pete's missing person's photo. And a picture of Chris. And the stories and photos of the missing recruits before that: Megan, G, Jeff.

I can assume what he's feeling, but I don't *really* know. I can't *really* tell what he's thinking. Which is unusual, because just a few hours ago, I *could* tell what people thought. When I was Zoe, I always knew what they felt. How they viewed themselves, the world. I miss that power, even though I know it was achieved with darkness.

"Tre," I say. "You're in there. And you can fight this, just like I did."

Slowly, he looks up to meet my eyes. His jaw tenses, his temples flicker and his lips purse tightly. "Ember," he says. "Where is she?"

"Are you asking as Tre or Damien?" If I had my Trinity powers, I would *know*. I would see. But the more I wake up, the more I carry around Ember's mind-altering stones, the less I feel Xintra's magnetic force and the rebirther spell.

"Tre. I'm Tre," he says softly. His eyes shift to a lighter blue, and he swallows. Pain colors his face. "I need to find her."

"How do I know that you're really Tre?"

He stands up and exhales loudly, frustration mounting. "Where is she?" He runs his hand through his dark hair and his energy is wild, like a bear caught in a trap.

"A quick test. Do you remember the first time I met you?" I ask.

"Yeah, you met me in the meadow. You asked me if I was hungry."

Good. One point for Tre. "Do you remember who you came with?"

"Come on, Zoe—"

"It's Nisha."

"Whatever. Yeah, I was with Lilly. Where is Ember? Is she okay?" His eyes are pained, and it's clear that he's there. Only I don't know how long he'll stay in control, whether Damien will re-emerge. When I woke up, it was fleeting moments between feeling myself and then Zoe.

"Sure, she's fine," I say.

"Where's Lilly? Pete?"

"She's here, in LA. An actress. Pete? You should know this. Pull from your Damien memory."

"No. No. No." He grabs hold of fistfuls of hair with each hand and shuts his eyes, remembering. "He's...a sab."

"But he's not dead." Zoe is still there, cool, collected, unfeeling—an ugly part of me. I put my palms together, shut my eyes, and take a deep breath. I want to be myself again. I want to be genuine, real, kind. That's who I am. Talented, smart, driven, hopeful.

He shakes his head, sinking into his real self again, and then it's as if he notices the room for the very first time. He scans it, running his eyes across the desk, the bookshelf, the ceiling, the view of the city from the windows. It's as if he just woke up in an unfamiliar place. At least for now, he's shed Damien like an ugly suit.

"I'm thirsty," he says, taking a step toward the desk, reaching his hand out to take the glass of water.

"No!" I yell, rushing in front of him and swatting it off the desk. Glass shatters and the water spreads onto the floor. A sizzling sound rises from the carpet, followed by tiny plumes of smoke.

Tre's eyebrows climb high up onto his forehead.

"Backup plan," I say.

He nods, gazing at the floor for a long moment before

blinking and looking at me. He puts a finger to his temple. "Why can I see visions?"

"You always had that ability, even before Trinity. But with Xintra's rebirther spells and the connection to Trinity's magnetic energy, you can see them even more clearly."

"Well then I need to get to Colorado fast." He picks up his suit jacket and heads for the door. "Because the vision I just saw scares the shit out of me."

13

EMBER

The man in the car must have been waiting for me to run, because his car hums just outside the garage—which is more like a carport with no door. The headlights shine on me, blocking my visibility, and he revs the engine and plows his car through the rain, headed straight for me.

My heart stops for an instant and I leap out of the way as the car crashes into the back of the garage. It misses me by just a foot. I clamber over a box, hitting my head on something sharp, and then scramble to my feet, tripping over a bicycle and slamming the far wall of the garage with my hip. A shovel hanging on the wall tips onto me.

Something warm drips down my forehead before dropping onto a white cooler. Dark red. I touch my forehead and my fingers slide over a gash oozing blood.

Outside the garage, the headlights of another oncoming car bounce in the distance. Maddie and Jared? Please God let it be Maddie and Jared.

I push off the wall with my elbows, clutching my containers and book, and climb over broken wood and other pieces of the house.

Sprinting into the dark pouring rain, I slip in the mud and squint as the raindrops pound my head. The madman guns the car— the sound is a flash the color of oatmeal— and the car backs out of the broken garage. Not again. A strangled moan spurts from my mouth.

I pick up the pace, my shoes slipping on the road. The car engine roars and the headlights flash.

With my eyes fixed on my only salvation, the headlights of the oncoming car, I run so swiftly that I cannot feel my legs. It's as if they have a mind of their own and I'm flying across the air, through the deluge of water. My breath is even, efficient and in sync with my legs, harkening back to my cross country days. I clench my stash and move stiffly for maximum speed.

The light from the headlights on the Mercedes skips on the ground at my feet, bobbing with the dips in the road. I glance back over my shoulder; the car is just thirty feet away.

I dive into the gully next to the road and the car misses me by inches, splashing mud and water on me and in my eyes. The warm breeze from the hot engine rushes over my face.

Lying on my stomach on the slick ground with rainwater gushing into my eyes, I move awkwardly to keep hold of the containers and the book. This extra time may be a fatal mistake, but I cannot help it. Somehow I know I need these rocks.

I scramble out of the gully, my hands and feet slipping

and clawing up the slope, just as the other oncoming car reaches me.

"Get in!" Maddie's periwinkle voice is a life preserver to me. She slows the car beside me and I stop to scoop up the black book that fell onto the ground.

"Hurry!" Jared yells from the passenger seat.

I run for Maddie's slow-moving car, and Jared throws open the back door. Clumsily, I toss the containers and wet book into the car and then hurl my body in after, landing half on my stomach. It takes my breath away. Maddie steps on the gas and I roll onto my side. The back door stays open, swinging wildly. Raindrops blow in through the opening.

Maddie drives toward Lodima's house and whips her little car around in a slippery U-turn to head back to the main road. "Stop! Mads, wait!" I yell.

She flips her head back to see me but doesn't stop the car. "What? For God's sake, what?"

"Stop!" I yell. "Please!"

She does but screams. "What?!"

"Axel!" As soon as the car slows, I jump out and scoop up Lodima's cat—nothing but four legs and bones covered by wet, matted fur and with huge popping eyes. He mews loudly, and the sage and amber colors sweep through my vision.

"A cat? We're saving a freaking cat!?" Jared shouts from the front passenger seat. I toss Axel into the car, jump in headfirst, and scoot on my belly across the back seat as Jared pulls the back door shut behind us.

"He's the man of peace," I whisper, pressing my nose into the cat's smelly fur and panting loudly.

The crazed murderer has turned his Mercedes around

and is driving directly toward us on the narrow road. He's playing chicken and is ready to slam directly into us in a head-on collision—all, I know, for "the cause."

"Oh-God-oh-God-oh-God!" Maddie yells.

The Mercedes gains speed, its headlights blinding us through the foggy rain. Windshield wipers whip back and forth. There's only enough room on the road for one car.

Then, at the last second, Maddie yanks her car to the right. The car jumps across the ditch on the side of the road, landing on one tire, then two. My head knocks against the window, and Jared lets out a loud noise. The Mercedes whizzes past, veering to follow us, but spins out of control in the storm, cartwheeling twice before landing wheels up in the ditch by the road.

Our car bounces wildly over the wet prairie, windshield wipers flapping furiously. After a minute, we make it out to the main road. I shake uncontrollably, squeezing Axel's wet, bony body.

"Brilliant!" Jared yells. "Keep going!"

"Oh God, oh God, oh God!" Maddie screams, repeating it over and over.

"Drive to the road. Just go!" Jared shouts, glancing over his shoulder at the wrecked Mercedes.

Maddie steps on the gas and, in the finale to the most amazing driving feat ever, gets us to the highway. She turns left and we go speeding west. Out of Crestone.

Away from the Mercedes. Away from Lodima's crumpled, dead body. Away from this place that was supposed to be different. Away from this place that was supposed to be a happy rainbow-colored bubble of protection. Not a nightmare. Not a murder scene.

I close my eyes and collapse sideways onto the back

seat, water dripping from my hair to the corners of my mouth. I press my cheek into the cool tan leather. My head throbs.

"She's dead," I whisper. "Everyone who knows how to stop this is dead."

14

NISHA

The airport is empty; the virus has kept people away. We park on the runway and walk to the white private jet. Aboard, the plane smells like a cocktail of coffee and leather and air-conditioner coolant. The captain smiles as we take our seats, and I study him for a couple seconds. He wears the typical pilot's garb, a white short-sleeved shirt with the official gold-and-black patches on the shoulders and a black tie. But his eyes dart around the cabin, and he fails to make eye contact. I can't see the charcoal fog of rebirthers anymore, so I worry for a moment that he's a sab who'll go on a suicide mission once we're in the air. *Will Xintra know I'm awake?*

Still, heart pounding, I sink into the large leather seat facing Tre. "Can you see the fog anymore?"

He shakes his head and then shrugs. He freaks me out for a second, when he sits up straighter and acts more like Damien, waving at the flight attendant, snapping his fingers. "Get me a cocktail."

But then I realize—he's just trying to act, in case these folks catch on about us.

I fold my hands in my lap, composed, trying my best to be Zoe. But anyone who is controlled by Xintra will see there's no charcoal fog over our heads and know immediately that we're awake. I need this plane to take off fast.

I try to relax, looking out the window, waiting for the plane to start moving. Hopefully a BMW will still be waiting for us when we arrive.

The plane rumbles and Tre talks to his MeToo device.

"My mom called me back forty-one times," he says. "I'm messaging her now." He talks to his phone. "Reply. 'Where are you, mom?' Send."

Pause.

"Reply. 'Why aren't you in Germany?' Send."

He nods, staring off into space. I still can't get used to these implants. It feels wrong to me, talking to a computer, telling it to reply and send your messages.

"Reply. 'Yeah, I suppose that was a stupid thing to say. I know it's been more than twenty years. Stay inside, Mom. Get groceries. Big weather coming. I'm coming to you. Promise.'" He pauses. "Yes, please send."

15

EMBER

I pet Axel, and a dam breaks inside me. Sobs shake my whole body, and emotion comes hurtling out in gurgles and tears and wails. I melt into the seat, panting, wiping the tears and snot from my face.

I cry until there are no more tears, no more gasps, and no more aching inside my throat and chest. "Please help me be strong," I whisper, asking for support from Lodima, from Mom, from the universe and from God. My trembling body stills at the request, and I'm able to take deep breaths that inflate my chest and my resolve. My ember is still lit.

Maddie glances at me in the rearview mirror. "Hey, Emb," she says. "You okay?"

I nod and wipe my face. Whatever Trinity is, it's lethal, and it's not going to let me go. But I'm not going down without a fight.

Jared turns around and squeezes my fingertips, and we stay that way for a long while. The car hums a bronze color, mixed with the indigo blue *whop, whop, whop* of the windshield wipers and the peppermint green of the spray of the water beneath the tires.

When I can talk, I tell them what happened with Lodima. I dig my hand into the waistband of my shorts. Only two of Mom's letters survived my attempted murder.

The envelopes are muddy and wet. I remove the first letter and separate the moist pages, careful not to tear them. I lay them on the seat to dry before opening the plastic containers and looking at the various shaped rocks. I touch a couple silver-colored stones and a black one. Another has a red tint to it.

"What's that?" Jared asks.

"Rocks," I say. "From Lodima's house."

"So some guy's trying to mow you down with his car and you're carrying a container of rocks. Why?" Jared turns to look out the front window.

"They're magnetic, I guess. Lodima said I needed them. But I don't know why."

"Let me see those," Maddie says, holding out her hand. I place a silver-looking one in her palm. She drives with one hand and glances at it. "Looks like a rare earth magnet. They've got neodymium, dysprosium, samarium, iron, and boron in them."

I squint at her. "You some kind of Rain Man when it comes to geology or something?"

"Yeah, how'd you know that?" Jared asks.

Maddie shrugs and hands the stone back to me. "I've had to take a lot of science classes. Plus, don't you remember when we went to that summer camp at the mining museum?" She makes eye contact in the rearview mirror.

"Kind of. But that was, like, in middle school. I don't remember anything about rare-earth magnets."

"They're super strong."

"Yeeeah, I'd assume."

"And.... they lose their magnetic properties when heated beyond one hundred and seventy degrees. Which is interesting because neodymium is used in welder helmets."

"Okay. Do they undo crazy witchcraft spells cast inside earth energy vortexes?"

"I don't know jack about spells, sister. Sounds like your domain. But don't you remember that cool experiment they did at camp? They connected a whole strip of neodymium magnets and then placed them in a circle around a metal top—you know, the toy kind you spin? They didn't touch the top, but the magnetism actually caused the thing to spin. It was cool. Nothing actually touched it."

"Don't remember," I say. For a long time, science was my thing. But maybe Mom was so into crystals and rocks, I just automatically rejected any knowledge about earth science.

I dig deeper in the plastic container and come across a long beaded necklace with a dangling ankh cross. I put it around my neck, and the silver pendant sits low on my belly. It's as if Lodima bought stock in a company that made ankh crosses. I pull out a couple other crystals that look like the ones on the necklace Lodima gave me when I was Oshun.

Laying them out on my lap, I type in descriptions of the

crystals into Google. *Shimmery red copper colored stone.*
Google's answer: goldstone.

I pull out another stone. A small royal blue one.
Google suggests azurite.

I put them back inside the plastic box and close the lid.

The Book of the Dead from Lodima's house sits on the
seat, open and facedown. Its pages are wet and muddy and
stuck together. I wipe the water off the black leather cover
—it's embossed with a gold Egyptian drawing of a man's
body with the head of either some sort of fox or horse.

"What's that?" Jared asks.

"Some book that was in her house. I felt like it was
important, so I grabbed it."

I flip through a few pages, listing what appear to be
spells, then some drawings and information about chan-
neling spirit entities and manipulating magnetic and electric fields. That has to be important. There's also more
about ancient heka ceremonies. Constellations. The Belt of
Venus. Ivory wands used to draw protective circles.

It's all a bit overwhelming and makes me feel like
spiders are crawling across my neck, like I'm back inside
the basement of Trinity. I shut the book.

Jared's phone rings and I catch a glimpse of the screen
when he pulls it out of his pocket. It says *Gram,* and there's
a picture of her, dressed in red flannel, proudly standing
next to her garden of pink tulips.

"Don't answer," I say. "She's going to make me go see a
shrink."

"Maybe. Maybe not," Jared says. He slides his fingers
across the screen to answer. "Yo, Gram."

I can hear Gram's voice on the line, but it's like those

old Charlie Brown cartoons where the teacher's voice sounds like *wah-wah-wah.*

"Yeah," he says. "Uh-huh. Really?"

Maddie watches him with wide eyes, and my heart pounds. Gram better not convince him to abort our LA trip.

"Okay, sure." Then he hangs up. He glances at me, as Maddie slows to a stop at a light. "Looks like we're headed back to Leadville."

"Why?" I practically scream. "Come on, Jared! You promised you'd take me to the airport. Maddie bought those tickets!"

"Yeah, but no need to go to LA when your boyfriend is in Leadville."

16

NISHA

Tre stands outside the passenger side of the car, leaning in through the open window. "She's not here," he says.

"Maybe that's a good thing," I say, sitting in the driver's seat. "Do you really think you're ready? Is Damien really gone for good?"

I rocked back and forth between the two identities for a long time. So did Ember. And I woke up a hell of a lot slower than Tre. I don't want him to slide back into Damien again, and I'm wary of the potential that I, too, might lose myself to Zoe and Trinity's power. It could happen, especially if Xintra discovers the stone I buried that disrupts her electromagnetic connection with the vortex.

A little wave of guilt sweeps through my chest. I put everyone in danger when I asked that intern to send out that email blast. When those rebirthers wake up, Xintra will feel it sooner than later. I need to figure out a way to give them more time to escape her grip and to use the financial resources she's given them.

Tre pats the roof of the car. "It's cool," he says. "I got this."

An old man with a John Deere baseball hat passes on the sidewalk across the street, head down, wearing a medical mask. Tre watches him shuffling down the hill toward the empty downtown. Not a single other car on the street. A couple of Victorian houses look tired and worn with broken windows; others look polished with fresh paint. But most of them stand empty—because of Xintra.

"Where're you going now?" he asks.

"Back to Trinity."

Tre looks at me, incredulous. "Come on. You can't do that."

"I have some things I need to do."

"Nisha... she'll know what you've done."

I shrug and place my hand on the gearshift.

"C'mon. You got out—you're *home*. Stay. We could go grab something to eat. That is, if she hasn't shut off my credit card yet." He squints down the street. "But doesn't look like much is open. Ghost town."

He turns his gaze to the turquoise house sitting up on the hill, ringed by a bent chainlink fence. "Never mind. I can't leave this place. Caius is after Ember. I saw it in my vision. But I don't know where they are."

"Yeah," I say. He stands upright and taps the roof of the BMW a couple times. He and Ember don't need Xintra's bullshit. They need to get on with their lives. The rest is for me to handle.

"Oh, and I sent that email to the feds," he says.

"Did you show documentation?" I ask.

"Yeah, of the Chinese collusion. Email strings having to do with the FDA payoff for fast-track approval."

"We'll see how much the storms affect everything," I say. "Whether federal investigators can really shut down MeToo—or if all their resources will be tapped."

"Let's just hope the storms die down." He sighs deeply.

I shake my head. "You'd think with the two of us being on the inside, we'd know how to stop them. But honestly, I can't remember jack—and I sure don't know how to reverse spells with that amount of energy."

"Me neither." He nods slowly, his eyes cast to the ground.

"You coming inside or what?" The voice is sharp, and I duck down to see out the passenger window. A gray-haired lady—Ember's grandma— stands on the porch. She wears a red windbreaker and puts a hand on her hip.

"I guess that's your cue," I say, putting the car into drive. "Good luck explaining everything."

"Be careful, I guess?" He frowns.

We gaze at each other for a long time. We were tied together in so many ways, but now we're free. It's weird to say goodbye.

"I will." I pull away and, in the rearview mirror, watch Tre say something to the old lady. He grins and tosses a hand in the air to keep things friendly. Good thing that boy can turn on the charm. This ought to be the biggest boyfriend test there ever was.

17

EMBER

The house looks dark and empty like usual when we drive up.

I fling open the car door before Maddie even comes to a full stop. "Ember Trouvé!" she yells. Mads is going to make a perfect mother someday.

The crooked sidewalk trips me, but I catch myself on my fingertips. When I look up, there he is.

Tre. Not Damien, but *Tre*. It's not the physicality of him that tells me; it's the energy of him. His softness, openness. His quick laugh, the way he throws his arms wide for me.

I just swallowed the sun, radiating warmth and brightness and everything that makes you feel like you can get up each day. He is alive. And he is Tre. I stumble with my arms outstretched, gasping and laughing and squealing as though the world was suddenly painted in gold. He jogs down the concrete steps to me, grinning. He is really here.

I fling my hands around his neck and press my cheek

against his broad chest—the only solid thing in this terrifying world.

"Ember," he whispers into my hair.

He cups my head with his hands, his thumbs grazing my temples, and our foreheads touch, his sky blue eyes fierce, our lips just centimeters apart.

"Oh my God," I cry out. My throat is tied off with invisible string. "I—"

My words vanish into his mouth. His bottom lip below mine, he kisses me. Once. Twice. A momentary pause, our mouths parted just long enough that it robs my breath before my lungs capture it again.

His mouth is soft and perfect and just what I remembered, and a swimming sensation flows along my nerves, and then I'm overcome with a profound gratefulness and torrent of emotion. Our mouths separate, and the tears drip down my cheek, my body convulsing in total relief. He's Tre. He's alive. He's in Leadville and in my arms. We made it. Us.

His lips brush my forehead and then drop to my temple along my hairline, and he runs his nose along my face and hair. I inhale the skin on his neck, pressing my lips against him, pressing my palms into the nape of his neck. His name is written, in bold screaming caps, on my heart. Underlined a thousand and one times.

"And you thought *we* were PDA." Maddie's voice reminds me that we have an audience. That not only is he here in Gram's front yard, he is meeting everyone for the first time.

A laugh slips through my tears, and I turn around and lean into Tre, wrapping my arms around his torso. He pulls me close, tucking his hand around my waist, firm on my ribcage. We face my brother and Mads, who stands with her arms crossed and that snarky smirk on her face.

"So he's *not* a figment of your imagination," Jared says, taking a few paces toward us with an extended hand. "I'm Jared."

Tre reaches out and shakes his hand. "Tre."

"I'm Maddie." She moves forward but brushes off Tre's extended hand and pulls him in for a hug, patented Maddie style—with me still attached to the other half of his body. "About time you showed up."

Tre and I sit on the green sofa in the living room, facing each other, holding hands. I'm a live wire. I can't stop kissing him, smelling his skin, tasting his lips. I giggle between our kisses.

We quietly talk about the shared terror of being a rebirther, powerful and powerless at the same time, about the creepy rebirthing ceremony, what went wrong, how Zoe dug up my demons, and how I stopped fighting. "I'm so sorry," I whisper, our foreheads touching. We kiss again.

He runs his lips along the side of my head. "We're out," he whispers, grinning.

"Do you remember seeing me on the rooftop?" I ask.

"Kind of, yeah," he says. "Everything went dark pretty quick, and I have a bad feeling about what I... er...Damien did."

I pour everything out about what happened to me— how I got hit by the car and escaped the vortex through the cave, how I found my mom's journal, met Lodima, and nearly got killed merely two hours ago. Tre's emotions rise and fall with my story.

"We have to stop Xintra," he says.

"Can we talk about that later? Right now, I just want to enjoy being with you."

I tilt my forehead onto his.

Maddie's voice breaks the moment. "I can't believe you're really from 1989." She sits across from us on a wooden chair, her palms pressed together, eyes bouncing back and forth between us.

Tre nods and laughs through his nose. We face her, and I lean my head on his shoulder, holding his hand in mine, our thighs touching, his arm around my shoulder. I can't get close enough. If I move away or blink, he'll disappear.

"Okay tell me, what was the top song that year?"

"He's not some sort of party trick," I say, lifting my head and scowling at her. "You can't do that to him."

"Punk or pop?" Tre asks, smiling.

"Pop." Maddie frowns. "Who even listens to punk?"

Gram stands in the corner, eating saltine crackers, listening, watching, sizing us up, untucking a piece of cracker from a back molar with her tongue. I wish I had a magic wand that could break through her stony gaze, her calloused hands and hawklike presence. She didn't believe me. It feels like she still doesn't believe me.

"You thirsty, Tre?" Jared asks, walking to the kitchen.

"Naw, I'm good, thanks," he says, craning his neck to follow Jared behind him. He faces Maddie again. "Well, I wasn't into them, but Milli Vanilli was popular. 'Blame it on the Rain' was a big hit."

"What even *is* that song?" Maddie taps on her cell phone and then shrieks with delight. "You're right! Wow.

Okay..." She plays a little clip of the song. It's horrible, loaded with serious '80s cheese. "Okay, how about this one. What movie—"

"Mads," I whine. Of all the important things hanging over our heads, this is the topic taking up airspace? A 1980s quiz? We have so much to talk about, so much time to catch up on. Mom painted a picture of him before I was born. He woke up. We both survived Trinity. *We both killed people.* We all act as if a few hours ago, some madman didn't just try to run me over. That Lodima wasn't murdered right in front of my eyes. I shiver. Yet at the same time, I'm swooning, over the moon happy that I have Tre on the couch like a regular, normal, amazing boyfriend. How can two feelings be colliding like this inside me?

I look at Maddie with wide eyes. "Could we, ahem, maybe have a minute?"

"Anyone?" Jared asks, walking into the living room with an open box of maple glazed donuts. He's like host extraordinaire.

"How'd you find donuts?" Maddie asks. "This place is a ghost town. I mean, who's even left in Leadville to buy them?"

"Exactly. Why do you think I got them for free from my buddy at Safeway?" Jared says.

I guess that's one good thing about the virus. Free donuts. But that's about it.

Virus. Xintra. Storms. The end of the world. Will my reunion with Tre even matter in three days when the Dark Day comes? I think back to Lodima, her spoon of curry hovering beneath her mouth. "*I have to tell you Ember, you're the only one who can stop this.*"

No. I have been through enough. Someone else can

stop this thing, stop people from disappearing into Trinity, stop people from dying. I'm seventeen. I need to live. Really live. Finally, the piece of my heart that was missing, that ached, is here. Right next to me, with his arm around me. Someone else can save the world.

18

NISHA

The sculpture of the ancient deity Weret Hekau is cold like ice. I touch the carving of the snake sitting on her head and run my fingers over the scepter in her hand before squatting down beside her and digging up the gold stone I had earlier tucked into the ground. Just burying it here isn't enough to entirely disrupt Xintra's control over the rebirthers.

After placing the stone on the dirt floor, I raise the hammer and slam it down onto the rock. The rock bounces around on the ground, but it doesn't crack. What in the hell is this thing made of?

I hit it again and again and again, grunting. I've got a stomach full of nerves, knowing Xintra could storm into this room and find me. One last strike and a small chunk the size of a quarter chips off. I tuck it into my pocket, then bury the large gold rock again.

Next, I slink upstairs and call to Bo and Blu, who lounge on the sofa watching TV. They follow me into the basement, their footsteps landing heavy on the stairs. Too heavy.

"Where are we going?" Blu asks. "Are you taking us to the Bath House again?"

"Not this time," I say, leading them through the dark hallways. The walls are stone and the moist air is cool on my skin. It feels like the change in temperature when you dive to the bottom of a lake.

"I don't like it in here," Blu says, rubbing her arms, so skinny they look like sticks hanging out of her white T-shirt.

I unlock the heavy wooden door that leads to the larger circular cabal room we use for ceremonies. Hundreds of candles still flicker along the edges of the room from the meeting, and the flames create shadows that skip across the walls and dirt floor. The steady dripping from the ceiling is something I never noticed before. Today, it feels spine-chilling. Eerie.

"Are these hieroglyphs?" Bo asks, touching the squiggly lines and shapes and drawings of people with horse heads and skirts.

I stop and squint, trying to remember their meanings. "Yeah, ancient Egyptian."

"How would they have drawn on the walls of a mansion here in the states? I don't get it," he says.

I wave them away from the carvings and lead them farther into the room. We need to move. "The ancient Egyptians, the Mayans, the Incas. They all discovered earth vortex tunnels and eventually found that they all met here in Trinity Forest. That's why their hieroglyphs and stories were similar despite the fact that they all lived in different places on the earth. Same with the ancient

Celtic Druids up north." I stop because I realize they're not following me. I spin around. "Hurry!"

"I don't get it," Bo says, sauntering over to me. "How did they find these tunnels?"

"They had help. Just like they had help with everything else. The pyramids, Machu Picchu." I spin my hand in the air and keep walking. I don't have time for a Trinity history lesson if I'm going to have to stop to coax them forward every five seconds.

"Help from who?" Bo asks.

"From aliens with advanced technology. They learned how they could harness the energy and magnetism of the vortexes for witchcraft. Just like Xintra does."

"Xintra?" Blu asks.

I sigh. "She's leading the show here. You guys, come on. Seriously. Quit with the questions. Let's just get the hell out of here."

Part of me wants to take that damn nose ring of Blu's and hook a leash to it, drag her forward like a bull on a chain. The sound of their feet squishing on the wet earth feels like it echoes. Too loud. Maybe I'm just nervous.

"Zoe, please tell us where we're going?" Bo stops again. When he talks, his dreadlocks bounce on his shoulders and he almost swaggers.

I put my hands on my hips. "Are you fools going to sit there and let Xintra make you murder people? That's what she does. She takes you folks, all sad and down on your luck, traps you in Trinity, and makes you into other people. Horrible people. She uses ancient spells to put her ancestors' spirits inside you. She plops you back out in the world and makes you do bad shit. Is that what you want?"

Their faces, lit faintly by candlelight, cringe. The two of them exchange a look.

"Is that what you want?" I repeat, a little more forcefully this time.

They swiftly shake their heads.

"Then come on."

Man, Nisha is back.

19

EMBER

When Tre and I are upstairs and out from everyone's watchful eyes, I shut the door to my room, turn around, and his lips are on mine. I sink into his kiss, and he pulls my hips toward him, backing us up into the wall. I pull on his waist, and a swelling wave of heat fills me.

"You didn't tell me," I say in between kisses, breathless. "How did you wake up?" There's so much I need to know.

He pulls away for a moment, our mouths inches apart. A current running between our lips. "My mom. I saw my mom." He kisses me again.

"You did?" I pull away, and our eyes lock.

He nods and then shakes his head. "I'll see her tomorrow." That's huge. He has to tell me where and how and what they said, what it was like to see her after being away for so long.

He kisses me again. His tongue moving along my lips, stealing the air in my lungs. I fall into the entangled heat of our mouths. He tastes like nicotine and cola, but our mouths are magnetic. Our hands and bodies crash together, winding around each other.

"I also saw you," he whispers. "Pictures of you, and I started waking up."

He spins us around like we're dancing, so I'm pressed against the wall and he kisses me again. One. Two. Three kisses. He reaches his lips to touch mine while quickly removing his jacket. His touch lights up every nerve on my skin.

Thump. Thump. Thump. Somebody knocks on the door, and I jump. I feel as if a hot poker permanently lives inside me. I wipe my mouth with the back of my hand, irritated. "What?" I say to the door.

Our faces are inches apart, our lips hovering. He runs his mouth up the side of my neck, his breath near my ear, sending a shiver through me. His fingers brush the hair on the nape of my neck.

Jared calls back. His voice is urgent. "Something's going on with Maddie. You gotta come downstairs. Now."

Tre and I freeze, gazing at each other wide-eyed for an instant before turning around and flinging open the door. We follow Jared, who takes the stairs double-time to the living room. The sound of the TV is a dusty maroon color, and a newscaster talks about the hurricanes and tornados bearing down across the United States and South America. "These storms are vying to be the worst in history."

Tre and I exchange a long, pained look, both of us surely thinking the same thing. Xintra. The storms are underway. People will die, and it's all because of Trinity. And us.

My body feels even more leaden when I turn to see

Maddie lying on the sofa, sweat beading on her forehead, her face the color of Gram's dirty white linoleum floor.

"I gave her some Tylenol," Jared says.

"I'm fine," Maddie whispers, waving her hand. "Just a little queasy."

She looks way worse than queasy. She looks horrible. Dark circles sucking her eyes into her skull.

"We should call someone," I say.

Maddie frowns. "Nooo," she says. "Just let me rest here for a few minutes. Ember, you didn't need to come downstairs."

Tre presses his lips together, shaking his head slightly. I can see it in his eyes too—a reflection of the visceral worry, fear and guilt that squeezes me so tight it feels like my skin is on inside out.

The TV is the only sound in the room for several seconds, while we watch her close her eyes. The newscaster's voice sounds urgent. "This has got to be the strangest system of storms we've ever seen, Harry. It's hitting everywhere. The winds are picking up in key places across the state, fueling the fires in Montana."

The TV is interrupted by a loud, hammering sound outside. It's the color of dead leaves. Through the dark curtains, Gram's shape is barely visible. She stands on a ladder by the window, hammering a piece of plywood over part of the glass.

"What's she doing?" I ask.

"She's boarding things up. Monsoon storms are coming," Jared says without looking at me. He kneels down by Maddie, who lies still with closed eyes. Her breath rattles in her chest.

Tre takes a step forward. "We need to call for help—"

Maddie bolts straight up off the sofa like a corpse rising from the dead. "Ember..." she says, wheezing, spit foaming at the corners of her mouth.

Then she begins to cough uncontrollably, choking. The noise is deep and labored, and it spins terrible colors of mud and thick tar into my Color Crayon Brain.

"Mads?" Jared asks, leaning in to her. My heart squeezes tight, and I know this is bad. Really freaking bad. I lunge toward the back side of the sofa, eager to stop the cough, to somehow breathe life into the body that suddenly looks so small, so weak.

I touch her back, and her body convulses; she gasps for breath. Her face turns a pale color, then gray. No. No, no, no, no.

I reach out to hold her shoulders up. "Breathe, Maddie!"

Her body goes limp, and she collapses back onto the sofa, slipping out of my hands. Jared moves in, hovering over her, shaking her, lifting her back up and cradling her head. She's limp, unresponsive. "Mads, hey. Mads?" He leans in close to her then straightens up to look at me. "Call 911!"

Without hesitation, I snatch Maddie's cell phone off the coffee table and dial. As I talk to the dispatcher, Jared leans over Maddie, pumping her chest, then breathing into her mouth. He stops, listens, then repeats. The movements are methodical, without any of the panic I might have brought to the job.

"Breathe, Maddie," Tre says, standing behind Jared. "I'll get her car. Where are the keys?"

The hammering outside and the TV news chatter begin to fade into white noise as I give details about

Maddie's condition and our location to the dispatcher. It's as if I'm not really the one on the phone. My attention is entirely on Maddie, on Jared doing CPR. He breathes, pumps, puts an ear to her lips to listen and feels for a response. Again, breathe, pump, listen.

Tre disappears into the kitchen and the back door slams shut, the sound a dull red in my Crayon Brain.

A terrible buzzing rings in my ears. Flat and gray like construction paper. Gram walks through the front door with a hammer in hand. "Why is the ambulance here?"

Paramedics flood into the small room behind her. Jared and Gram talk to the paramedics but I don't hear anything. The humming. Ringing. It's all happening around me as if I'm not really here. They place Maddie's body—my best friend—onto a stretcher, hook oxygen to her face and hustle to the ambulance out front. Jared is smooth and calm, but he's white as a sheet and his voice quakes when he talks. He races to the ambulance, and climbs inside, while I stand there flat footed, reeling like I'm floating a hundred miles above the action, a ghost who can't move.

My mind replays the same three sentences over and over. *No, this can't be happening. She can't die. No, this isn't happening.* Life was supposed to begin again. It *is* supposed to begin again. With her. With all of us.

Tre appears again beside me, placing an arm around my shoulder. He says something about following the ambulance to the hospital. But I can only sink down into the sofa and stare at the carpet. The same three sentences roll through my brain, eliminating all other thoughts, all other feelings. *No, this can't be happening. She can't die. No, this isn't happening.*

Gram's voice is distant, saying something about

meeting us there, but all I can see is a strange spot on the carpet that has me hypnotized, transfixed. A car door slams shut. An ignition starts and a car drives away. Tre sits next to me on the couch, breathing with me, holding me. Silent. Patient.

Axel jumps onto my lap. His mews are waves of sage green and muddied amber, and that's when I see it—a flash, another vision.

I am standing amid rebirthers who move like zombies toward me. Fear squeezes me like a straitjacket. And just like that, the vision's gone.

My eyes break away from the spot on the carpet to look at Tre's strained face. The virus. Maddie has the virus that's going to kill the world. *Xintra* did this to Maddie. *Maddie might die because of that bitch.*

If we don't do something, Maddie *will* die. Because Xintra won't stop until she wipes us out. All of us.

I hear the TV announcers again, speaking in black tones over video footage of rain and gray sky and wind blowing seawater onto the shore, knocking over a lamppost.

Lodima said it's up to me. I have those magnetic rocks, the weird book from her bookshelf in Maddie's car. But I have no clue what to do next.

It doesn't matter. I jump up from the sofa, anger scorching my skin, my mind, my soul, my heart. My blood pumps furiously through me and I grit my teeth and ball my hands into fists.

"Pissed yet?" Tre asks.

"Hell yeah!"

"Ready to go save the world?"

"Bring it."

Without a word, we know where we're going.

20

NISHA

My magnetic key still works. For now. Yet I know there's a chance I will leave with these two, and Xintra will know, will lock me out, will come after me. And I'll have no way of coming back here to stop anything she does. I can only leave the gold-colored rock beneath the Weret Hekau carving and hope that, after all it's done for me, it will be important to undoing her spell and stopping her control over the rebirthers. But I still don't really know it works, how I can use it against her.

All I know is I can save Blu and Bo. One little dig, one way to steal *something* from Xintra. We wind though a series of chambers and corridors so narrow that both my shoulders brush the stone walls, which extend a good eleven feet high. Despite walking in the pitch black, I know these winding paths by heart.

I open each door with the golden snake bracelet that wraps up my bicep on my arm. Relief flows through me as it triggers the magnetic pull in the vortex, turning the locks made of stone. The familiar click. The familiar hum. The grinding of stone on stone as the doors slide away. This was Xintra's father's discovery; he found the ancient caves that really got things rolling. Of course, James and his Annunaki ancestors had access to the other vortexes for centuries and used them to snatch people from their lives and turn them into puppets, harnessing the magnetism of these places for their spells. I played a hand in that for years. But when James and Xintra got access to Trinity, everything changed. It was the key that unlocked even greater power.

Blu's breath sounds shallow and rapid. "I feel like I can't breathe in here," she whines from behind. "I need to get out. It's, like, too, dusty. Too—"

I spin around. Sweat trickles down my forehead. "Are you serious? You pushed your momma all over the place in that wheelchair. Slept under bridges! This, girl, is doable."

"Yeah, suck it up," Bo says. He squeezes her neck and she nods. I can't really see her face in the light but I hear her take long, deep breaths.

We come to the final door—the exit that will take us to the hole inside the basement of the junker house owned by Xintra in East Los Angeles. I bite my lip, hold up the bracelet key. Blu and Bo stand too close to me, hovering just over my neck. I throw an elbow back at them.

"Do you mind? Some space?"

They both back off, and I hold up my arm to the lock.

The click. The hum. The stone-on-stone grinding. The door opens, slowly, and the cool air from the base-ment blows on my hot face. When the opening is large enough, I walk out into the dim light. The basement looks the same: stacked high with old furniture, kitchen chairs and truck tires, cobwebs and tall standing lamps. Junk.

Blu emerges from the doorway, then out comes Bo. The door, which is tucked into the concrete wall, slams shut like the jaws of an angry crocodile, and he howls. The rock door has trapped his right foot.

He screams in agony and falls to the floor. Blu lurches to help him up. "Shit!" she says.

"My foot! It's stuck!" Bo's face contorts.

Xintra. Does she know? Is that piece of magical stone in my pocket really just a regular old rock that's doing nothing to protect us? A nanosecond later and that door wouldn't have touched Bo. Thank God we're at least on the right side of the vortex.

I pull on his shoulders, my fingers digging into his silky Cleveland Cavaliers jersey, but his foot, caught mid-stride, really is stuck, blocking the heavy stone door from shutting.

"What do we do, Zoe?" Blu flaps her hands like a little kid.

"Nisha. Don't call me Zoe."

"What do we do?" she screams it again, louder now. Her breath smells stale and her hands are balled into fists.

I look at Bo. He grunts, his face taking on an ashen hue. I can tell he's in serious pain.

I crawl along the floor, untie his sneaker and—with a little effort—slip his foot out of the black shoe. The rock door slams shut, barely missing his foot, and the thud from it is so loud it makes my ears ring. The shoe disappears on the other side of the divide.

"There," I say, dusting my hands off on my jeans. "Let's get the hell out of here."

21

EMBER

Police lights flash behind us as Tre and I drive down Harrison Street, headed to Tennessee Pass—the way to Trinity Forest. I look at the speedometer on Maddie's car. I'm going sixty-five miles per hour. Way over the speed limit.

I look in the rearview mirror, groan, and pull the car over slowly. The rain pounds on the roof. "Shit."

"It's fine," Tre says. "Just be cool."

I exhale through rounded lips, trying to calm my nerves. "You *do* know that I am supposedly dead—or missing, depending on who I want to be—right?"

"Yeah," he says. "We'll need to spend some time getting identities straight after this."

The police officer arrives at my window and taps on it twice. I roll it down, letting in a rush of cool air and a gust of raindrops. The rain beats down on the officer and it's as if he's standing fully clothed in a shower.

"In a hurry?" he asks.

"Yeah, I guess." I can't see his eyes because of the flashing lights.

"You were going sixty-five in a thirty zone, miss," he says.

"My friend was—"

"License and registration?"

I look at Tre and he shrugs. "This is my friend's car," I say. "And... sure. Here's my license." I swivel around to retrieve the wallet that I was so desperately seeking earlier from the duffel bag on the back seat.

"Does your *friend* know you're driving her vehicle?"

I nod. "The ambulance just took her to the hospital. She has the virus. So I'm trying to follow." I'm surprised they even spend time patrolling Leadville anymore. So few people live here since the outbreak.

I hand the skinny officer my driver's license and wait, licking my lips. He gazes at it, using a flashlight, and frowns. Then, with one finger, he wipes beneath his nose.

I realize I should have just dyed my hair before I left. On my license, I look like Ember. But now, I look like Oshun.

My fingernails dig into the palms of my hands, and I can feel stress sweat dripping down the inside of my T-shirt from my armpits. Xintra is going to destroy the world, and I'm getting pulled over for speeding.

"This is expired," he says finally, handing the wet license back to me.

"Really?" I ask, squinting at it and wiping a couple drops of water off the front.

"Expired two years ago. And it doesn't look much like you. This girl went missing a long time ago. It was a pretty big deal around here."

"Well, it's still me. I'm back. I just haven't said anything to anyone yet," I say, shrugging. "I need to get to the hospital."

"Right. Right. Where did you get that ID anyway? Were you friends with that girl—Ember?"

"I *am* Ember." I open the wallet, my fingers shaky. I wasn't old enough to have any credit cards when I left for Trinity, but I have my debit card, my school ID, a couple of gift cards. "Here. I have these," I spread them in my hand like playing cards from which to choose.

The bubble wrap in my chest expands, and I struggle to keep down the rising panic in my throat. I need to get going.

He looks at the cards, clears his throat. "You really say you're Ember, huh? Because you look familiar, but not like her...."

I glance back at Tre. He bites his lip and pets Axel, who jumped in the car with us back at the house.

"Please, Officer. Maybe you can just let it slide this one time?" My voice is sweet and I bat my eyes. "My friend might be dying." Maybe he'll feel sorry for me, think I'm attractive, *something.*

He signals to another officer, who I assume has been in the police vehicle, and an older man with salt-and-pepper hair approaches the car. The rain continues to beats its fists on the roof of the car, a sound that emerges in my mind as faint forest-green starbursts surrounded by what looks like a swirling black hole.

The two of them talk quietly to each other. The skinny cop—whose badge says "Ron Neligh"—looks at me down his nose, frowns, and then turns back to the other officer, whispering something.

I consider just hitting the gas and making a run for it, and I glance at Tre to confirm my thought with a quick nod. He shakes his head before leaning over to me, talking softly.

"You'll make it worse if you run," he says. For such a rebel, he's become so damn practical.

The red and blue lights pulse, and scratchy conversations come in and out of the police radios, as the two cops talk for a good ten minutes. The older salt-and-pepper-haired officer turns his back to us and begins talking in a low voice on a cell phone.

"My friend is sick," I plead loudly. "I am who I say I am. Do I look like a criminal? Really?" I'm babbling. Trying so hard to be a friend, to be safe, to be the girl who they can't help but want to let go. But I'm not succeeding. I am a loony fraud, and they're suspicious.

"Who are you then, miss?" the salt-and-pepper officer asks.

"Ember Trouvé."

"Not Oshun?"

I feel like I just got knocked down the stairs. I'm tumbling, out of control, hitting my head on every single step. Dizziness sweeps me, and I shake my head emphatically—too emphatically. "No..."

He squints at me. "You sure do look a lot like her."

Of course he recognizes Oshun. For being a smart girl who was at the top of her class, I should have expected this. I should have planned for this. Should have looked at my ID before I got in the car. Should have used the hair dye. But I didn't do any of those things. My cheeks feel hot. The invisible bubble wrap expands and crinkles beneath my ribcage.

He stands at attention. "Please step out of the vehicle."

Panicked, I look at Tre for help.

"She's Ember. I can vouch for that Officer." He unbuckles his seat belt and opens the passenger's side door—but freezes.

"Stay right where you are!" The other officer says, approaching from the other side of the car in a defensive crouch. Holy shit.

"You can call my brother. My grandma," I say.

Tre leans in, clasping my hand over the console, and I squeeze it tight. This is going terribly wrong. Terribly, terribly wrong. Shit. Why did I have to speed?

"Out of the vehicle now!" The officer puts his hand on his gun holster.

My heart races, and slowly, I open the car door and stand with my hands up in the air. Officer Neligh takes my bicep and begins to lead me away from the car. Away from Tre. Away from stopping this war on the world. Away from saving Maddie. This can't happen. I've lost control of my life and my free will too many times.

I wriggle out of his grasp. "No." My voice is abrupt. "No...I'll leave the car here and walk to where I'm going. You don't need a license to walk, right?"

"Emb, we'll figure it out," Tre calls from the passenger's side of the car. "Just stay calm."

The officer squeezes my arm tighter, hurting me, and I glare at him.

He drags me away from the car.

"Listen, call my grandma. She'll tell you everything," I say. "Call her. Call my brother. He'll tell you everything, too."

Shit. Shit. Shit. This is all imploding.

The older policeman raises his brows and talks to me like a child. "You do know that faking your own death is called pseudocide. Not necessarily illegal, but you can be charged with fraud for a whole host of things. Fraudulent death certificate. Insurance fraud, if money is involved. Or... you could get one big bill for the false search-and-rescue operation. That is, if you really are the missing girl Ember Trouvé."

22

NISHA

Bo's foot is probably broken. He's writhing in the car, and as I drive, I catch him flexing every muscle as he tries to endure the pain.

"We really need to take him to the hospital," Blu says, leaning forward from the back seat. Her sapphire blue hair is damp with sweat and strands of it stick to her temple.

"We will," I say. "I just need to make a stop first."

"I'm getting him out. Let us out right here!" Blu shouts, shaking my arm.

I pull up to a stoplight, and the car hums. She puts her hand on the door to climb out, but pauses. Next to us: a white stucco house and a metal garage sprayed with bright orange and green graffiti.

Blu's face scrunches up as she takes in the unfamiliar landscape. "Where are we?"

"Los Angeles."

"But I came to Trinity from Sedona. And this is *not* anywhere near Arizona."

"What part of this don't you get?" I ask, turning around to look at her. "We were in a vortex. A time vortex. We came through an underground tunnel. With ancient carvings. Of course you're not in Arizona!"

"God, when did you become such a bitch?" she asks, sneering at me.

"Since I woke up and found out that I was gonna suck your life away. Then I save your ass, and you're asking stupid questions."

Bo shuts his eyes tight. "I'm okay."

"You can get out if you want," I say, but I don't look at Blu. I stare ahead at the stoplight, waiting for her to open the door.

In the rearview mirror, I catch her crossing her arms and slumping in her seat. She purses her lips and looks out the window. I guess she's coming with me.

I take us through the city on woven patches of highway, tailing other drivers, zigzagging through traffic. I don't remember all my days as Zoe, only vague recollections of driving through these streets on Annunaki errands. But I drive like I always have—more efficiently than everyone else, always seeing four cars ahead.

We wind through Los Angeles until I come to a red awning beneath the sign *Crystal Matrix*. I park and turn around to point a finger at Bo and Blu like they're small children. "Stay."

Just inside the store's front window sits a series of clay pots housing tall spiky white and amber crystals. The rest of the shop is filled with lines of clear glass shelves showcasing rocks of various sizes and colors—pink and green, turquoise and blue, red and gold. One fist-sized polished stone has been carved into the shape of a human skull.

A short, dark-haired woman wearing a pink tracksuit saunters to the front. "What can I do for you?"

"I need to know what this stone is," I say, pulling out the chunk of Ember's stone. "It has something to do with magnets."

She takes the stone and lifts a pair of glasses dangling by a beaded chain around her neck. She squints at the stone. "Iron. Has iron in it."

"Okay," I say.

"It has a high magnetic permeability. Ferromagnetism. It contains unpaired electrons, each with a small magnetic field of its own. They align with each other and persist even when the magnetic field is removed."

It doesn't make a damn bit of sense to me, but if it somehow messes up Xintra's spiritual connections to us, then I'm buying a shitload of them.

"Do you sell more stuff like this?"

"Sure do," she says.

After disappearing into a back room, she comes back with a shoebox full of the stones. I ask for 150 and she begins counting them out—just enough to block Xintra's grip on me and the others and give us more time before she knows we've gone AWOL. *I hope.*

The next quick stop is a Beverly Hills mansion. Its driveway meanders through a lush garden of emerald green moss, grass and palm trees. I pass a white fence with a horse pasture before arriving at the gray Spanish house on the hill.

I ring the doorbell, and a tall redhead comes to the door. She recognizes me immediately. "Zoe."

"Nisha, not Zoe," I say. "Just like you're not Ciara; you're Valerie. I'm done with the Annunaki. I'm assuming you are too. I'm guessing you got the email with the pictures and you remember everything?"

She blinks, licks her lips and then gazes out at the opulent grounds behind me. Valerie disappeared three years ago on a yacht in the Bermuda Triangle, and now she works as supermodel, seducing and framing high-powered people not favorable to Xintra's regime. This estate has to be worth at least thirty-five million dollars. She nods slowly. "Yeah, I'm... confused."

I don't know if she's fully awake now or dancing between two lives. When she does wake up, she'll need time—and a stone that can disrupt Xintra's connection to her. I drop a box with about fifty pouches containing the 150 stones I bought at *Crystal Matrix*. "If you're confused, this should help you figure it out."

"I don't get it." She sneers at the box at her feet and then picks up one pouch, dangling it between two fingers like it's covered in slime. "Why are you here?"

"When is your next meeting with the other rebirthers?"

"I'm supposed to go to a party tonight."

"There's a list of names in the box. Give each person on this list one pouch of these stones, along with their own list of deliveries," I say. "Ship them FedEx if you have to. Just move fast. It's crucial if we want to save their lives. Think of it like an old-school chain letter."

"What in the world is this? What will some rocks do to save people's lives?"

"They contain something magnetic that can disrupt

your connection with Xintra. You all can check in with me through that email address that's included in the list of names."

She puts a hand on her hip. "Why?"

"Xintra will destroy us all when she discovers we woke up—and it's my fault everyone is waking up."

"*You* sent that email to me?"

"Someone did it on my behalf. But it shook something loose in you, right?"

She nods slowly. Her eyes shift again, and I see Valerie, the chiseled statue of a girl who had deep cracks and insecurities when she came to the vortex.

"Report back to me. The more we stick together and communicate, the better chance we have of not becoming slaves to Xintra—or dying in the storms."

A half hour later, Blu ducks her small body beneath Bo's arm to help him stand in front of the hospital. The automatic doors to the emergency room entrance open for them, but they don't move. Blu gazes wide-eyed at me. This has got to be a trip for her.

"Thanks for the ride," Bo says. "Where are you going?"

"I've got some people to visit."

"I don't get what just happened to us. Who this Xintra is," Bo says. "But if you wait for me, we can help you."

"Just get your foot fixed," I say. He and Blu just need to move on.

The truth is, outside of waking people up and ruining Xintra's connection with her rebirthers, I really don't know *how* to stop the storms. So I just prep Bo and Blu, telling them to hunker down. I drove them to a hospital pretty far inland from the coast. I just hope they survive what's going to happen next.

"You two have your whole lives in front of you," I say. Bo grins, and I point at him. "Don't take it for granted. You've only got one life."

"You sound like a freaking motivational poster." Blu rolls her eyes. But Bo hears me. He puffs up his chest a little and gives a thumbs-up. Blu smiles, and they limp into the hospital.

23

EMBER

The interview room at the police station feels like a real jail cell. Hot and stuffy. White walls. Just two chairs and a table. The officers make me sit for a long time alone. They lied—they aren't asking me questions; they're holding me prisoner. I sit, leaning my elbows on the table, tugging at my hair with my hands. I tap my foot quickly.

"Hellooooo?" I scream. "I didn't break a law! A speeding ticket and expired license does not allow you do this!" Or at least, I don't think it does.

Finally, a woman in a dark business suit opens the door. Some sort of badge hangs off her lapel. Behind her in the hallway, Tre argues with a police officer and jerks his hands in the air.

"Give her a fine, whatever, but you can't just lock her in a room!" he shouts.

My heart surges. I can see that same rebel who helped tear down the Berlin Wall. Tre. *My Tre*, really and truly here. We briefly make eye contact. His blue eyes fierce, his jaw firm. "Ember!" he shouts.

The door slams shut and the woman blocks my way. She wears her blonde hair in a pixie cut that shows off elf-like ears. She's kind of pretty, probably in her forties.

I push her aside a little and reach for the handle. "I wouldn't do that if I were you," she says.

"Come on, I am not a criminal." I stay in her space, an inch from her shoulder, my hand on the door handle. "I could sue you for wrongful imprisonment." I have no idea if this is true, but it sounds good.

She touches my elbow, an effort to lead me back to the table. "Let's talk some, okay?"

I sigh and follow, sinking into the plastic chair across from her. I weave my fingers through the beads of my necklace, the one from Lodima's house with the ankh cross pendant.

"We wanted to get some fingerprints because there seems to be some confusion about your identity. There were a number of news stories about the connection between Oshun and Ember Trouvé that created quite a stir. The first one was written in..." She looks at her notes. "*Beats* magazine."

"You can't hold me like this. Looking like a star is not a crime." I brush the wet hair off my face.

"A dead star." She doesn't look up as she reaches into her briefcase. "And you *were* driving without a valid license and operating a vehicle that apparently does not belong to you. And speeding." She looks up and makes eye contact.

"It's my friend's car. She's in the hospital. I told you, I'm Ember Trouvé."

"The missing girl." She purses her lips and nods slowly.

"I was found."

"Right." She opens a brown folder on the table and removes some papers. She taps to straighten them in a pile on the table. "Well, we spoke to your grandmother as you requested."

I exhale. "Good. So she told you I'm Ember but I haven't been ready to go to the police and the press since coming home. That's fair, right? So I can go now? Just write me a ticket or whatever?"

"Well..." Her voice sounds like she's going to deliver bad news.

I lean forward, placing my palms on the table. "Well *what*?"

"Your grandmother said you've been talking about some things that are... unusual. You told her you went to a haunted forest. That you subsequently disappeared in a time vortex?" She tilts her head and bites her lip.

The expression makes me want to vomit. It's the kind of composed condescension reserved for powerless old people stuck inside nursing homes.

My heart twirls in my chest, a hamster on a wheel. Gram told me she wanted to help me, protect me. But she's basically buying the padlocks and handing these people the keys. Why would she do this?

"She *heard* how I nearly got killed by a car."

"Killed?"

I seal my lips tight. If I tell this woman about Lodima, will I be accused of murdering her? "I mean, how a bad driver cut...me...off." I give a small shrug. I don't know how to respond to all this. If I tell the truth, I look like a lunatic. Asylum guaranteed.

"And your boyfriend is someone named Tre? But you think he's really posing as Damien Pratt, the MeToo tech executive who died yesterday in a plane crash."

I clench my jaw and give a swift, tiny nod. "Yes, the guy who was in the car with me? Who's now out there in the lobby telling you how stupid you guys are for holding me?"

"Yes, the guy with you in the car is out in the lobby arguing with officers. But he said his name isn't Tre. It's Ted."

"*Ted?*" What is Tre even thinking? Unless he just doesn't want to get into the same kind of identity crisis I'm facing right now. That would mean two of us being withheld for questioning.

"You look strikingly like Oshun. The pop star? She was found dead, apparently."

I exhale, shake my head. "Lawyer please."

"We'd like to take your fingerprints," she says, pulling out an ink pad and a document with squares on it. "To help us settle all this."

24

THE REBIRTHED

Lilly

"Cut!" the director yells, snapping his clapboard shut. "Let's take two."

I lift up the life-size van, lightweight and made of aluminum, and slide my leg out from beneath it. The silicone rubber makeup makes my leg itch like mad. The makeup looks so real, for a half second I think my leg really is bloody and chewed up.

Normally, I'd feel proud of this zombie flick. I've worked to dull people's sensitivity to violence and gore for the cause for so long, to help prepare for the real genocide. The idea of it has always made me radiate, but today, looking at the fake gash that reaches from my kneecap to my upper thigh makes me feel gross. A sickly feeling, really. I don't ever recall feeling like this. It's sorta like I'm standing on a merry-go-round—dizzy and just trying to hang on.

"You're not going to run away this time, are you?" my assistant asks with a chuckle. He's some stupid skinny guy who, I think, calls himself Milt. He's been teasing me since yesterday. I was watching that TV show *Beehive Diaries* on reruns in my hotel room, and I suddenly felt...confused. Like I wasn't me anymore. It's a little fuzzy, but somehow, I wound up wandering around downtown LA. I felt so disoriented, I actually barfed in a planter for a palm tree. Some photographer got an action shot, too.

And then today, I got that email with the photos of the missing actress from *Beehive Diaries* who looks identical to me, and photos of her mother, all red lips and dripping with jewelry. The whole thing made my head spin, like I literally wanted to hide under my pillows in bed.

Why do I feel this way? Why does everything suddenly feel so uncertain? So untrue?

"Coffee?" Milt asks as we walk to my trailer.

"Yeah," I say brushing my hair out of my eyes. "And put some vodka in it."

* * *

Pete

The acrid smoke fills my lungs and I cough, stepping over the dead bodies and debris strewn from the train crash. A man in a suit lying facedown. A severed leg. A woman's red high-heeled shoe.

I stare at the shoe for a long time and tears pinch the back of my eyes. I shake my head. Ah man, that familiar feeling—it rips through me again, along with a few random memories. In one, I carry a skateboard in one hand, a joint in the other, tossing the hair out of my eyes as I climb the stairs of a basement that smells like, I don't know, flowery air freshener. *My old house.* A guitar riff from a Nirvana song. A name. *Pete Alaban.*

I shake it off and stumble away from the train wreckage, somewhere in the suburbs outside Boston. But I trip on something. I stop and look down. It's the other red high-heeled shoe, patent leather and shiny.

Just like Mom's.

Another memory hits me square in the jaw. Mom, standing in a black business suit, smoothing the skirt down with her hands, flashing an uncertain smile.

"Do the red shoes look like too much for a job interview? Too flashy?" she asks.

I eat Froot Loops at the kitchen table—oak, with little carved scrolls on the edges. The table was passed down from my grandma. "You look awesome, Mom. Just be yourself."

"Awww good advice. Who taught you that?" She gives me a quick peck on the cheek. She waves over her head as she leaves the house. "Wish me luck!"

The red shoe in front of me comes into focus. Its heel is broken, and half of it is covered by a piece of jagged white metal, the siding of the train. I lift the metal and see skin and splattered blood. A foot, just a few inches from the shoe.

I turn around and puke into the grass. I caused this accident. Somehow I know it's true, even if I can't remember how. Or why.

Shit. I've got to get out of here.

* * *

Chris

"Melinda." I nod at my secretary and head to my office.

"Mr. Culver, you have an urgent message for a meeting in Colorado. I booked a flight for 11 a.m. today."

I stop in the doorway. "What is it about?"

"The message just said, *Xintra*. Am I pronouncing that right?"

"Of course." The name makes me feel numb and woozy and a mantra reverberates in my head: *I'm here for the cause.*

In my office, seven people wait. Three women and four men, all of them rebirthers. The two non-rebirthers on the team were sent to Los Angeles on assignment to be eliminated by the tsunami.

I greet my collaborators with nods and handshakes, and we settle around the conference table as we would any other meeting. We start with the most pressing issues following the coup in the aftermath of the storms.

"We're freezing the twelve billion dollars in FEMA to minimize disaster relief efforts," says Rick Patton, the plump head of the Federal Emergency Management Agency. "But I'm getting pushback from some congressmen. I'm going to need your help, Lilith."

In her late twenties and wearing a pink business suit, Lilith nods. She runs NX News, one of the largest news organizations in the world—and under the Annunaki influence. She's in charge of propaganda for diverting the public's attention and fueling fear and division.

Seth Matton, the president's chief of staff, barks orders, but I don't hear all of them because my head feels heavy and I feel a little woozy. Seth speaks fervently, his head jiggling with each sentence, but his dark, slicked-back hair doesn't move. It stays stuck close to his head. "President Fein and Vice President Anderson will be scheduled to visit the disaster areas on separate planes on Friday," he says.

It goes without saying that each of those planes will crash via suicide sabs and, as Speaker of the House, Ralph Whittaker will take over as interim president. Even though he's a rebirther, Xintra put the snapdragon in his MeToo implant just in case he goes rogue.

"You're set on establishing the electric fences?" Seth asks, pointing a long finger across the table at Vladimira Get, the homeland security director. The sun shines in her eyes from the window and she squints.

"Yes, the crackdown will ensue amid the disorder, following Operation Fear," Vladimira says. Her voice sounds different, softer than normal, and she touches her fingers to her temples and frowns. I wonder if she feels nauseous like I do.

Lilith, who can make everyone in the TV business turn to jelly with her intense energy and gorgeous movie-star face, speaks up, leaning across the table to Seth. Her lip curls when she talks. "You *will* jail independent journalists who disseminate alternative information, correct? And all officials will stay on talking points."

He nods and shuffles his papers. "How many times do we have to reiterate that to you, Lilith?"

He turns his attention to me. "The fluoride dump is scheduled for water systems worldwide tomorrow. Your people will handle the details."

"It may take time," I say, "but it should have an analgesic effect on the survivors and should subdue the masses." *But why? Why are we subduing people?* "We'll have fresh water systems for rebirthers."

"Vaccination stations are still open in select neighborhoods, correct?"

I nod. "But there's an underground group trying to develop a legitimate vaccine and phase out our version."

"Eliminate them. Fast. A gas leak, a sab. Whatever. Just get it done." His booming voice makes me feel itchy suddenly.

I scratch my head and it sounds too loud. "Yeah," I say distractedly. "Will do."

The room and the faces of the rebirthers surrounding me suddenly go out of focus, and my stomach twists. I gaze at the glossy wood table, hearing bits and pieces of the conversations around me.

"—sabs set the forest fires in Montana and Idaho."

"—taking cover inside a vortex."

"—not entirely ready."

I press my fingers to my lips.

I'm not the only one feeling off. Vladimira blinks and then flips her head around the room, as if she just realized she was sitting here with us. She looks like she's choking on something.

"Let's take a break," I say, standing. "I need a moment. Why don't we all go grab something to eat, use the restroom. We'll reconvene in twenty."

They nod and file out of my office. I close the door, clear my throat, and turn on my laptop. For a few seconds, I simply gaze at the blinking cursor on the screen. I can't remember my password.

What the hell is my password?

I can't remember anything, for that matter. What am I

doing here in this moment? What's my name? Where am I?

My hands hover over the keyboard. I don't even remember how to type. Fear strikes me like a hot iron. I launch out of my chair and shake my hands out, let them hang loose down by my legs, as I pace around the wide-open office.

I light a cigarette and take a long exhale to calm the jittery feeling. Of course; I'm Jeff Culver. Head of the Centers for Disease Control. I've got this.

But a bizarre yearning sweeps through me, an itch I'm dying to scratch. I want to see those photos again. The ones someone anonymous sent me via email. I printed them out. I shouldn't have.

I want to see them. *No.* I want to see them. I need to see them again. *No.*

Electric nerves blast through my body. I scratch my head, though I can't get deep enough to reach the itch. My blood feels caffeinated. I'm like a drug addict.

Dammit. I lunge at my desk and rifle through a stack of papers until I find the photos I printed. A newspaper story with a headline: *Texan Oil Worker Missing in Colorado Woods.* A photo of a guy identical to me: Cowboy hat. Sad eyes. Weathered skin. A tattoo on his arm. My skin tingles. My scalp feels like it's peeling off—burning.

With my left hand, I run my fingers over the bumpy white scar on my right arm while I rummage through a desk drawer with my other hand. I pull out a magnifying glass, then peer closer at the photo. The tattoo on the guy's arm says *Taylor.*

Something cinches in my chest and I drop to my knees, kneeling beneath a heavy waterfall of memories that pound me, one by one, swift and hard—a stream of constant, heavy, rushing emotion. My son. Taylor. A flash of him waving his hands and talking to himself as he paces in our driveway. His dimpled smile, a cigarette hanging out of his mouth, as he climbs into his black Camaro. Roslyn's cherub face and her chubby body swaddled in nothing more than a diaper, lying on her back, kicking her feet in the air. Pain stabs my chest. I see her mom, Maggie, just nineteen years old, a breeze blowing her hair and the surprise and laughter coloring her face as we ride a roller-coaster at the fair.

I fold onto the floor, my forehead resting on the hard tile as memories of my real life drench me.

25

EMBER

I'm a caged lion running tracks into the linoleum floor. I wring my hands, ready for them to put me in handcuffs, tell me I'm accused of fraud or haul me off to some mental ward. But I'm ready to fight. I'll get out.

I try the door handle again. Still locked.

I stop pacing when the lock clicks and Tre enters the room. His eyes are wide and his head is tilted. *This is freaking crazy*, he says with his eyes.

I lunge for him and press my cheek to his chest. "Have you heard from my brother? How's Maddie?"

He shakes his head and my throat tightens. "I don't know anything."

"Tre, we have to stop this." Maddie could die. I can't give that thought any space in my mind. I need to get out of here and take down Xintra. That's my goal. That's my focus.

We hold hands, just inches apart. We're both rebellious. We're both fire. We're both ready to fight back.

"Even if we do get out, will we even be able to get into Trinity Forest again?" he asks.

"Why wouldn't we get into Trinity again?"

"My MeToo device was turned off. And... If Xintra knows I'm awake, my vortex key won't work anymore. And now, I'm afraid she'll use the implanted MeToo device to track me."

The ultimate irony. He pushed out those same implantable devices as Damien, and now he himself might be tracked. I pushed out the virus as Oshun, and now my best friend might die from it.

"Your grandma is fighting to get you admitted on a psychiatric hold."

"You're kidding," I sputter. I should have known—she really does think I'm crazy. "But...she *met* you. She heard Jared and Maddie... you, me, all of us talking about what's happening."

He shakes his head and shrugs. "She says she's worried about you. Unfortunately, I don't have much pull. I'm just a random guy who showed up at your house today."

"There's got to be a way to tap into the money we had as Oshun and Damien. Either get big-time lawyers in here or maybe even"—I lean in and whisper—"buy off the cops?"

He sits down at the table and presses his fingers to his temples. "Ember, a story surfaced online saying Damien died in a plane crash. I don't have access to anything from my rebirthed life. My credit cards, bank accounts— everything has been revoked. I'm sure you're in the same boat."

I sigh, sink down into a chair and put my forehead onto the table. I pop back up suddenly. "Okay well, maybe at least *you* can do some work on the outside. Maybe you go on TV? Say you're alive? Issue a warning?"

"That's a good idea." He nods and his eyes dart around the room.

Yet still, we're as clueless about how to truly stop Trinity outside in the real world as we've ever been. Who would believe Tre's message? Won't everyone just think he's a nut job? Worse, what if he was suspected of pseudo-cide and fraud like me? No wonder he said his name was Ted.

"Okay, so Lodima is dead. I've got a pile of magnetic rocks that I think are important and *The Book of the Dead*. I don't know what to do with them. Do you? You remember anything from being Damien?"

"Not a whole lot. But I do know that Xintra regularly called on spells from that book. So maybe I can get it from the car and look through it."

He holds my hand from across the table. His touch tingles.

An officer barges into the room. "We need to ask you to leave, sir."

Tre glares at the guy. "You know you can't keep her here like this."

The officer touches his gun in the holster on his waist with his right hand and jerks his head toward the hallway. "Out."

Tre grits his teeth and shakes his head before standing. He leans over to me, whispering into my hair. It sends a tingle down my neck. "We'll get you out of here, break down the walls if necessary."

"What are you, an Avenger?" I smile, looking up at him.

"A what?" He pulls back and frowns.

I laugh through my nose, forgetting that there are parts of this generation he really doesn't get, despite his time as Damien. "Never mind."

As Tre leaves, I call out to him. "Don't forget to feed Axel!"

The door slams shut with a thud.

26

EMBER

I'm officially booked into the psychiatric unit of the hospital. And now, the sun is up and I sit on a hard bed, where I seriously sweat buckets last night, unable to sleep, staring at the vanilla-colored walls of my claustrophobic room. I rub my hands over the pant legs of my blue scrubs, over and over, as if I could wipe this whole nightmare away.

"Knock, knock!" A nurse with a high ponytail and a pink smock opens the door with her back to me, holding a tray with two hands. I presume it carries whatever slop I'm getting for breakfast.

She kicks the door shut and spins around to face me. "I'm Cassandra—" Her face freezes in an openmouthed smile; her almond-shaped eyes grow bigger. *Oshun,* I realize. She recognizes me as the famous pop star.

"Oh," she says. "You're—"

"Ember."

She pauses, balances the tray on one hand, and looks at a piece of paper she produces from her pocket. "Right," she says, nodding quickly and stuffing the paper in her pocket. She's a video run on fast forward, swiftly setting the tray on a small built-in desk in the room and flashing an uncomfortable smile, then glancing at the door, pausing, scratching behind her ear. "Okay, then. I'll give you a tour, tell you what's coming up for your stay. We'll do the full psych assessment, and then we can spend some time outside before group therapy and lunch."

She waits for my reply, and her gaze drops to my foot. I can't stop my heel from tapping on the linoleum floor.

She tilts her head. "It'll be okay, Ember. I know this is a lot for you. But this is not a prison. We're here to help you. Really." She seems sweet. Genuine. Yet she *is* imprisoning me.

I swallow and stare so intensely, so furiously, I feel like my gaze could set her on fire. I bite my lip, glance at the window. I'm on the third floor. I could jump.

I look back at the ponytailed nurse, deciding to take a different tack. "You know who I am, right?"

"Ember Trouvé, according to your admittance papers. Do you think you're someone else?"

"I *am* the singer you thought I was when you first walked in. My name is Oshun. And I have a load of money I could sue you guys with. Because this *is* a prison. To me."

She sighs. "Okay. Well, I'm sorry you feel that way."

My shoulders slump. "I have to go home. Please." Third tried-and-failed approach: begging.

Cassandra walks me around the floor, showing me where I will spend the next several days. I follow numbly. We poke our heads into a small conference room that smells like peanuts and has eight folding metal chairs. Orange classical music plays softly from the speakers. She shows me a red padded room I can go into and hit and throw things if I feel angry. A game room with a ping-pong table with a broken net and a green card table stained with some sort of sticky brown substance. A big-screen TV plays the news with the sound off. The screen shows a long line of people with surgical masks waiting for a free vaccine. Words flash on the screen. *Pandemic. National emergency. Eight thousand people dead.*

"Ember." The nurse has a soft voice. She takes me down the hall, where we look out the window at an enclosed concrete patio three stories down. "You'll go out for fresh air at eleven o'clock."

I feel queasy. I know this place helps people who are struggling. I know the staff mean well. But I have to get out of here.

The nurse talks to another worker in the hall and I take a few steps toward the heavy metal door. The exit. I quickly trot in my yellow hospital socks, and then, after a couple strides, I dash into a full-blown run. My heart pounds. My ears ring. My nurse must not see me because I hear her golden laughter ripple behind me.

I pass a series of patient rooms before rounding the corner and throwing my body into the metal exit door with a thud, grasping the handle and tugging. But it doesn't budge.

I pull again, this time a little more wildly, a little more desperate, a little more crazed. Then: a buzzing noise, followed by the mechanical sound of a door unlocking. I straighten, shocked, and inhale, hopeful.

The door swings open. There, right in front of me,

stands Gram. Her brows twist and her lips shrink together. "Ember?"

Crap. I frown, breezing through the doorway, and find I'm stuck inside a closed room with lockers and another set of locked doors. I yank on the handles, but the doors stay firmly shut. Panic flaps inside my chest, and I feel as tortured as I did when I tried to escape the cliffs in Trinity. "I have to go!" I scream at the doors. "Let me out, Gram!"

I spin around, glaring at her. Something inside me unlatches. "You did this! You told me you'd *help* me! *This* is not helping! The world is falling apart, and I'm the one who can stop it. Blood will be on *your* hands."

Gram trembles and her mouth drops open a centimeter, as shock reverberates through her frail body. My angry rant pretty much screws me because two male nurses come racing around the corner, alert and eager to help. When they see me, they slow their pace, approaching as though I'm a tiger that's escaped from the zoo.

And I actually do feel like a tiger, wild and angry. Trapped. Each emotion spins a tiny tornado inside my head.

"Hey, hey, we've got some stuff to work on, Ember," one of the men says to me. His tone is so nice, his round face is so freaking kind, but it's all just so maddening.

I exhale, knowing I'm surrounded. "Please. I'll come back here if you want me to. But Gram, some really big stuff is happening out there in the world, bigger than you can ever imagine. Storms. Viruses. And my friend—"

"Tre," Gram interjects with pursed lips. She crosses her arms over her chest, holding her black leather purse tight to her side.

"Yeah," I say. "Where is he? Is he here?"

She tilts her head, and worry wrinkles her forehead. "Or is it Damien? Or maybe Ted? I told him to go home. We're going to get you help."

The two men walk slowly, nodding, smiling. "Let's go back to your room. Do you like to play cards?"

"I love cards!" says the other, a stocky redhead. "Let's go have some fun."

Just like Zoe said to me in Trinity, once. *"Let's just go have some fun."*

27

EMBER

Someone outside shouts. I stand and go to the window, smeared with drizzle. On the ground below, two security guards escort someone out of the building. The guy in their grip swears; his voice is unmistakable. Chocolate. Lovely. Even when he blurts out cuss words.

Tre.

God, no wonder I swoon over that guy. Smart. Savvy. My crusader for truth and justice. But the guards are rough, holding him up by the armpits as Tre's toes drag behind on the concrete.

My chest tightens. "No!" I whisper.

Tre cranes his neck to look up at the building as he's pulled away from me. I think he sees me up here, and I press two palms onto the glass and shout his name through the double-paned window. I bang my forehead onto the glass and yell until my voice goes hoarse.

He faces away from me again, and they take him deep into the parking lot before letting go. Gram must have told the hospital he was a danger to me, must have had his visitation revoked. Anger courses through me, and I shout his name again.

Two hands grab my shoulders and pull me back. Startled, I spin around. It's the male nurse with the cinnamon hair who calmed me after my attempted escape. His hazel eyes are serene, and he holds both hands up in the air to show he's not a threat. "Breathe," he says dramatically. "Everything's okay."

I nod. But Tre is gone and panic works its way through me.

"I need some time alone," I say. "Please leave me alone. *Now*."

His hands still up in the air, he walks backwards, facing me. "No problem. In an hour, we'll do an assessment. I'll knock when it's time."

When the door shuts with a click, I spin around and look out the window again, even though I already know Tre's not there. I sink onto the windowsill, deflated.

My open duffel bag sits in the corner of the room. Tucked inside is Mom's pink journal. It sits on top of a pair of flip-flops, next to the ankh cross pendant necklace they made me remove when I was admitted to the hospital.

I walk over, pick up the journal and open it to the middle, and catch a sentence that gives me goosebumps. *"And soon, something swept through me like a fiery, intoxicating dream, electricity swirling around us on the air, as if the chanting itself had transformed into something that was truly alive."*

The hair on the back of my neck stands on end. What kind of stuff was Mom into and how the hell did she get to Trinity—and get out alive?

28

DEZI

1986

The air buzzed around my head. It felt like lightning had struck a foot or two away—but it couldn't be real. I was just painting a picture, right? A girl's face—white as snow, with pale green eyes that drilled through the canvas and looked into mine. The red color I'd picked for her hair had a shimmer to it, with hints of fire orange, and the strokes spun the strands into a wild red hurricane.

"Five minutes, class." Mrs. Stengel's voice broke the spell like the snap of a whip. People bustled around me swiftly, stepping over supplies, cleaning paintbrushes at the sink, and delicately setting their canvases on the shelves to dry. My trance faded, and the picture I'd frantically painted came into clear view.

The girl on the canvas radiated as if she were full of demons and splendor and dangerous propositions. I'd never seen her before, but she just sort of came to me when I picked up the paintbrush, like a vision. I leaned back on the metal stool to take a look from a faraway position. With the back of my hand, I pushed a curl from my face, and promptly toppled backward off the stool, landing on the concrete floor.

"Despina Granger, are you okay?"

Why Mrs. Stengel had always felt the need to call me Despina, my stupid Greek name, instead of Dezi was beyond me. It made me feel like a child caught licking the frosting off the kitchen counter.

My paint pallet was pressed up against my smock, and pain pierced my back, but I scrambled quickly off the floor. "I'm fine. Fine. Thanks."

"Powerful portrait?" Mrs. Stengel deadpanned.

I heaved my body up off the floor and began the dreaded process of cleaning up my art supplies. The sounds of lockers banging shut, rushing chatter, and shrieks meandered in from the hallway as I rinsed my brushes, watching red and green water swirl like a pinwheel down the drain.

I passed a cacophony of animated students before stopping at locker #42. Quickly, I spun the combination lock and dumped my books at the foot of the locker while ducking under the cloud of hairspray from Guy Randal— the new guy who liked to spray his Mohawk between classes at his locker. I gazed at the yellow ski boots on his feet.

"Do you *sleep* in those ski boots?" Belinda Heart leaned her hip against the locker on his other side and smiled coyly at Guy, her latest crush.

"They're no fashion statement. They're for warmth." He pointed to his red kilt. "This? This is fashion."

"I like it," she said with a giggle.

I stared at her mindlessly, and must have mirrored her

hip-lean, just to see what it felt like to be so comfortable with guys.

"Uh, stare much?" she asked, and it took me a second to realize she was talking to me.

Embarrassed, I stood up straight again, training my gaze and attention to shutting the locker door.

When I entered the girls' bathroom, fumes flooded my nostrils. Around the corner stood four sophomores. I knew them but had never spoken to them. Dressed in stonewashed jeans and baggy blouses with thick belts, they gazed in the mirrors, going to town on their Aqua Net as if creating fine works of art. Jennie's method proved curious: she squinted while applying a wet spritz to a single blonde curl, pulling and stretching the strands as high as possible with her fingers.

I used to imagine those girls bald, without the shel-lacked, beautiful big hair framing their faces. I found they looked far less pretty in my mind that way, which always made me feel better about my own reflection. Sure, I had the whole big hair thing going on, but it wasn't quite on purpose. My dark nest of curls frizzed around my shoulders. Next to these girls, with their thick black mascara, blue eye shadow, and frosted pink lips, I looked like a kid.

"Did you see the new girl with that stupid name?" Jennie asked her friends.

I don't think she noticed me in the bathroom. I ducked my head and swept through the chemical stench to get to a stall. *Stay invisible*, I thought. I listened to their chatter amid the loud *tsss* sound of the aerosol spray.

The conversation continued.

"Her name was Lo....Lodima? Or something."

"I saw her! She's a flower child from the '60s."

"I kind of liked her coat."

"Ewww. Are you mental?"

Their shrill laughter echoed off the mint-green concrete walls. Yet another reason why I hated high school: gaggles of girls who judged. The way they moved in packs like shoaling surgeonfish, ebbing and flowing in formations through the hallways. The way they chewed gum with gusto and blinked slowly when they didn't understand you. The way they thought they were the only things that mattered on the planet.

I waited until they left the bathroom and then made my way outside, down the steep sidewalk from school to my house. My mind swirled with questions and curiosity. Who was this new girl, this so-called '60s flower child? If she was as weird as me, maybe I'd finally find a friend in Leadville before I graduated.

29

DEZI

"Despina, chop the firewood," Mama snapped from the kitchen. It was so like her, barking orders like a grumpy old soldier.

I ignored her, my hand sweeping across the paper with the charcoal stick. With a number of feathery circles, the vision in my mind began to take shape on the page. The lines gave life to a girl's face. Her straight hair ended in a blunt cut below her chin, and her rounded head looked like a dinner plate for the rest of the face. I drew her catlike eyes with rounded bottom lids, large irises, and corners that turned up at the outer edge. Somehow she looked inviting, perhaps even wise. The drawing gave me the same tingle I felt – the same daze—as when I painted the portrait earlier that day of the redheaded girl.

"Dezi, now!" Mama again.

Her voice sounded like shattered icicles, tinkling and jarring like a million pieces of light. It made me drop the charcoal on the table and push the drawing away quickly. Heaving a big sigh, I rose to meet her command.

Mama shuffled past me in her gray flannel shirt and worn jeans, reaching one callused, rough hand out to quickly grasp the handle of the microwave door. Her other hand clenched a package of hot dogs at her hip.

I accidentally stubbed my toe on the buffet table. It rattled.

"Despina!" Mama said. At least the buffet table was empty. When Papa was alive, every piece of furniture had been loaded with framed pictures. They all disappeared when he and Ricky died.

"Mama, are you ever going to put the pictures up of Papa and Ricky?" I asked, moving through the room.

She didn't answer.

I pulled on an old green parka and knit gloves and pushed open the door of our weathered clapboard home. The icy wind whipped my face and spun my hair out, turning me into a brunette version of Albert Einstein. I grabbed a gnarled stump from the pile around the corner, set it up straight on the dirt, and then heaved the ax over my head. The way the blade pounded down, with a heavy *crack*, always felt so satisfying—although it never broke the wood more than halfway. I was a two-chopper girl, always two hits on each piece of wood.

I thought back to the time those girls had peppered me with questions about wood chopping.

"Here comes Paul Bunyan," my neighbor Belinda Heart had sung in gym class. She had seen me chopping wood outside my house one day.

"Isn't her lumberjack face on the cover of paper towel packages?" Misty Gonzales asked. "Just kidding, Dez." She tried to pretend we were friends joking around. But she wasn't my friend; she usually only opened her mouth to tease me.

"But seriously, why don't you just pay for electric heat?" Belinda asked.

"My mama believes in using your own physical energy to heat your house," I had said quickly, before sprinting around the track, away from the questions. Mama thought that if you lived at 10,152 feet above sea level in Leadville, one of the highest cities in America, chopping wood was a badge of honor.

"Hearty souls," I'd whispered, repeating Mama's words. I had to work hard to believe that. Sometimes, I felt like I could just blow away in the wind and no one would see.

I firmly gripped the neck of the ax and lifted it again, with the stump still attached to the blade. I was just ready to smash it down onto the ground with great wood-chopping gusto when I caught something out of the corner of my eye.

A girl with blonde hair, straight as straw, stood on the sidewalk in a peculiar outfit: a brown and green tie-dye skirt and a heavy blonde fur coat.

I did a double take just before throwing the stump back down on the ground, breaking it in half with a swift thrust. Here she was—the girl from the drawing I sketched just moments ago in the kitchen.

My mouth felt dry. I had seriously just drawn her face at the kitchen table. I stood there, squinting at her, feeling like a rock sinking to the bottom of a pond—slow, heavy, dead weight. Stunned.

Hands in her pockets, she watched me from just beyond the chain-link fence. I dropped the ax, waved with a flick of my hand, and strode directly to her. Maybe this was that '60s flower child, Lodima. She did dress kind of strange. And just the way she stood silent, like a deer watching, unflinching, a blank face in the inky night air, I knew she wasn't like the other girls at school.

"You Lodima?" I yelled over the wind.

Her eyes snapped awake, as if she had been standing there, dreaming of a far-off place. Her mouth turned up slightly. "Yes, that's me."

I stuck out my hand, breathing heavily from my last industrious chop. "I'm Despina, but you can call me Dezi."

She took my hand, clasping it with both of hers, and her eyes came alive in the dim light outside. Her touch gave me the most comforting feeling. I realized that I hadn't really been touched since my brother died six years ago. "Ah," she said, "just like Despoina, the daughter of Neptune."

I had never heard that before. I just thought I was cursed with a dumb name. "Um, sure. So you go to high school here?"

"Yes, I do. Yesterday was my first day." Her voice sounded gravelly and low—a contrast to her round face and super smooth skin. She spoke slow and formal, like my literature teacher.

"Why'd you move *here*?" I asked. Half the people in the town hadn't had jobs since the Climax Mine slowed its production of molybdenum—the stuff used in steel and nuclear plants. Practically everyone was fleeing Leadville. Except Mama. Except me.

"My dad is a social worker," she said. "I guess social services is busy with so many people losing their jobs."

"Okay. So what are you doing *here*, in front of my house?" Mama always told me I was blunt. She hated that.

"Just going for a walk. I wanted to see Venus. See? You can see it shining right there." She pointed to the sky, and sure enough a star sparkled brighter than the rest.

"Today is Venus Friday; the planet that's all about the energy of friendliness and kindness and belonging. It's a feel-good day. From right here, I can also see the Seven Sisters—that's a constellation. When I was a little girl I used to talk to the stars in the constellation and believe that I had friends who lived there." She smiled.

I nodded. "That's weird."

"Yeah, I know." She laughed. "That's me."

"Hey, guess what? I just drew your face literally five minutes ago," I said. "How weird is that?"

I ran back into the house, retrieved the drawing and showed it to her.

She studied it in the dim light, tilting her head and smiling. "That's pretty good! Do you draw everyone you meet?"

"No," I said. "That was the first time. I still can't get over it. I must've seen you somewhere before." I paused, holding the drawing in my hand. I didn't want her to go. "So how do you know so much about constellations?" I asked.

"I read lots of books. I'm interested in all of it: nebulas, backward galaxies, global clusters." She looked at the sky, craning her neck as she spoke. "I love learning about how constellations affect the earth, people, horoscopes. I see stars as mystical lights, offering a window into the soul. My mind always wanders when I gaze at them."

"I count them when I'm bored," I said.

"Me too!" she said, smiling and leaning over the fence. "Want to walk with me? I can show you all my favorite stars."

I did walk with her. The first of many nighttime strolls. Two weirdos. Two mismatched socks. On a Venus Friday.

The night I met Lodima changed everything for me. And in a way, our friendship altered me, making me feel more dexterous, as if I had an extra limb.

After eating Thursday-night lasagna at her house and doing homework together on her bed, she walked me home down Harrison Street, showing me about fifteen new stones she'd purchased with her allowance at the local rock shop. She was obsessed with rocks and always told me about her new finds. She held up a small royal blue stone and leaned into me. "This is azurite. It used to be called Stone of the Heavens because it's supposed to awaken psychic abilities and help you with spiritual guidance."

"Sounds pretty fruity. If there's a rock for that, why do we have so many churches in this town?"

"We have more bars than churches," she said.

I punched a hole in the six-foot-tall snowdrift as we passed. Before Lo, those snowdrifts had always made me feel like I was being buried underground.

She shivered and stamped her feet. "I don't know if I'll ever get over this cold weather."

"There is no such thing as bad weather—"

"I know... just bad clothes. You always tell me that, but no matter how many layers I put on, I'm always freezing!"

A chilly breeze fluttered my hair. "Do you really believe that stuff—you know, powers of crystals?"

She shrugged. "It'd be cool if it was true. But I don't know."

She handed me a shimmery copper rock with rough edges and leaned her head into me. Her breath smelled like garlic, and the setting sun shone on one side of her face, like she was an angel. "That one is goldstone, symbolic of light that can always be found in the darkness. It deflects unwanted energies and is considered protective."

The sound of her voice actually made me tingle. Or maybe it was the stone. "Can I have this one?"

"Sure," she said. "All yours. I have more."

I put it in my pocket, and as we stepped off an icy curb to cross the street, she pulled a shiny black stone out of her bag. "This one is kind of creepy. It's black goethite. It digs up wounds buried within the unconscious."

"Who makes this stuff up?" I asked, laughing. We came to my little house on the hill. "Okay, so see you tomorrow morning for Golden Burro breakfast?"

"Friday morning ritual," she said, turning and waving goodbye.

Inside the front door, I took off my scarf and turned around to find Mama standing in her dirty brown work boots, fresh from her shift at the mine— one of the few people left with a job. Her nose was smudged with soot. "You're never here anymore," she said.

"Sorry," I said, breezing past her to the kitchen. She turned to follow me.

"I think you need a curfew. Maybe four o'clock."

I spun around. "What?"

"Well, where have you been? You're never home." She stood, her legs stiff and parted in the doorway. The idea of her cutting me off from Lodima was worse than death.

So I lied.

"I got a babysitting job, working for a new family in town."

"Who?"

"The Hamiltons."

"The Hamiltons," she repeated, crossing her arms over her chest.

"Yeah, and they need me a lot. It's good money."

She stared at me with a flat, unflinching face that I'd grown to resent ever since I was nine. It was the same look she gave me the day I came home from school not long after my brother died.

Mama had sat in a plastic kitchen chair, smoking a cigarette. Her brown hair had looked messy, her hand jittered, and her eyes were slits. She'd said, "People say I should put you in an orphanage." I remembered how it had felt like she'd just stuck her knuckle into a bruise. "I think they're right," she had added.

After that day, I decided I would never depend on her again. And since then, I had been a lone raft floating down a river—until I met Lodima.

After I lied to Mama about the babysitting job, she asked no more questions about my whereabouts. Once, when I was getting ready for bed, she even indulged in my fantasy family, mentioning one afternoon that she'd seen Mrs. Hamilton at the store. I froze, with my toothbrush in my mouth and a lump in my throat, assuming I'd been caught. But Mama went on to talk about the Hamiltons like they were real people.

"She said you've been a huge help," Mama said. As if she wanted to believe my fictional babysitting story so much, she'd added to it.

One Wednesday that spring, Lodima and I huddled in the school library, where I tried to memorize acid-base reactions and terms like *equilibrium* and *driving forces*. But God, I hated chemistry. The only reactions I cared about were when two colors of paint combined to make a perfect mosaic on a supersized canvas.

"Hey, let's go over to the Old Ruby Garden tonight after school," she said. We always hiked through the snow to the same spot way up above town to talk. I liked it because it was so peaceful I could hear the trees whisper above our heads. When it was warm enough, I'd lie back on the grass and count the clouds. It also meant time away from the suffocating energy of Mama's chores and her shuffling and grumbling about unswept floors and bills to pay.

"That sounds fun." I shut my chemistry book and began drawing on a blank piece of paper. My pen moved without my permission, and I fell into another trance, frantically trying to capture my vision.

I drew my own face, full lips, round cheeks, big eyes gazing into a reflection in the mirror inside my bedroom. Tight wet curls framed my face, and a bath towel with frayed terry loops draped across my shoulders. A feminine hand held a few strands of my hair from above. Encircling the girl's smooth, lean wrist was a bracelet. I drew with swift movements until the sketch showed a bracelet of a dark snake. I drew the color, thinking that perhaps it was made of black goethite. *Digging up the unconscious.*

"Pssst," Lodima whispered, leaning across the table. Her gravel voice pulled me out of my daze. She pressed her lips together and looked like she was bursting with excitement to tell me something important.

"Pssst," I said back.

"I have a secret." Her eyes darted around the library like a spy.

At the next table, Steve Trouvé was asleep, his head flat on the table next to us, his cheek spread flat and his mouth open. Misty Linford, the most annoying girl in school with her ten-foot-tall blonde bangs and big shushing mouth, sat behind Lodima. Every few minutes, she frowned and policed the volume of our conversation.

"What's your secret?" I asked Lodima.

"I hear things. And I see things."

"Yeah, so do I," I said. Blunt. Sarcastic. "I hear you right now. And, guess what, I see you, too!"

"No, I hear things and see things differently than most people. Like, I know right now that Steve over there is dreaming about driving a racecar." She looked up to the corner of the room as if she were watching it on a screen. "Yes, it's a red racecar and he is loving the ride. Ah, but now the seat is starting to recline backwards and he can't see. He feels drunk... as though he's going to crash."

Steve's mouth moved in little twitches before Lodima leaned forward across the table and whispered, "*Bam.*"

Steve sat up with a jerk and gasped. Lodima smiled, so proud, I swear, that it filled her up from chin to forehead. I shook my head, thinking somehow she had played a trick on me.

"Go ahead, ask him," she said, reading my face.

Steve wiped his mouth and pulled on his jean jacket.

With a swift shake of his head, his dark, curly mullet fell on top of his collar. He was the oblivious kind of boy who had no idea how cute he was, even when he drooled while he napped. I'd always loved the way he did things like open doors for me, let me cut in line, and give me pieces of gum. He was a throwback to the days of chivalry.

"Hey, did you just dream about a red racecar?" I asked too loud for the library.

"Shhhh!" Misty again.

His eyes grew wide and his face flushed red. He bit his lip. "Yeah... why? Did I talk in my sleep or something?"

I giggled. "No, you didn't talk in your sleep. What happened at the end of the dream?"

"Huh?" He picked up his books and cradled them in his forearm, pushing his chair away as he stood. His face had brightened with the conversation, and he sauntered over to our table.

"Did I shout something?" he asked. "Sometimes, I mumble. My mom told me I once walked in my sleep and tried to pee in the litter box."

Lo and I both laughed and I clapped my hand over my mouth before dropping my gaze to the table. "No, seriously," I whispered. "What *happened* in your dream?"

"Did you lose control of the car?" Lodima asked.

His eyebrows clipped together. "How'd you know that?"

I glanced sideways at Lodima and she giggled.

"Come on, seriously, how'd you know?" he said slowly.

"How exactly did you lose control?" I asked, looking at Lodima and taking him in with quick glances.

"Well, my seat fell backwards while I was driving. But it

was a killer racecar." He grinned and stood there, slightly bowlegged, with his books in his arms.

My mouth dropped open and a chill ran down my neck. Lodima and I beamed at each other. "No way! That's what she *said* happened in your dream!" I turned to Lo. "Are you psychic?"

"I told you, I see things. I see people's dreams!"

"Come on," he said.

"It's true," I said. My pulse quickened. Could my best friend really be psychic?

"Right, right, whatever. You guys..." Steve took a step to walk away and then stopped, hesitating. "Hey, um, do you like music?"

"Sure," I said. My cheeks felt hot and I couldn't look at him anymore. I kept my gaze on Lodima's round face.

"Because I started a band, and we're practicing in Nick's garage. It'd be cool if you came and listened sometime."

"Oh, cool." I felt as if I was made of helium and starting to float off the ground, yet I still couldn't look at him. He stood there for a couple minutes, and from my peripheral vision I could see him bobbing his head, telegraphing nervous energy. After a moment, he started to shuffle away. "Uh, cool. See ya then."

"Why didn't you look at him?" Lodima asked once he was gone. "You do like him. That, I know."

I shrugged. Why would he like *me*? Next time, I thought, I'd talk to him. Maybe I'd listen to his band.

"So how did you do that?" I asked. "The dream thing?"

I considered that maybe Lodima had paid Steve to tell me what she wanted me to hear—as some sort of prank or a way to get me to talk to him. But Lodima was the most gentle, serious person I knew; her body was absent of all sarcasm or bawdy humor. In fact, Lodima had always been different—a turnip in a flower garden. While other girls practiced cheerleading or glided on the Nordic ski team, Lodima collected rocks and crystals and read books about animal symbolism. She talked about the moon and herbs used to treat wounds in medieval times. Not your usual girl. That's why I liked her.

"The dream thing happens all the time lately," she said. "I'll hear voices and realize people aren't speaking. I see flashes of memories, ideas, dreams. People who live in faraway places, visions of people I don't even know. I think I'm an empath."

With my elbows on the table, I covered my eyes with my hands, and excitement pulsed through me. "What's an empath?"

"It's a name for people like me who feel the world rather than seeing it like everyone else. So yes, kind of psychic. An indigo child. I've always felt like I was different, but it wasn't until I moved here that I started having dreams and seeing things and actually hearing other people's thoughts."

"Right," I said, "hearing people's thoughts... Okay. So what am I thinking right now?" I closed my eyes, as if that made it easier for her to read my mind. She didn't respond, so I opened my eyes. I laughed, incredulous.

Her expression beneath the stick-straight bangs didn't change. She had the innocence of a plush kitten. "No, Dezi. It's not on command. It's something that comes and goes— and in a way, it's a *feeling*."

"Come on," I said, rolling my eyes.

"Sometimes, it appears to be out of my control. When

it started happening, I began studying more about my Celtic heritage."

"You mean, what, like, in Ireland?"

She took a thick library book from her backpack and slid it across the table. "People from Hill of Tara in Ireland, where my ancestors are from, would follow celestial patterns—"

"Of course, because you love the stars."

"Yes. They were called Celtic Druids—soothsayers skilled at reading dreams."

My heart raced. Just knowing how unusual Lodima was, it was plausible. Perhaps even more to the point, I believed it because of my own experiences. I mean, I had drawn a picture of her face without ever meeting her or even catching a glimpse of her in town. Was I an empath too, or maybe some sort of Venus Friday turnip like Lo? She always called me Neptune, always reminded me that my name, Despina, came from one of Neptune's daughters.

"I think I'm supposed to help the world," she said.

The bony librarian, Ms. Stuben, walked past us—all six floral feet of her, jiggling and shushing us with one finger.

I leaned forward and whispered, "Help the world? That's a lot of pressure for a girl. Like, help them by waking people up before they crash cars in their dreams?" A wry smile crossed my face.

She smiled with her eyes again, exhilaration practically spewing from her pupils, spinning through the air across the table and landing atop my frizzed-out head. My body felt just as electric.

"I'm not talking about superhero antics." She paused. "But I think you have something special in you, too."

A few beats passed and my eyes bounced back down to my chemistry book again. Maybe I didn't reply immediately because I wondered deep down if that might be true. But there was no way I could see or hear people's thoughts. I could never know what Steve was dreaming about—though sometimes I was curious to know. I liked being a mismatched sock with Lodima, but I didn't want to be *that* different from everyone else.

"You're crazier than I thought, Venus Girl," I said.

"You're more gifted than you think, Neptune Girl."

A mixture of uncertainty, nerves, and denial crashed inside me with her assertion. I wasn't gifted, or even anything special. But I *was* different.

Behind her, a girl entered the library from the hallway. She must have been the new girl everyone was talking about. Her long, swooping red hair bounced as she moved —graceful, head held high, shoulders back. A queen without a court. When she got closer to our table, she looked incredibly familiar to me: very pale skin and green eyes so light you could see through them, as though looking to the bottom of a calm ocean. It wasn't until she flipped her hair behind her shoulder that I understood why I recognized her.

"Hey," I whispered across the table. "I painted that girl's picture in class earlier this year, but I've never seen her before."

I watched the girl move through the library, feeling heavy like I had the time I first met Lodima in my front yard after drawing her face.

"See, you do have some sort of extra special gift," Lo said with a wink. "Her name is Xintra."

I nodded slowly. "The painting was kind of spooky,

really powerful. When I finished, I fell off my stool. In the painting, she was prettier, more mature. And somehow, like, more powerful. Different. Right now, she seems... nice."

Lodima nodded and then looked down at her book on Celtic history—not chemistry. I never understood how Lo could ace all her tests without studying. Perhaps she simply read the minds of all of us who did study.

My eyes followed the new girl as she moved through the library. It was as if she floated, moving the energy in the entire room, possessing a similar enrapture to the one she had in my painting. People turned their heads as she swept through the room.

Maybe Lodima was right; I had some sort of empathy stuff going on here. Maybe this new girl had some significance in my life, I decided.

I wiggled three fingers over my book as a friendly hello. She smiled warmly and bit her bottom lip, as if she was excited for us to meet as well. Surely, she would soon be my next mismatched Venus Friday friend.

30

DEZI

Xintra was a magnet. Everyone in school wanted to be near her. A few days after seeing her in the library, after the last bell, I passed her in the hallway. Half a dozen kids surrounded her by the senior benches. I tried to pretend I didn't notice her, but she called out to me.

"Hey!" Her pretty British voice lassoed me in, like it did everyone else.

I stopped. "Hi."

"You like art, right?" She exuded cool, chewing gum and wearing high-waisted jeans and a flowered blouse.

I nodded.

"You should see the stuff at my house. My father has a collection. We're all headed over there after school. If you want to come."

Of course I wanted to come. Of course I wanted to see his art collection. Of course I wanted to hang out with Xintra. "Sure."

"It's up on Ridge View."

Snob Hill. That was the nicest place in town.

After school, Lo and I did hike over to Xintra's ginger-bread house, a two-story purple place with a tall, rounded turret. When we knocked on the door, Xintra called to us from inside.

"Yessss, come in…"

When the door swung open, we found her lounging on the hardwood floor, surrounded by Jennie Kitner, Greg Summers, Misty Gonzalez, and Jeff Sanders—some of the coolest kids in town.

Lo and I stood shoulder to shoulder in the doorway, snow on our wool knit hats, nerves fluttering. There was too much to take in. Xintra and the other kids took long swigs from wine coolers and leaned into one another, laughing. I'd never said two words to those kids outside of school, and here Xintra was having a picnic with them on her living room floor, just four days after she'd moved here. It was if they'd had her popular girl slot open, ready and waiting for her.

The house was impressive too—a museum. Carved wooden Aztec masks, with turquoise headdresses and large white teeth and slanted eyes hung on one wall. An ivory figurine of a man stood four feet tall by the staircase. Above the crown-molded mantel hung a painting of an Egyptian phoenix with three-foot wings. Strange and beautiful art packed the entire room.

Lodima and I didn't move. We gaped and leaned forward through the doorframe to take in the bizarre landscape. "Wow," I whispered.

"Are you coming in? Or are you going to just freeze us out?" Xintra's voice made me jump, and we quickly stepped inside.

For several moments, I focused on quietly taking off layer after layer.

"You two look like Sprite girls," Xintra said, standing up.

"Yes, we are," Lodima said, answering for us. Xintra took a long drink of her wine cooler before standing to get us sodas, and for a second I wondered why, exactly, I looked like a Sprite girl.

Lodima and I stood in silence, shoulder to shoulder, studying a line of huge oil paintings. We gazed for a long time at one by Claude Monet: a garden with vivid pinks, purples and blues and greens.

"It's just thick dots," Xintra said, standing behind me with her arms folded over her chest. She handed me a can of soda. "I don't get why he's so famous."

I looked back at Xintra, who tilted her head and scowled at the painting. "The way everyone knows his name, you'd think he did something really big. But he just painted some pictures. Blurry ones at that."

I debated how to answer. She was seriously wrong, but just her presence, as she stood a good six inches taller than me, felt intimidating. If I gave the wrong answer, I could be shooed out of her house. If I gave the right answer, we might be friends.

"But look," I pointed. "The irises are darker where the sunlight is blocked, and in the middle, where the sun pierces through the trees, the colors of the flowers just pop. It's like you're standing in his garden in France."

Xintra squinted and leaned in to examine the painting. "From close up, it's just a big mess." Then she looked at me, really looked at me, turning her head to the side. She put her hand on my shoulder. "But you're pretty smart, you know? I like you."

I beamed inside. It was like those three words—*I like you*—had turned on the furnace inside me. I felt a lot warmer, a lot more comfortable.

Still, I didn't say much. For hours, Lodima and I sat close together at the edge of the circle, sipping our Sprites while listening to Xintra hold court with the others. She talked about her father's house in Hawaii and the sushi there, and told wild stories about visiting Stonehenge on foggy nights in Great Britain and exploring old churches in Berlin. Normally, with a group like this, I would have felt like my presence didn't matter, except Xintra kept looking me in the eye when she finished her sentences and smiling at me when other people talked. She was so inviting.

Near the end of the night, she bet Greg and Jeff they couldn't scoot a penny across the hardwood floor without using any of their limbs. Greg flattened his muscled body on the floor and shoved the penny with the top of his head —like a bull—and Jeff wound up pushing it with his nose. When Jeff stood up, proud of his accomplishment, we all rolled with laughter because he had dirt in the shape of an exclamation point on his pointy nose. Exactly how she'd planned it.

By midnight, it was just me and Lodima left at the house, and Xintra gave us a tour. She showed us her father's antiseptic bedroom with its rows of suit jackets with leather patches on the elbow and crisp white shirts that hung in a straight line in the closet.

"Where is your dad?" I asked.

"He travels all the time," she said, quickly ushering us

out of the room, glancing around as if someone was watching.

"Where's your mom?" I asked as we walked down the hall.

"She's a loser," she said, opening the door to her bedroom, which had slanted walls due to the peaked roof. "*This* is my room."

On the wall opposite her four-poster canopied bed hung a poster of The Cure, and on another wall hung a framed photo of Russian dictator Joseph Stalin. I figured she must have been a history buff. On her blue dresser stood an old silver brush and nesting dolls in the shape of Egyptian mummies.

Xintra fell face-first onto her bed with her arms spread out wide. She rolled over onto her back, far less poised. Her blouse and red hair were stuck, twisted beneath her left side. "You need to drink with me next time, guys," she said. "We'll have so much fun."

She patted the bed with a hand on either side of her, and Lodima and I glanced at each other, smirking. But inside, my synapses went haywire. Lodima was sugar. She was wise and she was safe. But Xintra was like tasting exotic Indian food for the first time. She was electricity and enthusiasm. I wanted to be her friend, and that night, I knew I would be.

I picked up her wine cooler off the dresser and took a long gulp and then dove onto my stomach on the bed next to her, giggling as the fluffy pillow smothered my face.

31

DEZI

Since we three had become friends that spring, Xin was the one in charge. It worked for me. She was the kind of friend you appreciated because you didn't have to think when she was around. You could just show up and she handled the details.

My friendship with Xin was also nothing but blunt.

"No offense, Dezi, but I could make you far prettier than you are now," Xintra told me one day in her lilting British accent. Her "far" sounding more like "fah."

She stood over me as I perched on my disheveled bed with the lacy white comforter. As soon as Xintra and Lodima had arrived that Saturday morning, I felt ashamed of the state of my room, which hadn't yet evolved from that of a little girl to a teenager. I hadn't even painted over the large, starry-eyed unicorn on the wall by my bed. I'd always loved the magic of unicorns and everything unexplained.

"I'm not sure how to take that, Xin," I said, crossing

my arms.

"I want to fix you," she said. "As my father always says, we can help you shed your skin and find the light inside of you."

I shrugged. I had nothing else to do that day and was happy someone like Xintra was even paying attention to me. "Sure."

"First off, throw away your brush," she said, pinching my bristled hairbrush with two fingers and dropping it in the trash can. "You need to use mousse and your fingers to style your curly hair. Otherwise, you'll only continue to get this giant triangle of frizzy hair you seem to fancy."

"Oh," I said. My cheeks flushed. That was me: an ugly triangle head. I always watched girls spritz and spray their hair and use curling irons, but I'd never wanted to give my hair much time. Still, if Xintra thought I needed help, then maybe, I decided, I *should* care. "Okay, sure, sure," I said finally. "Fix me."

We giggled as she washed my hair. No one had wash my hair since Mama used to do it when I was a little girl. Even then, it was rough and rushed, Mama tugging on the strands so hard it made my eyes tear up.

Xintra wrapped a towel around my shoulders, and when I saw my reflection in the mirror, I gasped.

"What?" asked Xintra.

My wet curls. The towel on my shoulder. My eyes shining with enthusiasm. Xin's hand adorned by the bracelet with the black stone snake. It was the same thing I had drawn that day in the library when I first met Xintra. Surely this meant our friendship was destiny.

"Did you seriously just gasp?" she asked.

"No."

She pulled out some kitchen shears from her bag and prepared to cut my hair. I wasn't sure it was destiny to let your untrained friend lop off chunks of your curls. My face must have said everything I was thinking.

"Dez," she said, "I've done this a million times. Trust me."

I bit my lip and let her snip bangs and layers into my hair. She used her fingers to style my curls, creating long ringlets that grazed my shoulder. It really did look better.

"I've got an idea," she said, swinging the scissors around. "Let's be blood sisters."

I may have liked unicorns, but that sounded like something we might have done at age twelve. Not in high school. But Xintra was convincing and soon, Lodima and I were holding out our fingers to be pricked by Xintra's scissors. We dropped blood onto a cloth the way Xin told us to, and then we all three promised to be loyal to each other.

"Blood sisters forever," we whispered.

As I put on my Band-Aid, I caught a glimpse of Xintra tucking the rag with our blood into her purse.

"Ewww," I said. "Why don't you throw that blood-soaked thing away?"

"Because you never know when I might need your blood!" she said in a Dracula accent before grinning and slapping my shoulder. She unzipped her makeup bag. "First, eyeliner," she said, pulling out a long kohl pencil and swiftly leaning in to draw on my face.

I craned my head back. I did not want a sharp pencil near my eyes.

She threw her hands in the air. "Come on, Dezi! Are we doing this or what?"

Slowly, I let out a long breath and leaned forward to let

her put the eyeliner on my top lids. This was her art, I decided. Let her be creative. I trusted her.

As she lined my eyes and then applied blush, eye shadow, mascara, and lipstick, her hot breath grazed my face and her free hand pressed into the side of my cheek. I felt so grateful she was spending time on *me*. No one had been this close to me in years.

"Promise, you will look gorgeous," she said. I loved the sound of her voice and the way I felt around her. She was honey and I was the bee. If she wanted to make me over, perhaps maybe I could be more like her.

Once finished, Xintra moved to reveal my reflection in the mirror. I looked immensely better, hardly recognizable even to myself. My eyes shone brighter. My skin glowed, and my hair looked like something I might actually claim. She had painted a new me, and I loved it.

"Wow," I said.

Lodima gazed up and smiled. "*Now* will you talk to Steve?"

I grinned at the mention of his name, but a glare on Xin's face shrank the feeling. She shook her head and raised her eyebrows, a mother scolding a child.

"No," she said. "You could not at all possibly be interested in *him*."

"He's nice." My voice was weak and I glanced at Lodima, who sat with legs crossed on the floor by the windowsill.

"Please. What a dork. You can't go out with him. You can do so much better." She waved off the conversation. "Because..." she said, as if a drumroll should have accompanied her statement, "I have some more stuff for you." She shook a plastic bag, dumping a pile of jeans, blouses, bright socks, and hair bands onto the bed. "It's my old stuff, but you can have it."

I had truly won the clothes lottery. Mama never saw the value in fashion, whether it was ruffled blouses or stonewashed jeans. She only cared what would last the longest. For years, I had stepped on the bottoms of my jeans for months until they actually fit.

"For me?" I asked hesitantly, holding back an excited squeal.

Xintra grinned so big I thought it might make her head explode. It was as if my own transformation had lit up some part of her. It made me feel so happy that I could make her feel that way.

She clapped and spun, searching the room, her eyes landing on Lodima. "Your turn, Lodi!"

"Do I have to?" Lodima asked, a wry smile crossing her face. She appeared intrigued but not entirely convinced.

"Yes! Yes!" I said, pulling her to stand and steering her to my chair by the mirror. I couldn't wait to see Lodima transform into a butterfly, too.

Turns out, Lodima's thin, straight hair didn't bend much or take to a curling iron. And she politely refused to wear any makeup or change her '60s retro wardrobe. So she stayed Lodima.

Xintra let out a silent sigh, heaving her busty chest a bit, but Lodima didn't care. She went back to the windowsill and was soon engrossed in the stones she'd found by the river.

Meanwhile, Xintra turned her attention back to me and began a lecture about how to wear my new outfits.

I ate it up. She was going to be the best thing that could have ever happened to me.

32

DEZI

Xintra had this way of holding herself. The fiery red hair, the way she walked down the hall with her hips moving in a sexy sway—it caused the boys in our school to really pay attention. Not just to her, but to all three of us when we were together.

After the makeover, I became someone who, somehow, finally fit, rather than just being a mismatched sock, an isolated twosome with Lodima. Now, I was someone who mattered. By the start of junior year, we had become a threesome. We were noticed, powerful, and invited to all the right parties.

Xin could talk people into anything: buying us movie tickets, getting us alcohol, hosting parties at their houses. With one conversation, she landed the lead in the school play. She regularly had guys buying us lunch. She got the language arts teacher, Mr. Howard, to make her editor of the yearbook without any experience because she said she wanted to start fresh.

One Friday, we stood in the lobby of the movie theater with no money. But we wanted to see *The Princess Bride*. Xintra's target for manipulation that time: Greg Summers.

"I like that outfit you've got on, but your shoes don't really match," she said, assessing his checkered sneakers and stonewashed jean jacket. His chest puffed up. He should have been insulted, but instead he seemed charmed by her backhanded compliment.

A couple minutes later, she spun around, grinning and flashing three movie tickets.

"How did you do that?" Lodima asked with wide eyes.

"You play on their insecurities," she said. "It's about control, pushing him to earn my approval. He ends up thinking he *wants* to buy us tickets. But I'm the one pulling the strings."

"Do you like him?" I tried to keep up with her long-legged stride as we headed to the bathroom to spray our hair.

A girl in a black dress, with straight dark hair down to her waist, passed us, and Xintra bumped her with her shoulder. "Hey," the girl said, turning to face us with a grimace.

"Freak," Xintra said, moving into the bathroom and giggling.

"Who's that?" I asked.

"Alessandra. My personal shadow." I watched Xin in the mirror, as she flipped her hair over her shoulder and leaned in to apply pink lip gloss. "She's a bitch."

"So do you like him? Greg?" Lodima asked, standing behind us. Lo didn't even cast a glance at her disheveled stick-straight blonde hair. She just craned her neck to follow our conversation.

"I've had my pick of the Leadville hick boys here, but, Dezi and Lo, you two need some practice." Xintra pressed her lips together and then put the tube of gloss into her leather purse. "You'll make your move on some guys next weekend at Nick's party." She ruffled my hair. I hated when she did that.

I didn't want to tell Xintra that I'd never even held a boy's hand, let alone kissed one. No one would have noticed me without Xintra.

Lodima nudged me with her shoulder and caught my eye in the mirror. "Steve?" She sang his name.

Xintra ignored her. "I think you'll get with Chris Gomez."

"Oh I will, will I?" I asked with a laugh.

"He likes you." She turned to leave the bathroom, and we followed her into the silver-wallpapered hallway.

"How do you know that?" Lodima asked.

"I'm going to put a spell on him!" Xintra turned around, wiggling her fingers and tossing her head back for a loud, cackling laugh. We walked into the lobby, the smell of popcorn welcoming us.

"Right," I said, rolling my eyes.

"Seriously, though, I did find a bunch of cool stuff in an old book about witchcraft. I'll take you to the store where I got it sometime." She handed Lo and me a ticket each and then beamed at the theater employee—tall, handsome—who tore them up and pointed us toward the theater. Greg Summers, her so-called date, trailed behind us.

She turned to look at me. "And really, Dez, you're hot now. Don't act like guys haven't noticed."

Those last two lines pumped me up, and I felt like I might explode inside. Xintra thought I was pretty.

Turns out, I did make out with Chris Gomez the following weekend. I don't know whether it was because of a spell or the power of suggestion—or just Xintra's mind control over me. But it was one more step toward my losing myself to her.

33

DEZI

The kitchen was huge—with dark wood cabinets and really nice Formica countertops. I tossed my head back and took in the empty room. "It's like you live alone," I told Xin.

She shrugged. "My father is always off on business."

We sat on the kitchen floor, eating animal crackers from a big plastic tub.

This time, we didn't invite Lodima; Xintra had confided that Lo could be a buzz kill at times. I'd agreed but felt bad for not including her, like I was cheating on a boyfriend. Lo was the sanity and security in my life. Before Xintra, she was my family. My other half. But I liked having Xintra all to myself, too, like eating the last of the ice cream in the middle of the night and not sharing a bit of it.

"What's his business, anyway?" I asked, examining an elephant-shaped cookie. We'd eaten half the barrel.

"I don't know really," she said. "He did tell me that

when I was old enough I could join him on his ventures, whatever that means. But it's cool because we have houses in Hawaii, Peru, Egypt, London..."

"A house in Hawaii? God, you're so rich! And here you are, sitting in Leadville eating animal crackers on the floor with trailer trash like me." I giggled. I wanted her to tell me that sitting on the floor with me was better than being in any worldly mansion.

"Yeah." She snorted. "But these are only the highest quality animal crackers, and where else can you eat animal crackers and sit among freakazoid art?"

Above her head was one of those weird ancient Egyptian paintings—a man with the head of a horse, wearing some sort of skirt.

"Why *does* your father have all those weird masks and Egyptian totems?"

She shrugged. "He's eccentric and believes he's part of some ancient force."

"That sounds weird. Do you *really* have a father?" I was joking but I wasn't. "It's like you made him up."

She shrugged, but I thought she was lucky. She had this huge house all to herself with no curfew, no rules, no chores.

"What's he like?" I don't even remember mine. Memories of Papa come to me in specific, brief moments. The rough feel of his cheeks when he kissed me goodnight. Me tugging on his Denver Broncos T-shirt, begging him to spin me around in the front yard. His hand expertly sketching realistic eyes on a cat in a notebook. The time I went fishing with him and he told me I talked too much for the fish. I was so little when he died, sometimes it feels like those memories are just stories I told myself. Just ideas of a papa I don't really remember.

"My father wants me to win, that's all," Xintra said.

"Win?"

"Yeah, like, I remember being maybe ten or eleven years old, and I took second in a school race. I was so happy, holding that red ribbon, and Father looked at the ribbon and then handed it back to me. He said, 'Second? You lost.'"

"Oh my God!" I said, laughing.

"But it's true, though." She looked serious. "The last thing I want to be is ordinary. You might as well be dead."

Something in the way she said that made me believe she really meant it. I hoped *I* wasn't ordinary. With Xintra, I didn't think so.

"You've got to find out what he does to make all this money."

"I'll do some reconnaissance for you." She winked and kicked my foot.

"Do you miss your mum?" I asked. I liked using her accent.

"No." She didn't look at me, but flipped her hair off her shoulder. She put a cookie in her mouth and talked with her mouth full. "But I do have a brother."

"What? You didn't tell me that. Where is he?" I opened a cupboard and stuck my head inside, pretending to look for him. "Do you keep him locked up?" I smiled.

"Stupid," she said, kicking my foot again. "He's my half brother. I never met him. He's with my mum—wherever that is. That's what my father says."

"So are you gonna find him?"

"Maybe," she said.

"That'd be cool." A dash of jealousy whistled through me.

"I want to find him, but part of me feels like when I do, I'll just want to torture him."

"What?"

"I can't get over the fact that Mum chose him over me. She *picked* him. Sometimes, I hate them both for that," she said. You'd think she was joking, but she was dead serious, and I swore I could actually feel the iciness of her words.

She sat up straighter, picked up an animal cracker and studied the shape. "Father says he's worthless because he's not his son. He's another man's. Mum was a traitor. She had the genes, the potential, too, a special gift. Father says he and I have a destiny."

I giggled and leaned into her. "Destiny!" I said, mimicking her accent like an actress on stage. She didn't really laugh.

I put an elephant-shaped cookie in my mouth, hoping the dry tasteless bite would drown out thoughts of Ricky and Papa. What had been *their* destiny? Just to be dead?

"What about you, Dez? Tell me about Ricky."

Had I ever mentioned Ricky's name to her, or even told her I had a brother? I didn't remember saying anything, but she could have heard about it from someone in town. She rested the side of her head on mine, a bookend.

"He died of pneumonia when I was little. I didn't really get to say goodbye. They just swept him off to the hospital."

"Who?"

"Doctors. My mama."

"They just left you alone?" Xintra asked.

"Not really, but Mama stayed for weeks while he tried to fight off the pneumonia. In the meantime, I was stuck in a dark house with Mrs. Randolph."

"Who's that?"

"She's this neighbor lady. She seriously never opens her curtains. Ever. She made me sit at the table while she cut out paper snowflakes. Meanwhile, my brother was dying. When Mama came home, she didn't talk about it. She just set out a black dress on my bed and told me the funeral would be the next day."

"Dude."

My throat felt suddenly tight, just thinking about it all and seeing Ricky's face in my mind. He'd had golden curls and big brown eyes that looked like almonds and a quick smile. I'd entertain him by drawing pictures of whatever he wanted. His requests got weirder all the time—he was trying to stump me, I think. A red fire truck with purple pom-poms. A dinosaur with dog ears playing the piano on a beach. He covered an entire wall of his room with those bizarre-o pictures. It got old after awhile, but seeing his expression when I drew what he wanted was worth it.

"He had such a great imagination," I said. "And you know, we were, like, kind of a team after Papa died and Mama went dark. I mean, MIA. So we became each other's cushion. You know?"

I was peanut butter and he was jelly. When mama checked out after Papa died, I had stepped in, making Ricky breakfast, brushing his teeth, reading him stories and helping him build snowmen. When he ran circles in the kitchen and Mama swatted at him with her hand, I would pick him up and take him outside to play chase.

Talking about him after all those years brought up

emotions I didn't even know I still had inside. Hot tears poured down my cheeks, and when I felt them drip onto my lap, it surprised me. Xintra leaned into me, putting an arm around my shoulder.

She made me *feel* again. And she made me feel *seen*.

34

EMBER

Someone knocks on the door, and I snap the journal shut. Thoughts have been banging together in my mind as I read Mom's words. I hate that Mom calls her Xin. It's so familiar, so friendly, and it makes my stomach sour.

Plus, Mom was so *different* on these pages than she was with me. She radiated sunshine when she served Jared and me waffles and sticky syrup. She became a storm cloud, though, when she curled up from sadness. But mostly, she was enthusiasm and weirdness and curiosity and love. I wanted to see a stronger girl in that journal.

The girl in these pages didn't think for herself. She *liked* Xintra, the girl who took my life, trapped me, turned me into a wicked star and murdering machine, and then tried to kill me to boot.

Yet in a way, Mom and I were so much alike. Both of us were lured by Trinity's power. The difference was that she wanted to be seen in high school, and I wanted to disappear. I wish I had known this story a long time ago; if I had, none of this would have ever happened, and I wouldn't be sitting here in this hospital room.

A tall man dressed more like a teacher than a doctor enters the room, introducing himself as Dr. Bartlett. His large physique makes a thwumping sound as he sits in the chair by the desk. He opens a folder and flips through its papers.

"I'm going to do what's known as an assessment. Get to know you better." His voice is monotone and coffee-colored. He's not really the kind of person you'd want to open up to.

Thoughts and worries jostle for position on a tightrope in my mind. I'm stuck here. I'm captive.

Just like in Trinity.

Now, it's not just about reclaiming my own life, swimming to the surface of reality, it's about millions of people's lives. I can't just sit here, knowing their lives are going to be turned upside down, destroyed, stolen. This is a whole other level of being trapped, and I want to scream.

"Did my grandma ban my boyfriend from visiting me?" I blurt.

"He can visit you," Dr. Bartlett says. "But not if he's going to be aggressive."

"Agressive?"

"He wouldn't relent with the questions."

"Since when does asking questions count as aggression?"

"We asked him nicely to stop. Multiple times." He doesn't make eye contact but instead looks at the pages in my file.

"I say that's determination. He wants answers."

"We all do, Ember." His gray eyes meet mine. He kind

of looks like my dentist. "That's why I'm here. Let's do a little intake, just to see where we stand."

How many other ways can I explain I'm not ill? "I don't need to be here. Really. Do I seem delusional?"

"What do *you* think?" He strokes his chin.

I lean against the wall, picking at the blanket on the bed.

"Why do you think you're here, Ember?"

"Because my grandma wants to torture me."

He jots down some notes. "Has your appetite, weight, or eating pattern changed?"

"No."

"Trouble sleeping?"

"No." I roll my eyes. "Outside of the fact that this bed sucks."

He strokes his chin and nods. He has pockmarked cheeks, and when the light hits them just right, they look like craters on the moon.

The list is long and takes a while. He goes through my past drug use. My depression. He asks if I smoke. If I drink. If I experience headaches. If I have diabetes, cancer, liver problems. *Seriously?*

The questions persist. Do I hear voices? Do I see people others cannot? Do I feel like people are out to get me? Do I ever feel like something is crawling on me? Do I experience electrical sensations? Do I believe that someone outside of myself controls me or influences the world?

I answer *no* to everything. *Everything.* And after an hour, the doctor places the papers back into his folder and pauses. "You know, Ember, we'll make more progress if you're forthright."

"What I'm telling you is the truth."

"Okay." He scribbles in his folder and stands up, shakes my hand. "That's enough for today. I'll be back and we can talk more."

I roll my eyes and flop onto my side on the bed. When he's gone, I pull out Mom's journal and read again.

35

DEZI

The first time I saw Xintra's father, it was super brief, and really, I didn't even get to actually meet him. We stopped by her house so she could get her mittens and hat, and he was in the living room smoking a cigar.

We dashed through the ornate room and Xintra flashed him a quick wave and gave no introduction. I couldn't help but feel like she was embarrassed of me or something. When I passed, I remember being so shocked. He was the most youthful father I'd ever seen—and cute, too. He had auburn hair, piercing hazel eyes, and a lean, long face.

Once I got a good look at him, my skin tingled and my breath caught in my throat; I'd painted his face earlier in the week. In my painting, he was standing amid this colorful meadow with tall cliffs. By then, I had decided to keep my mouth shut about my visions and art, mostly because I was afraid Lodima would claim I was seeing the future like her. And I didn't want to be that weird anymore.

But the trances still happened. Just the day before, I had gone into a daze and painted Lodima as a middle-aged woman with smooth skin, her face lit by a fire in a forest. She wore two long gray braids and an ankh cross, and she sat across the fire from a young girl with curly hair—who, eerily, looked a lot like me.

The week before that, I painted a fuzzy scene of a figure standing next to a tree. A girl with long dark hair and a black dress was facing me and Xintra in the forest in some sort of confrontation. I had a red cup in one hand, and the other hand on my hip. The sky was moonlit and cloudy. Rain trickled down, and dark shadows reached across the girl like giant hands. A lightning bolt flashed in the upper left corner of the painting. By the time I had finished, the image made me shiver.

But I kept all this to myself.

In the expansive living room with all the weird, magnificent art, I stopped and gazed at Xintra's dad. My head felt flooded with blood, and I wanted to go to him. He was like a beautiful flower you wanted to pick and smell. Like Xintra, I supposed, but even more so.

He nodded at me with liquid eyes, and Xintra yanked on my arm like I was being pulled offstage with a cane. We went to her room, where she pulled out drawers looking for her hat and gloves. Her favorites—the ones with the fur-lined edges.

"*That's* your dad?" I asked, laughing. "He's, like, so young. What was he, five years old when he had you?"

She shook her head and bit her lip, ignoring me. She became incredibly flustered about finding the gloves.

"We're just going to Lodima's house, Xin. You don't even need gloves."

She shook her head. "No, I need to take you to Trinity Forest."

"What?" I asked. That came out of left field. "Why? People say that place is creepy. And Lodima already rented *RoboCop*."

"My fath—" She stopped and pushed my shoulders down so I sat on her bed. It was so soft I wanted to throw my body back into the fluffy pillows and roll around like a cat. "Stay," she said. "I'll be right back."

She disappeared down the hallway and I sat still on her bed, feeling like an obedient child—and sweaty in my parka and knit hat.

After a couple of minutes, I stood up and slunk down the dark hallway to the top of the stairs. I could hear Xintra talking to her father in the living room. She didn't sound like herself. She sounded submissive, like a little girl.

"I'm sorry, Father. I didn't expect you to be home."

I heard his deep voice, but I couldn't make out the words exactly. I scooted closer to the edge of the stairs, leaning in to listen.

Xintra must have been closer because her words rang clearly. "I'll take them there. But I need more energy to really make it happen. More people."

A deep murmured response.

"Yeah, I have the blood," she said.

Blood? I took another step and sank down to sit on the polished wood step.

Xintra said something about her mom and immediately she was interrupted by his booming voice. It made the hair on my arms stand on end.

"Your mum didn't meet expectations, didn't meet her

highest potential," he said. "Do you *want* to be your mum?"

I couldn't tell exactly, but from up there on the stairs, it sounded like Xintra was whimpering. "Please, Father. Please..."

There was a clanging of some sort. A pot, maybe? And then footsteps and a door slamming. I stood up straight and scampered back to Xintra's bedroom, resuming my position. Xintra came back smiling, breathless, back to her regal self.

That night, when we pulled up to Lodima's house, Xintra announced that we were going to Trinity Forest and she was going to get someone buy us beer.

"Seriously?" It almost seemed as if her father had told her to do that. But what kind of parent would send their teenager into a forest to drink beer? "But I've never seen *RoboCop*."

Xintra raised her eyebrows and flicked her hand. "Shoo. Go get Lodima and let's go."

When I went inside Lodima's house, she was in her slippers and sweats. I told her the new plans, and she crossed her arms over her chest. "Go without me."

"Come on, Lo, just come with me." Her three-bedroom house smelled like lasagna and garlic bread, and it was tempting to stay. It reminded me of the old days when it had just been me and Lodima, when I had spent nearly every day at her house after school. Homemade lasagna had welcomed me every Thursday, and on Friday nights we had a standing appointment to watch *Dallas* on TV. We hadn't done that in so long.

"I rented Robocop." Lodima hated changes of plans, and staying in with a movie was one of her favorite things. A bowl of popcorn sat on the buffet table behind her.

"Loooo," I whined, stamping my feet. "Don't make me go alone."

"You can say no."

"I can't." I didn't know why I felt like I couldn't. Maybe it was easier to disappoint Lodima than Xintra.

"Well, I don't feel good about it. I dreamt that something weird happened in Trinity Forest," Lodima said.

"Oh pleeease. Like what?"

Lodima shook her head, her eyes wider than normal. "I don't want to talk about it. But we shouldn't go."

The horn honked outside, and I felt a dopamine rush. "Come on, it'll be fun."

She stood stiffly and shook her head.

"I need you," I said, tugging on her arms. "It won't be the same without you."

Her body relaxed, and it felt like the old me and Lodima. I put my arm around her shoulder.

Ultimately, she did get in the car. We made a campfire at Trinity Forest that night, to warm our hands. Xin and I drank beer and got into a deep philosophical conversation about the world and how screwed up it was. Lodima, meanwhile, used a stick to draw in the dirt, as if she was somehow on another planet that night—again.

I couldn't shake the fact that the more time we spent with Xintra, the more Lodima faded into the background. I missed our time together, just the two of us. But Xintra was... I don't know, enigmatic. I was a moth. She was the flame.

"Someday," Xintra said, "the world should be, like,

wiped clean. We should start over. Like Noah's Ark. You know? Start with the best people."

"Well, that sounds brutal," I said. "Who gets to decide who the best people are?"

She shrugged. "I don't know. But the very best would stay. It'd be like natural selection. My dad said that once."

Xintra held her black fur gloves out over the crackling fire and pointed at me. "Oh! Guys, you're never going to believe this. I finally found out what my father does with his time."

"What?" I asked eagerly, and even Lo seemed curious.

"For one thing, he comes to this forest. Often," Xintra said, leaning forward, a dramatic flare to her voice as if she were telling the best ghost story ever. "And when he comes, he holds some sort of chanting ceremony. Like a secret society. They wear robes."

I frowned, and a heebie-jeebie feeling traced across my skin. It wasn't anything real, just a feeling. Lodima's face also shifted. Maybe she felt it, too, but I wasn't sure.

"Oh," I said. *Creepy,* is what I meant. A chill had sunken into my bones. I wanted to go home. "We should go soon, okay?"

Lodima's eyes widened. "Yes, that would be good," she said. "Maybe we can go paint at your house, Dez."

Xintra leaned her torso over the flames of the fire to hand me another beer. I knew I shouldn't drink another, but I wanted it.

If Xintra was going to keep drinking, then maybe I would, too. I didn't want to go home, really, and maybe the beer would make me warmer. The can hissed as I opened the top. My fourth beer that night, and it was getting a little harder to focus. My lips were a little looser, my personality a little bigger. I liked it this way.

"Are you sure you should be drinking so much?" Lodima asked. At the time, I thought she was trying to be such a know-it-all goody-goody. I rolled my eyes. "You drive."

She shrugged. "Sure, I can do that Dez. But I need to get home soon because my mom and dad want me to help them make pies tomorrow morning for the local—"

"We all know." Xintra swatted her hand at Lodima. It was true. We'd been around Lo's parents so much, witness her dad fixing cars in the driveway or mowing the neighbor's lawn, watching romantic comedies with her mom. Perfect, just like Lo. He and her mom were local social workers, feeding the poor, raising money for books and shoes. Glittery, happy monks. A little nauseating, no offense to Lo.

Lodima sat up straight, smiling as we laughed about how perfect they were. Xintra waved her hand. "Sorry, Lo, what were you going to say?"

"We're making pies for a fundraiser. You know, you two joke that my parents are so perfect," Lodima said. "But it's hard. If you have a selfish thought, even for a moment, you're in for a half hour lecture from my mom. She's exhausting."

"You actually have selfish thoughts?" I laughed and turned my attention again to Xintra, who looked up to the inky black sky, sprinkled with a million stars, and then slowly let her gaze fall on me.

"I don't want to be anything like my mum." She lifted her beer to her lips.

I don't want to be like mine, either, I thought. I took a chug of beer too.

36

DEZI

Looking back, I should have seen things more clearly for what they were, how we were together. One day, the three of us climbed into Xintra's car at her house, and from up on the hill, I could see a girl with long black hair walking along the side of the dirt road. She was pretty far away, a good half a mile.

"Oh my God, there's Alessandra," Xintra said, pushing a cassette tape into the stereo.

I squinted. "How can you tell?"

"She follows me." Xintra backed out of the driveway, swinging her car out wide, and then headed down the dirt road toward the girl. She smiled. An old song by the Rolling Stones, *Sympathy for the Devil,* played.

"Watch this."

I was just opening my purse to get out some lip gloss when the motor revved and the wind whipped my hair through the open window. "Xintra!" I yelled. "What are you doing?"

I leaned over and watched the speedometer tick up from thirty to fifty-five miles per hour. The car bumped over the dips in the road and actually flew in the air at one point. I screamed—a swirl of joy and fear.

"Slow down!" Lodima yelled. The car picked up speed and soon, the car was screaming at sixty miles per hour.

"Yeah, seriously. Slow. Down." I clutched the handle on the door and pressed my foot into the floor, as if I could control the brakes from the passenger side. "Oh my God!"

Xintra bared her teeth in a freaky smile, and the music blared way too loud.

A few feet away from her, Alessandra swiveled around and saw us, then leapt out of the way and into the roadside ditch.

I covered my mouth, half-shocked, half-laughing at Xintra's audacity. I turned around and Lodima's eyes were huge. I think I could have seen all the way to the back of her eye sockets—they were that big.

I caught a glimpse of Alessandra, climbing out on all fours, her black hair obscuring her face, mud and snow covering her dress.

Xintra's lilting laugh was wicked and kind of delicious, and it became a sort of frosting over the Rolling Stones song.

"What the hell were you thinking?" I screamed, delighted, afraid, and completely dumbfounded by what had just happened.

"She's a stalker," Xintra said.

"She's just walking down the street," Lodima said. Her voice was sharp like an adult's. I glanced back to see Lodima's chin jutting out as she glared out the window. I hadn't seen Lo look like that before. She turned to me. "We should go back and see if she's okay."

Xintra swatted her away. "Oh, please. She's fine. She deserved it."

I didn't say anything. Xintra turned up the stereo.

Xintra's favorite store was about ten miles southwest of Leadville. From the outside, it looked like a wooden house shaped like an igloo with small, octagon-shaped windows. Crystals dangled like icicles from string tacked onto the overhang above the front porch. We ducked beneath them and rang the doorbell.

"Why are we here?" Lodima asked again. *Always with the questions.*

"Because I have some stuff I wanted to look at," Xintra said. "It'll be cool." She turned and gazed at Lodima with a look that could melt steel. "Or are you opposed to cool?"

Lodima shrugged.

A hunched woman answered the door. Her long gray hair hung in chunks like yarn. "Store's in the back," she said.

We followed her through a dark living room, every single inch covered with clutter and junk. It smelled like paper and mildew and dust. A hoarder's home. Three-foot-tall stacks of newspaper formed a path to a back doorway, covered only by a silk purple curtain.

I hesitated, the toe of my sneaker catching on the edge of a newspaper, and glanced back at Lo. In the dim light, she looked like she'd seen a dead body.

Candles flickered inside the room, shaped like a C with rounded walls. Tables draped with tapestries and wooden shelves were covered with objects for sale. Crystals and stones, stacks of tattered books, lit candles, figurines of gargoyles and monkeys, pyramids and lions, jars filled with various herbs. Xintra browsed them, curious, while Lodima and I hung by the door.

Eventually, Xin picked up a thick black book with a red pyramid on the front. The title read *The Book of the Dead*. "It's Egyptian," she said.

"I thought we were going shopping," I said. "Like, for clothes?"

"I need some way to deal with Alessandra."

"Seems like you already dealt with her," Lodima said, holding up a yellow tapestry.

"She's a liar. She spreads lies about me, and wherever I go, there she is. It's like that song by the Police. '*Every breath you take, every step you take, I'll be watching you.*' She's freaky."

"That sucks," I said. Xintra was cool, and I supposed all cool people probably had freaky stalkers. I picked up a red-and-black tapestry, feeling the silky texture and studying the tiny Egyptian symbols along the edges. "What's that book about?" I asked.

"It has secrets on how to unlock the power of the earth and how to use spells." She shook her head with wide eyes and a silly grin.

"Ahhh, of course. Everyone needs one of those books," I said, peering over her shoulder at the words. There were strange squiggles and drawings on the pages. I caught some words. *I am Atum, the power and impending of all that is to be. The magic is older and greater than all the gods together.*

"Weeeeird...." I sang, picking up a golden elephant figurine. I wondered the meaning behind it.

"Can we go now?" Lodima asked. "I have homework."

"Yeah, me too," I said, but still I lingered, wanting to be there with Xintra. Plus, I couldn't take my eyes off the piles of weird objects in there, lit by flickering candles.

Xintra saw Lodima looking at a book called *Circle of Stars Almanac.* "Oooh, that looks good," Xintra said.

"I'm interested in anything to do with stars," Lodima said. They huddled over the book for a long time. Xintra wound up getting *The Book of the Dead* and another one, *Art of Connectivity Souls: Earth Matters Bible*, while Lodima bought her star book.

While they made their purchases, I ran my fingers through a bowl of powder. A tiny label beside it said, "cat's claw and moth's wing." Disgusted, I dropped the powder and took a step back. "Let's go," I said, suddenly eager to get out of the shop. The whole place, the whole day, had left me with a creepy vibe.

I should have paid more attention to that feeling.

37

DEZI

"Party at Trinity tonight!" Xintra announced as we walked through the hallway at school. It was a Friday and the school was amped over the bash that Xintra was organizing. She was buying the booze and selling red plastic cups to everybody out at the forest. A true entrepreneur.

"Will people really come if that place that is supposed to be haunted?" I asked, walking faster to keep up with Xintra.

"Of course they will. Who wants to look like a chicken? Plus, that's the lure—going where you're not supposed to go, seeing if anything crazy happens."

We passed Brett Davis, who was busting out of his shirt with those football muscles. Xintra said every girl in school wanted him, but he liked *me*.

"You coming?" I asked Brett as Xintra and I passed. I felt like she and I together were giants holding the world in our hands. Lodima, who by then was becoming a third wheel of sorts, trailed behind the Xintra-Dezi power couple. Everyone appeared to bow to us now: even the Aqua Net girls of last year looked at me entirely different, squealing at the idea of a bonfire and keg in the woods.

Brett met my eyes for an instant and then scanned my body, lingering on my breasts, then my waist, clearly outlined in the tight pink sweater loaned to me by Xintra. "Hell yeah," he said.

My whole body lost oxygen for an instant. I offered him my best sexy smile and then ran to catch up to Xintra, who was strutting down the hallway toward her locker. "Hey, Brett's coming tonight!" I whispered.

"Of course he's coming," Xintra said, batting her long eyelashes with a smug look on her face. "I told you. Everyone will come."

Lodima stood there for a moment without a word, and then seemed to vanish in the flood of people.

Xintra shoved her books into my abdomen. "Hold these." While I waited for her to open her combination lock, people passed us in the hall, nodding to me, smiling and giving me high fives.

Two years ago, those people barely glanced at me as I shuffled down the hall. When I gave speeches in class, they same people would turn and talk to each other. When I got the guts to actually talk to them in the hallway, they gave me brief, false smiles, politely answering questions about a social studies assignment or the weather, but their eyes always darted behind me, looking for someone better to talk to next.

Xintra was the cocoon that had turned me from hairy caterpillar into a butterfly. I loved being next to her. I couldn't get over how lucky I was.

A few lockers away, Alessandra sat on her haunches,

pushing a pile of books into her locker. Her straight black hair was so long strands had gotten caught between her bent waist and thighs, which were clad in green striped tights.

Xintra smirked when she saw her. "She's practically slept with the entire town of Leadville," she said. "No wonder she looks like the walking dead. She's disease-ridden."

As we passed, Xintra bumped Alessandra with her knee so she tumbled over onto the floor. "Oops," Xintra said, shrugging.

"What was that for?" Alessandra cried, swiping a hunk of black hair from her mouth and popping up off the floor to her full height of maybe six feet. Black army boots protruded beneath the long black cotton skirt and her face was pale, painted with black lipstick and thick eyeliner. A long beaded necklace dangled from her neck, and a looping ankh cross pendant bounced just above her belly.

Xintra turned around and walked backward, shouting down the hall to her. "Wow, great makeup, girl. If laughter is the best medicine, your face must be curing the world."

A smile inched onto my face but I knew that was wicked mean. But really, Alessandra was just as hateful. "I wasn't born with enough middle fingers to let you know how I feel about you," she shouted at us as we marched down the hall.

Xintra leaned into me, and I felt strong in her presence.

"How do you get the balls to do that?" I asked.

"Just hate." The crowd of kids parted like the red sea for us. "What do *you* hate?" she asked, glancing at me before swiftly turning the corner toward the front doors.

When we got to the exit, she stopped, waiting for me to open the heavy metal door. I did.

"I don't hate anything. Maybe sauerkraut? Physics?"

"I hate waiting for things," she said. "And I hate my mum."

The wind whipped around us, sending a chill through my skin. "Come on, you don't *hate* your mom. You don't even know her."

She stopped at her car, turned around, and looked me square in the face. "Yes, I do hate her. Someday, she'll *feel* just how much I hate her."

Standing in the parking lot, flooded with kids racing to their cars, I could taste her bitterness.

At the party that night, I clenched the plastic red cup in one hand and snaked my arm around the crowd of kids to get a refill from the keg. I needed to slam another beer and put on my very best Xintra-inspired performance for everyone.

I sipped the foam and licked my lips, and then spotted Lodima sitting on a stump watching the scene alone. She drank a Pepsi.

"When are you going to drink? Be like us?" I asked, flopping onto the ground next to her. My beer splashed onto my leather bomber jacket, another stylish item loaned to me by Xintra.

"I don't need it," Lodima said. "I believe it muddles my brain, and I like to be sharp."

"You talk like you're ancient sometimes, you know?" I teased her, but I meant it. Sometimes it felt like she really was from the Seven Sisters constellation. Sure, I was from there too. But this was a new role for me, something I was trying on for the time being. Xintra made it easier, giving me the costume, the lines, and the places to be.

"I miss the days the two of us spent together, before Xintra," she said finally, sifting leaves between her hands.

Me, too. We spent so much time together, and she was my first best friend. I couldn't help but hitch my wagon to Xintra's star, yet I didn't want to lose Lodima. There had to be a way for us to connect again. "Okay, tell me someone's dream. You haven't told me about your empathy stuff in awhile," I said.

"*Empathic* stuff. Not empathy stuff. You wouldn't understand. It's very hard to explain." She patted my arm to lighten things up, a signal that I was clearly trying too hard. "Did you see that Steve is here? He's over there sitting on that log." She pointed.

I looked across the crowd of people and Steve glanced up. We locked eyes for a moment. There was something special about that guy, and I could feel it. Nervous, I turned my eyes down with a bashful smile. My heart fluttered. I thought about going over to talk to him, but Xintra stepped in front of me.

"Brett is heeere," she sang with glee.

I hesitated. Xintra thought Brett was the guy for me, and she hadn't steered me wrong yet. I took another gulp of beer. "Yeah, but what do I say to a guy like Brett?"

"Ask him how he enjoys football," Lodima said. She sounded like someone's mother.

Tipping my cup back, I swallowed the rest of my beer in one long pull. My sleeve became a napkin, clearing the dribbles from my chin. Pulling out some lip gloss from my coat pocket, courtesy of Xintra, I stood and marched over to find beautiful Brett by the bonfire.

Steve's eyes lit up as I walked in his direction, and for an instant, I considered changing course and talking to him. But instead, I marched toward the grown-up powerful energy of Xintra and Brett.

Laughter and chatter rippled through the air, bouncing off the flames of the bonfire to the stars and back. Two Aqua Net girls stumbled around the campfire ring, leaning into each other and giggling. Another two people wrapped their bodies around each other kissing, oblivious to the crowd. Elbows bumped them, beer splashed on them, but their kiss had transported them someplace else.

"Get a room!" I shouted, emboldened by my newfound place on the planet.

Finally, after weaving through the crowd of people, I found Brett. The world looked a little slanted. Slamming three beers in less than an hour could do that to you.

"Heeyyyy," I said, turning my head down, offering a coy look that was intended to look attractive. But really, inside my heart, I knew it was all a costume. It felt better than being the Neptune Girl who sat on the sidelines.

"Hey Dezi," he said, slowly reaching a hand out to touch my arm. With eyes half-mast, he ogled me up and down. "Don't I get a hug or what?"

"Um, yeah," I said, throwing my arms wide open. I rarely hugged anyone. Not even Mama. But this was one big embrace, our bundled-up bodies pressed tight together from thigh to head.

"Mmmm, you smell good," he whispered, his hot breath blowing into my hair.

The comment flattered me. Surely I was now a butterfly. The costume was on, the beer was in the system, but I had never been great with people. So I wondered, what to say to a boy you have nothing much in common with besides school?

"So... did you study for that Spanish test?" I asked. Loser question.

Brett leaned in toward me to whisper something in my ear when Xintra yanked my arm, spinning me around and away from him. "She's here. Can you believe it?"

"Who?" I asked.

Xintra pointed into the trees. Alessandra stood near a pine tree in a long dark skirt, her straight black hair blowing in the breeze. She didn't talk to anyone; she just stared at the party, looking like a ghost in the flickering light of the bonfire.

"Watch this." Xintra took my hand and together we approached Alessandra. About five feet from her, Xintra crossed her arms. "Get out. You weren't invited."

"This isn't your property," Alessandra said. "It's sacred land. Of *my* people."

"What?" I whispered to Xintra, leaning into her and nearly losing my balance.

"She has some ridiculous belief that this forest belongs to her family," Xintra explained, loud enough that Alessandra—and the rest of the party—could hear.

"The Incas and the Egyptians," Alessandra clarified, "and all of the world's ancient civilizations. We're charged with protecting it. And you're trespassing." The crowd quieted down, and it was as if a spotlight shone on Xintra and Alessandra.

"Incas? I think you're in the freaking United States," I

said, my chest puffing up from the rush of defending my friend. I crossed my arms and tilted my head.

"You think you can get what you want by pulling the energy of these people to unlock Trinity. But you'll be sorry," Alessandra said.

"I doubt that," Xintra said.

I didn't have time to comprehend what they meant, because just then, blue and red lights flickered behind Alessandra. A smug expression crossed her face. "Guess your party's over."

Someone shouted, "Cops!" and the crowd dispersed, inciting commotion and movement around us as people ran through the trees.

Xintra scowled and then, in one quick turn, she spat at Alessandra. The dollop of saliva hit Alessandra squarely on the cheek, and she screamed out in disgust. I think her mouth dropped open, though I couldn't make out her full expression with the blue and red lights flashing behind her. She wiped her face. "You bitch!"

I gaped because I couldn't believe Xintra had just *spit* on Alessandra. Xintra had more balls than any guy I knew, and I half expected them to throw down and start pulling hair. I stood with my hand over my mouth, watching the scene as if it were in slow motion.

Xintra heaved her chest forward and jutted her chin before a wicked smile inched up her face. She whispered something across the dark space to Alessandra, something I couldn't really make out. It sounded like, "Got the energy, bitch." But I couldn't tell for sure.

My eyes were glued on Alessandra, her dark hair blowing in the wind and her silhouette lit by the flashing lights behind her. Her face twisted, her nostrils flared, and it almost looked like she might cry. Her bottom lip quivered and she bared her teeth like a hissing vampire.

The sight of her with that black lipstick on her lips made me yell out. Part freaky moment and part delight. I could see a police officer built like a bowling ball coming tottering toward us, calling for us to come with him.

I couldn't let Xintra get into a brawl here in the forest— or get arrested—so I grabbed her hand and pulled. We ran, laughing, dropping our drinks and taking off through the dense pine trees.

"Lodi!" I yelled, turning around to search for Lodima and her blonde fur coat. I spotted her twenty yards away and waved. Soon, I could hear her wheezing asthmatic breath and pattering footsteps behind us.

Xintra led us to the barbed-wire fence. The lights of the police cars still pulsated, and their vehicle wasn't too far away from Xintra's BMW. A police officer leaned against his green and white car with his arms crossed, smirking with his arms, watching the other kids dart out of the forest.

We ducked down in the bushes and followed the barbed wire until we came to an opening where no one could see us. We snuck into Xintra's car and slunk down low in the seats for a while. Then Lodima and I got out and pushed the car slowly down the road, with the engine in neutral, before hopping in. Xintra gunned the gas to get away.

"Oh my God!" I screamed. This was like living in a movie. "We got out!"

Lodima giggled from the backseat, clenching her chest tight with her palms. "That was close!"

Xintra was laughing too, but then as she glanced in the

rearview mirror at the police lights, her face turned stony. "She called the cops. You know she did."

"Who?" Lodi asked.

"Alessandra," I said. "Probably because someone got scared when they saw her face." I blurted out a forced laugh.

Lodima reached up from the back seat and touched my arm. "Dezi! That's *so* mean!"

I shook her hand off me. She could be so much like a mother staring down her nose at us—or at least that's how I felt then. I leaned into Xintra, glee filling me head to toe, cackling.

"I can't believe you spit on her!" I said finally, gasping with disbelief. I spun around to look at Lodima. "Did you see that? She totally spit on her."

Lodima pursed her lips like a disapproving old lady, so I turned back to Xintra. A small smile inched up her lips. Headlights from the oncoming cars on the highway lit her face white.

"She'll be sorry," she said.

The next Monday, I pulled a book out of the library stacks and saw Lodima on the other side of the bookshelf, talking to Alessandra. Their voices came in murmurs, but looking at the back of Alessandra, I could tell the conversation was an emotional one. Her rounded shoulders shook, and Lodima frowned and patted her arm. Alessandra whispered something and took off her ankh cross necklace and gave it to Lodima. They hugged.

I frowned; it felt like a betrayal to Xintra. I watched

with disgust when Xintra popped up behind me, squeezing my sides.

I spun around, trying to block the hole that made Lodima visible.

"I found the best book ever," Xintra said, grinning. She pulled a book out from behind her back, proudly displaying its title: *A Female Guide to Proper Poo: Etiquette for Public Lavatories.* We busted up laughing. "I'm checking this out and never returning it," she said.

I immediately forgot about Lodima and Alessandra. But the following month, Alessandra wasn't at school anymore. It was like Xintra's words after the party, that wish, had made her vanish into thin air. There was no police report or search or news coverage. It was like she and her family just picked up and left town.

Or at least that's what I assumed.

38

DEZI

The cold wind rushed past me when I opened the front door. I felt groggy, awakened suddenly by the thundering knock on the door. I couldn't imagine who would be at my house at midnight on a Tuesday.

It was Xintra, standing in the frigid April air with no coat, hat, or gloves. With her hands crossed over her body, she jumped up and down from the cold.

"Hey," she said, stepping inside immediately.

"What's going on? Where's your coat?"

She beelined directly to the potbelly stove in the corner and held her hands up to the heat. I stood there in my cotton nightshirt wrapping my arms around my chest. "You okay?" I asked.

She glanced at me over her shoulder and then focused again on her hands, frowning and biting her lip. Clearing my throat, I inched closer to her. Her eyes looked glossy, as if she were on the verge of a breakdown.

This was *not* how our relationship worked. She had

always been this tall, impenetrable tower—utterly unbreakable. Made of steel. The one with the plans. The one with the knowledge about how things ought to be. But in this moment, a crack became visible in that tower. I needed to comfort her. But I didn't know how.

"Hey... what's going on?" I asked, resting my fingers on her back. I could feel the indents of her ribs. God, she felt skinny.

Xintra shook her head and then slowly sank down to sit on the floor. She gazed at her thin, lace-up leather boots. "My father. He revealed everything tonight and dumped it on me."

"Dumped what?"

"He wants me to take over his operation."

"Operation? Like, his business?"

"Sure." She shrugged. "But it's something he wants me to do *now*. Which means I would have to change a lot of stuff, a lot of me. And, I don't want to be like my mum...I don't want to be ordinary. And I..." The words stopped in midair and then, without warning, tears rolled down her smooth cheeks. She looked perfect even when she cried, unlike me, whose lips would puff up and cheeks blotched red.

"You what?" I asked.

"I feel like maybe he's right. It's destiny. But I'm scared."

I laughed out loud, my way of getting everything to lighten up, for her to bounce back to being Xintra again. "You're seventeen. *Destiny*? I'm just trying to get through trigonometry."

She laughed airily and wiped her tears. "You know Gilman?"

"Yeah," I said. The government had shut off all public

access to the mining town about twenty-five miles away because of toxic pollutants.

"My father had people high in the government shut the mine there down," she said. "He wants to buy it."

"Okay..."

She sniffed and waved her hand at me. "Never mind. Will you... go with me to check this opportunity out?" She bit her lips together and begged me with her eyes.

"Where? Gilman? It's hard to get down there." The old mining ghost town sat on a hillside so steep off Tennessee Pass that was so steep, frankly I was surprised it hadn't been swept away by mud and snow already. I hoped this "opportunity" instead meant checking out some of the places her dad worked—Hawaii, Egypt, Peru.

"Trinity Forest."

Those were not the words I expected. A deep, hearty laugh exploded from my throat. "For another party?"

She didn't laugh with me or even answer my question. So that meant that she was serious. I stood up and walked into the kitchen. "Want some tea or something?"

Sitting cross-legged on the worn carpet, Xintra looked up at me, her green eyes wide. "Please will you come? I'm scared."

She could be so convincing, no matter what her demeanor. "What is his business anyway? Why the forest?"

She shook her head. "Our family has worked for centuries on this. I'm talking back to our ancestors."

"Ancestors? I don't get it."

"My father finally got ahold of a key that could unlock everything... could change everything. I mean, everything, Dezi. Life as you know it. But I don't know if I want to... I don't know if I'm ready."

"Then why don't you just say no?" I asked. Xintra usually had no problem doing that.

She shrugged with one shoulder. Her entire body grew still as she gazed off to the corner of the room. I cringed, wondering if maybe she noticed all the dust and mildew and balls of cat hair stuck to the floorboards.

"Father says the world will be better off. That it all depends on me. I need to do this." Her eyes broke from their stupor and she gazed up at me again. She pushed her palms together as if in a prayer. "Please say you'll do this for me?"

Xin had pulled me out of the depths of obscurity in school and changed my whole life. I owed her. I inhaled deeply and exhaled my answer. "Sure."

Her father was right. She had a knack for leadership, destiny, whatever you wanted to call it. A genuine grin spread across her face and a good warmth filled me.

Her eyes looked gentle. "I'm glad I found you, Dezi." After a moment, she added, "And let's make sure Lodima can make it too. I want it to be the three of us. Like a trinity."

"Okay," I said, and she stood up.

She hugged me tight. "Three," she said again. "Like Hectate, the three-headed goddess of witchcraft."

I rolled my eyes and told her to get some sleep.

39

DEZI

My teeth began to chatter. Winter had slowly faded away and spring was around the corner, but in the Rocky Mountains it was still freezing cold at night. Xintra, Lodima and I huddled together in our parkas.

"What are we doing here again?" I muttered.

"Just give him a few more minutes to get here," Xintra said. The full moon created an even glow on the three of us. Patches of snow dotted the ground amid tree roots, rocks, bushes, and rotted logs.

Lodima took a ragged breath before catching my eye. She gave a little shake of her head. "I...I would rather be eating popcorn and watching recorded soap operas at your house, Dez."

"Let's build a fire while we wait," Xintra said, breaking away from our huddle. Without her, the air became colder.

"Let's just go home, Xin," I said with a whine and a few cold stamps of my feet. "Let's go drink wine in the car and then eat popcorn and watch soaps. Like Lodima says."

"I didn't say the drink wine part," Lodima said.

"You never do." I grinned. "Besides, Xin, we'll never find dry wood to build a fire. This is stupid."

As soon as I said this, Xintra started gathering dry branches and pulled out some paper and a box of matches from her backpack. She assembled the sticks and lit the kindling, puffed air from her cheeks, and after a few minutes we had a fire. Xintra was an on-demand Boy Scout.

Lodima and I reached out to warm ourselves by the fire. I guessed we were staying. The flames stayed low, but it gave off some warmth nonetheless.

"So does your father care that you have your two side-kicks here?" I asked.

"He loves that there are three of us. And he loves that you two are... um, gifted."

Lodima and I exchanged goofy looks of surprise.

"Gifted?" I asked. "Does that mean we're freaks? Because we are." A belly laugh shot straight from my gut.

"Yes, we're Venus Friday friends," Lodima said with all seriousness. "Dezi is the Neptune Girl, and I am the Venus Girl. "

My face contorted into a half smile, half grimace. I felt as if I'd grown out of the whole Venus Friday thing and the description defined a lonely, younger me who had been trying to find somewhere to fit. So really, Neptune Girl didn't describe me anymore. But I didn't have the heart to tell Lodima that.

Still, Xintra liked the whole planet thing. "And *I'm* the sun!" she screeched, jumping up with delight.

I laughed. Of course, she was the sun. Xintra must have seen me roll my eyes.

Lodima frowned. "Come on, Dez, don't you believe in the power of the constellations? In astrology, the sun is symbolic of the self that is expressed outwardly to family and friends and makes us visible to the world," Lodima said.

Apparently, now we were in for a dissertation on astrological signs.

"Do I believe it? Not really," I said before putting up a hand to Lo. "Sorry, no offense."

"Well, I love it," Xintra said, eyeing Lodima with a shared grin. Jealousy flashed in me. I was the one with the connection to Xin, not Lo.

"In ancient Celtic and African cultures, the sun is feminine power. Life. Power. Strength. Energy. Self." Lodima ticked off the attributes with her fingers.

"See? I should *really* be the sun," Xintra said, nodding and laughing.

I stared at the flames and changed the subject. "So why did you think we were gifted?"

Xintra shook her two hands covered in fur-lined gloves. "Because you see things."

"Yes, I do see things," Lodima said, suddenly bright. "I hear things and see things. I would say that yes, perhaps it is a gift."

Xintra looked to me. "And you, Dez, you paint stuff. Visions, right?"

"Well, I haven't really painted in awhile," I said, trying to stop from blushing. "Who told you that I saw things when I painted?"

"Lodima. When I first met her," Xintra said.

"Oh," I said. Lodima shared my secret. I felt like I'd just

been stripped naked in front of them. I looked at Lodima. "What made you talk about that?"

"Lo and I just talk about stuff like that," Xintra said. Lodima's smile extended full and wide, showing all her teeth. She loved this sort of stuff. But it left me feeling like I was on the outside, and that was an ugly feeling on the inside.

The fire flickered and popped, and Xintra took a step closer to warm herself by the flames. "Anyway, I've been wanting to tell you guys that I want to do a fun little game here. Something that will make use of your gifts."

"Sure," Lodima said. She stood up straight and her face glowed as if she had waited all her life for someone to ask her to use her superpowers. "What's that?"

"Okay," Xintra said, clasping her hands together. She slowly unraveled her story like a ball of silky yarn. "There's a hidden energy source in Trinity, something deposited here long ago. It's magnetic. Magical. Not of this earth."

Perhaps her father wants to mine this area, I thought. He must've had an awesome business deal here.

She held up *The Book of the Dead* with two hands. "We have our special gifts because of our ancestors, the Sumerians of Mesopotamia. You, Lo, came from the Celtic Tuatha Dé Danaan tribe which were alien deities."

My mouth dropped open slightly and then I laughed out loud. The bold, obnoxious kind of laughter that Mama always hated. How had my stylish, popular friend turned into this nighttime storyteller of ancient gods and magical places? I couldn't imagine where she had come up with this stuff.

Xintra set *The Book of the Dead* down on the ground and moved behind us, firmly placing her hands on Lodima and then me, directing us into positions around the fire. Lodima and I exchanged smiles. How far would Xin go with this silly little charade? I waited for her cackle, the tuneless laugh, for her to tell us what her dad really had planned there.

Instead, she handed us each some sort of coin. I couldn't see what it was, but I assumed it was a quarter. I put it in my pocket.

She picked up a long walking stick and dragged it slowly along the ground, outlining the three of us. The lines she drew created a triangle. At the base of it, between me and Lodima, she traced something else into the dirt and snow. A snake with a dragon's head.

Lodima and I watched silently, and I started to feel weird about it. Xintra didn't crack a smile or stop. She moved her whole body, her hair swishing, while she drew the creepy-looking dragon.

"Xin," I said, suddenly feeling much colder. I shivered, my teeth chattering faster as the fire crackled and popped. I felt wildly uncomfortable, like something was crawling under my skin, breathing on my neck.

She returned to her place at the top of our triangle around the fire, held her stick with two hands high above her head, and began chanting words I did not at all understand.

I couldn't get over how bizarre this was, seeing my friend do this, in this dark weird forest. I liked it so much better when she talked about boys and makeup and parties. This howling young girl didn't feel like my Xintra. She wailed the words so loud that I swore if anyone were to see us, any kind of social life I had managed to develop in Leadville would surely be destroyed.

I glanced around the forest, wondering if maybe this was a prank and people were watching, waiting to see if we'd join in, follow her. Her expression was serious, though, enrapture written plainly on her face, from her lips to her eyes.

I became concerned, and I opened my mouth to stop her. But the words didn't come out. No one cut off Xintra.

As her fury and chanting continued, I became warmer. The air lost its chill. She took a breath, and for an instant snapped back into my friend Xintra, grinning big and waving her arms up and down. "Come on, come on, go with me on this. Chant, you two, chant!"

From across the fire, Lodima looked to me with wide eyes, and then the two of us started mumbling and fumbling the foreign words, laughing and joking and playing along. I stopped and looked at Xintra, tilting my head. "Really? Come on..."

But Xintra didn't stop. She kept reciting the same words over and over, and I could feel something shift. My skin felt so warm, and a little buzzing feeling swept through me, pulsing, like electric energy circling back and forth, in and out.

I took a step back from the fire, and the energetic buzz diminished. I took a step forward and it increased. I *liked* the pulsing energy. So I moved forward another step into what felt like a hypnotic embrace that I wanted to stay nestled in.

Lodima bit her lips together, took a step closer to the fire, too, and her eyes bounced back and forth between me and Xintra. Eventually, I could understand Xintra's words, and something I saw in her from across the fire compelled me to start chanting them with her, over and over.

Maybe it was her hair that blew in circles when there wasn't a breeze, maybe it was the Xintra costume I wore, the way I mimicked her mannerisms and even caught myself copying her accent. It was *Xintra*—that's all I can say to explain it. She was transcendent to me, especially in that moment.

"*Novus ordo mundi.* Hail Ki. Hail Tuatha Dé Danaan. I call on earthly powers. Connect us now and in all energies. Connected we shall be!" We chanted this over and over. Louder and more powerful. Lodima joined in, too. We closed our eyes, raised our hands.

I was not a religious girl. Mama had stopped taking me to church after my brother and Papa died. This felt creepy, dangerous, and bad. But somehow, I could not stop myself from continuing the chant because it was also surprisingly delicious and invigorating. The hair on my arms felt electric.

Xintra pumped her stick up and down with each beat and motioned to us that we, too, should raise our arms in the air. We did, albeit hesitantly. She closed her eyes and began to sway in something of a spiritual enrapture. The chanting grew stronger, louder, more hypnotic, like an African drumbeat or a bewitching séance. And soon, something swept through me like a fiery, intoxicating dream, electricity swirling around us on the air, as if the chanting itself had transformed into something that was truly alive. A tornado building in the air.

I loved every minute of it. The power. The fury. The dark rapture of its energy.

The next instant, a huge bang interrupted my words and my eyes snapped open. A bright bolt of electricity shot up from the fire and lingered in the air between us, the flickering blue-white streak rising like a fountain. It crept out and around us, encircling us, touching the ground, as if we stood in a triangular bubble of electricity.

I stopped mumbling words. My tongue felt like it might choke me. Lodima looked dumbfounded, too, as she gazed openmouthed at our electric enclosure.

My hands slowly dropped to my sides as Xintra's lone voice boomed loudly and she pumped the stick high in the air like a captivating witch. She opened her eyes, more beautiful than ever in the firelight, her hair swirling in a hurricane of wind and electricity. The fire lit her snow-white face and her green eyes just so, and immediately, she became the exact replica of the portrait of her I painted in a daze last year. I sucked in a breath.

"Xin!" I yelled. She looked unearthly, possessed almost.

From across the fire, a grin spread over her face, combining delight and pure, raw power. I could not deny the power of the chanting, the swirling red hair, my painting prophecy and the—*holy crap*—electric bubble around us. This was real. Her power was real.

She dropped to her knees, bringing her head to the ground in the most vulnerable position I'd ever seen her assume. With that submissive stance, the electricity disappeared and the mystical magic of the moment dissipated. Slowly, she gazed up with innocent eyes. It took me a moment, but I realized the look was not intended for me and Lodima. She fixed her eyes on something else— behind us, in the trees.

Lodima and I turned to follow her gaze and saw a man clad in a long dark robe standing near the trees. He emerged from the forest, clapping slowly, almost sarcasti-cally, as if she were auditioning for a part in a play.

I recognized him immediately as Xintra's father.

"Very good, my dear," he said once he arrived near our triangle. His deep voice boomed like a British military general. "You three have helped increase the geomagnetic field of Trinity. This. Is. Destiny."

He removed the hood of his robe with two hands, revealing the auburn hair, the piercing eyes. He nodded slowly from me to Lodima. "Will you join us to reach your highest potential?"

"Heh," I said with a breathy laugh that evolved into a hysterical giggle. I had heard of people laughing at inappropriate times, especially in times of stress, and I supposed this was that. This was all so crazy.

Lodima must've felt the same because she giggled too.

My laughter petered out when I noticed for the first time that a fog had swamped the forest, moving slowly across the ground as if we stood inside a cloud. The hair on my arms stood, and it felt as if the oxygen stopped moving through my body.

Lodima took a giant step closer to me and clasped my hand in both of hers. I nudged her shoulder with mine as the fog rippled in like a river, then swirled around the two of us, entwining us like mummies until we couldn't see anything beyond our own noses.

Then, as if things could get any weirder, a light began to make its way through the fog. Blinking fast at first, I squinted to see a tall wrought-iron gate that led to a day-lit colorful meadow. Xintra and her father floated to the gate and swung it wide open.

"Come on, guys," Xintra said. "You two are the other parts of me. Let's go in together and do a *real* makeover. On the whole world!"

She glanced up at her father, who towered over her, and gazed at him as if she were a small, eager child. He did not look back at her, but stood incredibly still, like a statue made of stone.

"Please, guys, you owe me," Xintra pleaded, sounding like my real friend, the one who had plucked me from obscurity. She picked me, the turnip in the flower garden. I did owe her. And that meadow behind her looked amazing —and just like my drawing. *Destiny*.

Lodima must have seen something different. She crossed her arms. "No," she whispered close to me. "This is not good. I can feel it. This is what I dreamt about. We shouldn't have come."

Lodima pulled on my arm to leave, but I wondered what would happen to me at school if Xintra went off with her father on some adventure and disappeared. I wondered whether I would be anything without her. Xintra had already offered me a better version of myself. I was curious to know what was behind that gate.

Xintra tilted her head and waved me into the meadow. "It'll be fun."

And with that, I gave Lodima's hand a squeeze and let go. Glancing back at her as I trotted toward Xintra, I yelled over my shoulder, "Tell Mama I'm sleeping over at Xintra's tonight."

And I ran through the gate and grabbed Xintra's hand.

A decision I would forever regret.

40

EMBER

The journal ends there. Just like that. I shake my head. Mom took part in a creepy, dangerous séance. And she *enjoyed* it. She may have even fueled Xintra's power. I guess in a way, it's a relief to know I'm not the only one who fell for Trinity's allure, but it still makes me feel like rocks are rolling around inside my stomach.

I lie on the bed in my room, on my belly, gazing at the empty pages left in the journal. Something happened to Mom there in Trinity. I expected her to write about it. But she didn't, and now she's gone. An anchor hangs on my heart. Every once in a while, the realization that she and Dad are gone for good still physically hurts.

And now, Lodima is gone, too, murdered in front of my face. And Maddie could be gone, as well. My best friend. It doesn't make sense. Maddie and I were ready to start again, now that I was back and finally *alive*.

An invisible belt wraps around my chest and arms,

cinching tighter and tighter. All my answers remain with the dead.

I sit up, take a bite of green Jell-O from the tray of food left for me, and consider new escape routes. My throat feels so dry that I jump up and stick my head under the faucet to gulp water. A nurse comes in to check on me, asking me stupid questions about whether I've filled out the questionnaire—which I'm assuming is about medication—and then picks up my tray, tidying up the bare room, lingering too long.

When she leaves, I notice the newspaper she left on the built-in desk. I pick it up and just below the Denver Post banner are headlines about the virus epidemic, the forest fires in Montana, and the hurricane barreling up from the south. Xintra made the front-page news.

Then, in the far right-hand corner on the bottom of the page, I catch a glimpse of a photo. My stomach twists, seeing him again: his sunken cheeks, crooked nose, shaggy hair.

It's a mug shot of Zach. Above the photo is a headline: *Leadville man sentenced to eight years.* The story says he was busted for selling heroin to high school kids.

Feelings and memories come screaming back, surprising me, stealing my breath. A flash of Zach, smelling of peanut butter, pouring the white pills into my hand, the two of us standing in tall grass behind our high school. The feeling of the metal button on his jeans cutting into my leg while I lay half-naked on the seat of his truck. So vulnerable, so weak, so robbed of everything. Revulsion twists inside me. I shiver. *It wasn't your fault.*

The fact that he got nailed for some other crime makes me feel better. But still, it's like dropping an ice cube into a glass of warm water. It helps, but it doesn't make a big enough difference. The truth of the matter is he took something from me, a piece of me, carving it up for himself. JT was no better, cutting out a little divot from me each time he pocketed my cash in exchange for my escape pills, the first bump in the road to my demise. All these experiences have become thick scars on my soul that will never go away. New skin may grow over them, covering them up, dulling the discoloration and the irregular bumps. But the marks will always be there.

I pick up the newspaper and rip it up. Gritting my teeth, I tear up Zach's face, twisting everything—his story, the past—tearing it into tiny pieces. Rip. Rip. Rip. I pull and squeeze and dig my nails into the paper. The satisfaction of destroying his face and, as a result, destroying the thoughts of him in my mind, that time in my life, feels so incredibly cathartic—like taking a gasp of air after holding your breath at the bottom of the pool. I've been fighting for survival since I got to Trinity Forest, and I never stopped to really process what happened. What Zach did.

A knock on the door makes me drop the sweaty ball of newspaper in my hand.

The door opens and I see Tre and Jared—two reminders that not all guys suck.

Visiting hours! I leap off the bed and fling my arms around each of their necks. "Uhh my God, I need out of here!"

The nurse from earlier returns and bustles around the room, wiping off the counter and so obviously eavesdropping, so the two of them remain pretty subdued.

"How's Maddie?" I ask.

Jared shakes his head. "Same."

I cover my mouth with my hand. "Is she coherent?"

"Not really," he says, sitting down. He squeezes his lips with his hands, just like Dad used to do.

Tre runs his hand through his hair and paces the room. He sits on a chair that's been bolted to the floor, while the nurse fusses in my room, peppering me with questions about feeling "comfortable."

"Do you have Axel?" I ask. That poor cat saw Lodima die and then was abandoned by me.

Tre nods. "Yeah, I've got him covered."

At last, the nurse leaves us alone. The moment she shuts the door behind her, Tre leans forward and speaks urgently. "Okay, we've got a plan," he says. "I met this girl downstairs in the cafeteria who'll help us get you out."

"Who? How?"

"We gave her forty bucks to help us," Jared says.

I'm thrilled they have a plan, but bringing in an outsider makes me wary. "Why would she want to help us?" *Can we trust her?*

"I just started talking to her," Tre explains, "and she offered to help. She's about your height, dark hair."

Jared takes a balled-up black T-shirt, a baseball hat and a pair of jeans and throws them at my head. "You'll dye your hair brown. If you guys are dressed alike, the nurses won't notice. I'll go out there and chat with them, distract them with my charm."

"Charm," I deadpan.

"Listen, I'm the people person of the family. I'll figure out what the nurses dig and chat them up. After a few times of the girl coming and going, you'll be the one to emerge wearing similar clothes, a baseball hat, and jeans. You'll use her visitor's badge to exit."

"Okay, that's sounds good."

"If she stays in your room a little longer, she can pick up a bonus—a gift card to Applebee's I'll leave downstairs in the cafeteria. Then, voilà, she'll come out, looking like herself. Not you. Cool?"

"God, you're like a spy on a TV show," I say.

"It's always mission impossible with you," says Jared.

"How long have you been planning this?"

"All day," Tre says.

"So you guys will be downstairs waiting?"

Jared shakes his head and stands up. "No, I'm giving Tre the keys to Gram's truck, and he'll be downstairs waiting. I have to head back to Maddie's room and stay with her, so I can't come with you guys."

"I want to see her," I say. Jealousy pricks at me. She was my friend and suddenly now she's Jared's girl. How did that happen?

"You better hit the road if you don't want to spend the whole week up here in group therapy. Plus, Tre says you have some big witch to take down or something?"

"Yeah." I stand and hug him tight, his chin pressing into my upper back. I turn and hug Tre next, so happy to have him here after what went down yesterday.

"Thank you. I thought for a little while that you were on Gram's side," I say, looking at my brother. I thought I was alone. I really did. But they're coming through.

"You've definitely got trauma, Emby, and probably years of therapy ahead. But I don't think you're crazy. I think you got caught up in some crazy shit."

I nod, my heart swinging wide open. I. Am. Not. Alone.

41

EMBER

The girl is short with dark hair but that's about where the similarities end. She has a long hook nose and droopy eyes. "Hey. You must be Ember."

She walks into my room without knocking and tosses the box of hair dye on my lap before taking off her baseball cap and leather jacket to reveal a short-sleeved black T-shirt. She looks around the bare room, grimacing.

In the hallway, Jared leans on the countertop at the nurse's station and laughs. "Ah man, right from the beginning, he had a tough first inning." His voice sounds beige. "He battled through eighty pitches!"

The girl's eyes land on me again. She crosses her arms. "I'm Chloe."

"Thanks for doing this."

She shrugs and bites her fingernail. "I've been down in the cafeteria for three fucking days waiting for my wicked stepmom to die. So at least it's something to do."

"Oh... I'm sorry." I perch on the edge of the bed.

"She's pretty much a bitch anyway."

I really don't know what to say to that, so I study the box of hair dye. It has a picture of a woman with shiny brown hair and an openmouthed grin. Somehow I doubt that's what I'll look like after squirting that stuff on my head.

Chloe wrinkles her nose and tilts her head to get a better look at me. "Wait a sec. You look like that one chick..." She takes a couple steps toward me before nodding and shaking her finger at me. "Yeah, Oshun. You look like that Oshun girl."

I flash a hesitant smile. "Yeah, I know. That's why I'm dyeing my hair."

I feel her eyes linger on me while I read the instructions on the hair dye box. *Step 1. Prepare the room. Step 2. Condition your hair.* I can't do anything but pour the freaking hair dye on my head over the sink. I don't have the necessary stuff: petroleum jelly, shampoo, a towel—nothing. I pull off the bed sheet to use as a towel.

"So do a lot of people think you look like her?"

"Yeah," I say, walking into the bathroom by the closet. I lean over the sink and turn on the water, and drop the sheet at my feet.

Chloe follows me and leans on the doorframe. "So why're you in here anyway? Are you, like, some kind of sicko who boiled her ex-boyfriend's cat?" She giggles.

"Just a miscommunication," I say before dunking my head under the water. I squeeze my dripping wet hair dry in the makeshift towel and then quickly squirt the cool dye on my scalp, before rubbing it through my hair. The chemical smell makes me feel like it will burn my scalp off.

"Are you on, like, meds or something?"

I roll my eyes and brush past her, then start loading my things into my backpack. The seconds tick by slowly while I wait for the dye to take effect. "Didn't my brother promise to pay you forty bucks if you kept going in and out of the room?"

She shrugs.

"Would you mind doing that?" I ask.

She sneers, then snorts a little, before pushing off the doorframe and walking into the hallway.

For several minutes, she leaves and comes back, leaves and comes back, very unconvincingly. Rolling her eyes, she crosses her arms over her chest and juts her hip when she's back in the room. "There. Happy?"

"Yeah." I rinse out the color and then with water dripping into my eyes, grab the sheet and pat my hair dry as best I can. In the small mirror, brown smudges ring my hairline and drip stains line my cheeks like exclamation points.

Chloe opens the door again, sees me, and grimaces. "Whoa. You should not ever become a hairdresser. Ever."

The water drips on my arms and neck. "Okay, will you go out there a couple more times in the black T-shirt and baseball hat? Then I'll wear my brother's hat and you stay here."

She sits down and picks up the empty hair dye box, flipping the lid back and forth. "I don't know..."

"You don't know?" How do I tell her that the world is coming to an end if she doesn't do this?

"I mean, what if, like, I'm stuck here and then it's a *miscommunication*." She puts her fingers up in air quotes over the word. "And, like, they won't let me go? Besides, what if you're a total psycho and I help break you lose?"

I exhale deeply. "Listen, it's not a prison. I'm not crazy. And I really need your help."

"Is that your boyfriend out there?" she asks, throwing her head to the door.

"Jared?" I really need to hurry. I really, really need to hurry. Maddie is dying. The storms are coming. I have to get out of here.

"No, the guy with the dark hair I met in the cafeteria."

"Yeah," I say. "Why?"

"He's hot."

"Yeah." I shrug.

"I'll help you, won't tell on you. But I like your boyfriend."

"Me too."

"I want to make out with him and then, my lips are sealed." She mimes zipping her lips and throwing away a key.

"What?" Irritated, I throw my head back. What a whackjob. Why did Tre and Jared stake my future—and the world's—on this freak show? "Please." I roll my eyes. "No."

Jared peeks his head in the room and then slips inside, gently closing the door behind him. "Ready?"

Chloe tosses her head in a weird shoulder shrug. She picks up the hair dye box again and starts flipping the lid back and forth, back and forth.

"Yeah, we're ready, right Chloe?" I ask.

"Whatever. Ember said she's going to introduce me to her boyfriend. First." She looks at me in the eye. "Because I've been known to do stuff, like yell really loud. Especially when I see rules being broken."

I gaze at her, pressing my tongue against my teeth. "Oh

for the love of—Jared, give her another forty dollars, please?"

"I don't have forty dollars." He pats his pockets and looks at Chloe. "Listen, I told the nurses you have a bladder infection and have to pee all the time, okay?"

"Gross." She hangs onto the "O" in the word.

"Well, it eliminates nosy questions and suspicion." He shrugs. "Emb, dry your hair as fast as possible." I squeeze my hair through the sheet wrapped around my head.

"Chloe, head out real quick, okay?" Jared says. "I'll grab your duffel bag, Emb."

Chloe stands up slowly, drops the box on the bed with two fingers and looks at me with a hand on the hip. "Introduce me?"

"Sure," I say, nodding. What are my options here, really?

"Now."

"I'll go out and get him as soon as I leave."

"I have a loud voice."

I force a cheerful smile and widen my eyes. "He is the *best* kisser. You'll love it. I'll run and get him immediately." Her smile is wicked and weird.

Jared goes back out to work his charm, and I put my finger to my lips. "Shhh... Be right back." We look nothing alike and she's a good two inches shorter than me. But whatever. Dark hair. Black shirt.

I pull Jared's gray baseball cap down low over my brow, straighten the T-shirt, and inhale deeply. Chloe sits on the bed watching me with raised eyebrows. She scratches her head and then gestures like she's pulling an invisible zipper across her mouth.

I cross my fingers over my heart and point downstairs. "We'll wait for you in the cafeteria," I whisper.

A smug grin twists on her face. She hands me her visitor's badge and shakes my hand firmly. "Pleasure doing business with you."

I flash a hesitant smile and exhale through a rounded mouth, then pull open the door, ready to do my best impersonation of this whack job, Chloe. I walk with my butt sucked in, shoulders slightly slumped, head down. I don't look up as I pass the orderly at the nurses' station. Through my peripheral vision, I only see a figure. A thin body, pink scrubs, head down, reading a magazine. I pass him and head for the hallway.

"Have to pee again?" His voice is sea-foam green, friendly enough. But it makes me stop dead in my tracks, my heart pounding like a bass drum.

I pause, trying to decide if I should try to mimic Chloe's voice. It's dull and the color of wet cement, and I honestly don't think I can pull it off. So I wave my hand in the air and trot with knees together like I have to pee, until I disappear around the corner.

42

EMBER

So maybe charging around corner in the hallway wasn't the smartest, because I slam right into Cassandra, the bright ponytailed nurse who met me my first morning here. Surprised, she apologizes for the collision, but then pauses with her mouth open and her head tilted. She points a finger at me but I don't give her time to talk, speed-walking past her, headed for the double doors. My heart pounds loudly in my ears.

"Ember?" she calls.

I bolt to the doors, past a line of patient rooms. Cassandra's voice follows me, calling my name. At the exit, my fingers feel like thick hotdogs as I fumble with the keycard and reach up to the card reader on the wall. The door responds with a series of clicks. I grin.

Chloe shouts from down the hallway. "Ember stole my keycard and locked me in her room!" The sound of her cement-colored voice sends a jolt of electricity through me. *Shit.*

The door buzzes, releasing the lock, and I yank on it, pulling it wide open. I dart into the vestibule and touch the second set of doors—until a pair of cool hands latch onto my arm, stopping me cold. Pulling me away from my destination, my freedom.

"Hey, Ember, it's okay." The soothing sound of the male nurse with the cinnamon hair who got me last time.

I groan and wriggle against his firm grasp, thrusting my keycard up to unlock the doors. "Get off me!"

Yet he pulls me away. One inch away. Then two inches. Then six inches. I cry out and twist and reach my fingers, wiggling them toward the door, but before I know it, I'm in the middle of the vestibule several feet from the exit. This time, the cinnamon-haired nurse holds me a little more forcefully, and his fingers bite into the flesh of my arms and waist.

"Hey, you dyed your hair," Cassandra says, as if this is a normal conversation, as if some guy is not completely restraining me. "It's a good look. But really, Ember, you'll go home. You will. Once you acquire the skills you need to deal with your situation."

"I'm not supposed to be in here," I say. "The world is going to end if you don't let me go! I'm serious. Just *trust* me."

"I know." Her voice is soothing. "But I think the world is going to be *just* fine. We're having group therapy now. Maybe you can tell everyone about it, okay?"

They guide me back down the hall, and I struggle against them, thrashing about. "You have to let me go! Ask my brother!"

"Your brother has been asked to leave the premises." Cassandra dips her head down to look me in the eye, her hands on my shoulders. "Sweetie you need to calm down, otherwise we'll have to use restraints, and we know you don't want that."

The idea of being wrapped up in a blanket hold or put inside a locked "quiet room" makes me freeze. I relax with a huge exhale and bite the inside of my cheek until I taste blood.

"There," she whispers. "That's great."

The keycard is extracted from my hand, and I'm escorted down the hall, past that bitch Chloe, who's covering her eyes and obviously fake crying. She and I make brief eye contact, and a small smirk creeps across her face. "You were gonna break your promise. I know it," she says.

43

EMBER

Five people sit in a circle on folding metal chairs. A couple of them glance up when I enter. A girl with long wavy hair stares with wide eyes and then points with an extended arm. "Dr. Charles, will she keep the confidentiality?" Her voice is loud and has a pink rattle.

A woman with a pointy bird-like nose nods. She wears black slacks and a white silk blouse. "Thank you, Olivia. We will let her know that this is an expectation and ask if she feels she'll be able to do so." The woman introduces herself as Dr. Charles, and she outlines the rules and expectations of the group to me. Maintain confidentiality. Attend all sessions. Communicate with words, not actions. Participate.

From her folding chair, Dr. Charles nods at a guy next to me with hulking shoulders, a wide, flat forehead, and narrow lips. "Ember, Jesse here was just describing the beliefs he had about the Day of Judgment. Please continue, Jesse."

"I was meeting famous artists from the past, because I'm an artist," Jesse says. "I'm also pretty religious. So it all seemed plausible. Right?" He sniffs. Wipes his nose.

His voice becomes a distant whir, the color of a manila folder, and I watch a boy across from me with long shoulder-length black hair, tap his forehead. Small red sores dot his face, like he's picked at his skin relentlessly. I wonder what his deal is.

Next to him is a young guy, my age, with his head down. He wears glasses. When he looks up, I freeze. So familiar. The freckles. The Howdy Doody look to his face and the wavy hair. It's Ben Alackness, one of the missing people from my notebook. I saw him in the basement of Trinity before I was rebirthed, too.

I shift in my seat, try to meet his eyes, but he gazes at the linoleum floor in the center of the circle.

Olivia's pink voice pulls me back into the group conversation. "For me, having a delusion or hallucination is like eating a piece of chocolate cake. At first, you really like it and you don't ever want it to end. Then you get a little full, but it's still good. By the time you realize you overdid it, you get a total stomachache and puke all over your best friend, and all of it—all the things you see and believe—comes to a halt. But you were having so much fun you didn't see the signs. You ignored them because the cake tasted so good."

Jesse chimes in. "Yeah, it's hard picking out real reality from my fiction sometimes. I mean, every day I was seeing proof that the end of the world was coming. The buildings were crumbling. I swore it. I stepped over dead people on the sidewalk."

"But it wasn't true. It wasn't reality, correct?" Dr. Charles asks.

He shakes his head. "No. It wasn't. But some days, I still feel like the end of the world is coming. I do."

"I think others in this group might have had a very similar experience, a difficult experience. It's frustrating and scary, not knowing what to believe if you can't believe your own thoughts." Dr. Charles looks at me. "Ember, would you like to tell us more about why you're here?"

I look at the woman, debating how to handle this. If I tell the truth, if I'm forthright, then I'll be stuck here. I need to prove to them that I'm stable. I need to get myself out of here. I press my lips together and clasp the seat of my chair with both hands.

Dr. Charles pauses and then leads me. "We noticed the newspaper in your room that was torn up into bits and pieces. Is there a reason why you did that?"

My frantic pace of running and escaping Trinity and its hold over me screeches to a halt. My mind stops spinning like a beater on high. Everything slows. Thoughts. Emotions. Time. The past. For the first time since leaving Trinity, everything is still and I actually take a minute to process what I've been through. What became of me. What I lost. What I could have been.

God, I was lost. So so lost.

I look up at Dr. Charles. Tears pool in my eyes. Without my consent, I'm talking.

"The newspaper had a picture of a guy I knew."

"It sounds like there's some pretty powerful anger toward him there."

"Yeah," I whisper, and it's as if I can see those memories of me and Zach through a pair of binoculars. Like I'm seeing someone else from far, far away. The old me—that ash-colored ember. But now, I'm fire. Stronger, better, more determined. Scars and all.

"Care to share?"

"I don't know why, but it feels like I was someone else when...when I knew him. Like it was a different life." *Just as much as Oshun was.*

"What happened?"

"I didn't used to be able to face the world, so there was a short period of time I was using drugs. And when I did, I had some run-ins with assholes. Date rape."

"Rape?" Dr. Charles sits up straighter and glances around the room. Olivia covers her mouth with her fingertips and Jesse frowns.

"I didn't stop him, but I wasn't really coherent. So yeah." I touch my fingers to my hair, smoothing a messy damp clump on my shoulder.

She steeples her fingers. "Maybe we should save this for a private session, Ember."

I nod, not wanting to talk about it anymore anyway.

"Is this what prompted your feelings that life was becoming unmanageable?"

I pause. "No. I was looking for an escape."

She nods slowly and her eyes fill with concern. "And why was that?"

I recall the guilt. The acidic guilt I felt back then. So vivid I can actually feel it in my throat and chest. The way I was so mad at Mom before the accident. The way I hated her back then. The way I felt those times when I got so high of the Percocet, how I shut down. The way I used to feel like I killed my parents.

"My parents died."

"Mine too! Mine too!" The girl with long wavy hair stands up, throwing a fist into the air.

"Olivia, we'll come back to you in a few minutes to talk about how your parents are 'dead' to you, but please let Ember finish."

Olivia collapses into her chair with a loud *thwunk*.

"Ember, please go on."

"I met some kids."

I remember Trinity and how peaceful I felt and then reliving the panic that swirled inside me when I found out what a fraud it all turned out to be. Everything that happened there—Lilly, Pete, Chris, Tre, Zoe. All of us trapped. Waking up as Oshun with little control over my own body. Later, nearly being sacrificed, burned to death, then running in the lightning from Xintra, my near-drowning in the cave. Escaping from the man in the Mercedes, seeing Lodima dead at my feet just moments after we talked. Maddie, her face pale, her body unconscious. The heap of all of it rains down on me.

"Where did you meet these kids?"

Truth or fiction? *Whatever gets you out of this place.* Fiction then. "Trinity Forest." And I'm speaking without my own consent once more.

Ben Alackness looks up at me. His face carries no real expression outside of the eyes. He doesn't blink. His eyes almost bulge. I gaze at him, trying to communicate without words. Trying to say, *"Me too. Xintra took me too."*

I point at him. "Ben, you had a similar experience right?"

"How'd you know my name?" The sound of his voice isn't what I expected. From that round face, I expected a high-pitched little-boy voice. But instead, he has a deep voice—the color of polished cherrywood.

"Because I know you went missing. I remember. Years ago," I say.

Dr. Charles intervenes. "Let's stay focused on you, Ember."

"I did. I did go missing," Ben says. He sits up straighter. "She's right."

"Me too. I was gone for three years, but at the time I was transformed into a pop star. Oshun."

"I remember you!" Olivia stands and darts across the circle, grabbing my shoulders, her fingernails tearing into my flesh. It startles me and hurts, and I pull away from her.

"Olivia! The rules! Express yourself with words!" Dr. Charles says, standing up.

"But I remember her, Dr. Charles! I love Oshun's music. I just want to touch her. To say I've met a rock star."

She tears at my shirt, and I push on the floor with my feet so my chair scoots and squeaks on the linoleum. "You've touched me. Mission accomplished?"

"Olivia! Enough," Dr. Charles shouts.

Olivia lets go as if my skin is a hot stove and returns to her chair without a word.

"Ember," Dr. Charles says. "Everyone here has something they're working on. Sometimes, what we see and believe is dictated by our brains and the natural chemicals inside them. It's nothing to be ashamed of. It's just like if you have asthma and you need to take medicine to help your lungs work properly. Olivia has requested that she not take her medicine today. So we're allowing her to do so."

Dr. Charles clasps her hands together. "And Olivia, how do you feel without the medication?"

Olivia stares at the wall. "I think I need it."

"That's fine. Sometimes, we just do." Dr. Charles turns to me. "Tell us about the time you spent as Oshun."

The memories bounce between dream-like and reality and I know I should stop, know I'm not helping myself here. But suddenly it's as if the truth is poison, and if I don't get it out of me, I'll die. "It's fuzzy to me," I admit. "But I was doing bad things. I was hurting people."

"Why were you hurting people?"

"I was under the influence of..."

"Of...." Dr. Charles slowly turns her hand so her palm is face-up before her.

"...of a corrupt system that kept me under its thumb." Poison, poison out. "When I wanted out, I had a breakdown."

"Did you like being a star?" Ben asks.

I pause, looking directly at Ben. I want to pull him aside, ask him what he remembers, if he wants to take down Xintra like me and Tre. But instead, I answer his question. "Kind of. I always wanted to sing professionally. But I wasn't under my own control when I was a star. So no, it was horrible. It was being a prisoner in your own body."

Ben nods slowly, minutely. He understands.

"How so?" Dr. Charles asks.

"I had to find myself. My inner strength and fight to escape." I look at Ben. "You know, right?"

His lips part but he doesn't answer. His nostrils flare.

"Okay, then." Dr. Charles takes a sharp inhale and looks at her watch. "It looks like we need to wrap it up.

Does anyone have a sense of what they want to take away from today's group?"

"We know that we're not alone," Jesse says.

"Good. That's good." Dr. Charles makes eye contact with each of us and nods, a virtual handshake.

We stand and begin to file out the door. I reach a hand through the others to touch Ben's shoulder ahead of me. He turns to look at me and freezes, like I'm a wild animal ready to attack.

"Ben, we have to stop Xintra," I say.

He shakes his head swiftly. "I don't know what you're talking about." He darts out the door and down the hall ahead of me.

"Ben!" I attempt to follow him, but Jesse takes up most of the doorway and doesn't appear to really care that I want to get out. I turn the corner to follow him down the hall when the nurse, Cassandra, catches up to me.

"Hey Ember," she says. "Wanna eat lunch with me?"

"I need to talk to that guy." I point.

"Come on. I bet there's a hamburger in the kitchen with your name on it," Cassandra says.

I sigh and follow her, deciding that now is the time I have to prove my stability, show them it's time for me to go back to the real world.

44

EMBER

The hamburger is good. Like, really good. I feel like I haven't really eaten in days. It's been this treadmill of commotion and action, and I'm grateful that Cassandra made me eat. We sit alone in a private office, just me and her, eating hamburgers from a local restaurant.

I relax for the first time in months, taking large bites. Cassandra tells me that she grew up in Nebraska on a farm. She woke up every day at four o'clock in the morning to milk the cows with her dad. She talks a lot, and I know she's trying to get me to open up, trust her.

I realize how badly I fucked up back there. How opening up, draining that stupid poison, only made me seem crazier. Maybe if I were really here for the drugs, for what happened with Zach, maybe then this place would have been good for me. Maybe I could open up and begin to heal. But what happened to me, no one would believe that. Not Gram, not the police, and certainly not the doctors.

"You know," I say through a mouthful, "I'm okay. I don't think the world is coming to an end. I think I just worry about the environment. It was all misconstrued. Really, it's just one big mistake." I wipe ketchup off my lip.

"The environment?"

"Icebergs. Polar bears. Yup." I nod and swallow.

"Your grandmother didn't seem to think that was the case." Cassandra bites a french fry.

"She didn't want me to leave with my boyfriend. That's all."

"Hmmmm." Cassandra frowns and nods. "That's it?"

"Yeah, I'm good."

"Odd."

She looks at her plate and drags another wiggly french fry through a pile of ketchup.

"Why?" I ask, smiling. Too cheerful. It feels like I'm acting in a play.

"Well, your police statement shows that you believe Trinity Forest is a powerful vortex and at the helm of a dangerous group. That they're plotting to take over the world with powerful storms."

I swallow, and the hamburger bun sticks in my throat. I take a sip of water.

"And there's video footage of you as Oshun having a breakdown on stage. Some stories about you experiencing various fugue states. Confusion."

I take a long drink of water, gulping, gulping, gulping, buying myself time to respond. I put the glass down and wipe my mouth. "No, no, that's not true. Misunderstanding."

"Ember." Cassandra puts her fingertips on the edge of

the table and leans toward me. "It's okay. We're a safe place with people who care."

"I know you are." That's the truth. I know they care. I do seem like I'm delusional. Of course they want to keep me here—so I'm safe. But none of us are safe if I don't get out.

"I'm tired. I think I'd like to go lay down now." I stand up.

"Thanks for having lunch. I'm around if you need me." She smiles and nods to a nurse to escort me back to my room. The last open door we pass in the hallway—the door right next to my room—happens to be Ben's. He's reading a book and looks up when I pass. When he sees me, he kicks his door shut.

Another day passes and for one brief second, lying on the bed gazing at the ceiling, I actually question reality. If maybe I am delusional, if maybe I really did make all this up. I remember what Tre told me that first night in Trinity. *"Einstein once said that 'reality is merely an illusion—albeit a very persistent one.'"*

I'm called to another group therapy session. This time, the spotlight is on Freddie, the guy who picks his face. Ben Alackness doesn't show up this time, and no one acknowledges it.

Group is followed by another private session of therapy, where I actually cry, where I actually relive all those painful moments, my guilt and my parents' deaths, with what happened with Zach and the self-destructive behavior.

When I'm finished, Dr. Charles hands me a tissue and tilts her head. "What do you know in your heart, Ember?"

"That the accident wasn't my fault." I nod. "And I always know there's help."

It was the therapy session I needed four years ago. We walk back to the room, and I wait for the next scheduled activity by lying again on my bed, staring up at the textured white ceiling.

I'm just about to doze off when something rattles, a silver sound. Like a rhythmic scraping—something turning, twisting. Coming from the ceiling.

I look up, listen carefully. There's the metal grinding, followed by a heavy *thunk, thunk, thunk.*

Someone is removing the metal air-conditioning vent in the ceiling! I watch it slide away. Watch as two denim-covered legs drop down from the ceiling. Watch as a boy's body empties onto the floor. Dark hair. Black leather jacket. He touches his fingers to the ground when he lands to keep his balance. He rises, and a thrill rushes through me.

Grinning, Tre wipes his hands on his jeans.

I squeal quietly and run to him with open arms. I rest my head on his chest. Solid. Familiar. Sane. Verifying that I am *not* delusional. That my reality is not an illusion. That Tre is imprinted on my heart.

"They might come in any minute," I say.

"I'm breaking you out. This time—"

"This time our future won't rest in the hands of a girl like Chloe?"

"Not a chance." He grimaces. "Sorry."

I look down at my scrubs. "I want to change first." I pull a T-shirt and jeans out of the duffel bag—which was confiscated from Jared and returned to my room after the last failed escape attempt—and Tre politely turns his back to me.

Once I'm dressed, I tuck the ankh cross necklace into my back pocket. I don't want it to get caught as I crawl through the vent.

My heart pounds as we gently scoot my bed a little to the corner of the room, just below the air-conditioning vent. Tre stands on the bed, places two hands on my waist, and lifts me up to the opening like a cheerleader. I claw my way up and inside, pulling myself up to my elbows, legs dangling in the air. Finally I'm able to scoot on my stomach farther into the vent, which smells of air-conditioning coolant and dust. It's pitch black and I have to exhale to keep my nerves calm.

Everything sounds tinny, an electric yellow color, and every movement sounds like it echoes. Tre uses the bed as a trampoline to get enough air to reach the vent. Hanging by his fingertips, he does a pull-up, raising his chin, then shoulders and elbows up through the hole. It's as if he's been training for this.

After a couple seconds, he's inside the tiny vent with me, carefully replacing the metal cover.

"Go that way," he says, nodding his head toward me. We scoot along the vent, me first, in the dark on our hands and knees, each movement reverberating a bending tinny sound. It's milky green. We move gingerly and cautious to ensure we don't crash down through a weak piece of sheet metal.

I pause over another vent located next door to my room. Ben's room. "Wait!" I whisper. "We have to take Ben with us."

"Who?"

"Another rebirther who woke up. He's here! In this room." I point to the vent.

Tre leans in close to whisper to me. "It's too much a risk. Even talking up here is a risk. If he reports us or hears us now, it will blow our chance."

My nails dig into my palms and my heart pounds. Stopping Xintra, that's our priority. If I don't leave now, no one will be there to stop her. It has to be me, according to Lodima.

"We'll come back for him," I vow. "After we stop her, we'll come back for him."

Tre breathes a sigh of relief and nods.

We move fast through the vents, using only hand signals, crawling for what feels like the entire length of the hospital. We come to a T-shaped corner, where the vent goes straight but also splits, heading to the right. I stop and sit, breathless. "Where do we go?" I whisper.

Tre climbs over my lap to the other side of me, grinning and sweeping his face centimeters from mine, sending a rush of heat between our mouths.

He places a hand on my thigh and leans in close to me. Our noses touch and his lips graze mine. I can't help but kiss him. My body hums, and his lips taste salty.

He smiles. "This way goes to a closet by the front lobby." He points down the dark vent. "There's a trap door and then we'll be outside the secure area of the ward."

He makes his way down the vent a few paces ahead of me. After a good hundred yards of us scooting and me cringing—it's too freaking loud and I'm sure we'll be caught—he stops, unlatches a hinged door on the bottom of the vent, and disappears through it.

I crawl quickly to the opening and peer down. He stands on the ground below me with arms outstretched. "I'll catch you."

I drop down, and his hands slide up my torso, lowering me to the floor. The storage closet is tiny, and a broom falls off the wall and hits me in the head.

Tre carefully peeks out the door, waiting until it's clear, before we slip into the hallway and step inside an elevator. My heart thumps so loud in my head I'm sure the doctor standing next to me in the white coat will know we're escaping and report us.

When the elevator door opens to the ground floor, we patiently wait to exit behind a guy in a wheelchair and a mother holding a child's hand in one and a bouquet of flowers in the other.

In the lobby, Tre and I walk silently, eyes straight ahead, melting into the handful of people moving through the lobby. Our shoes squeak. One foot in front of the other, until we step outside where drizzle coats the air. Tre takes my hand and we walk briskly then trot to the parking lot.

Inside Gram's rusted pickup truck, we look at each other and grin.

"We did it." We both exhale.

45

EMBER

Gram's rusted F-150 truck is no getaway car. The broken muffler roars, appearing as burnt orange swirls in my Color Crayon Brain, and the empty gun rack on the back window rattles loudly. We hold our breath for a few seconds until we've made it onto I-70 from Vail. Tre takes my hand and squeezes, and I lean into him and kiss him on the cheek. He smells like some sort of spicy cologne.

"Man, that was intense." His voice is huge chocolate dots in my vision and the color of it makes me tremble with gratitude. His voice is home, and I feel like I'm finally free—yet again.

"Do you think they'll come after you?" he asks.

"Why would they waste their time? Plus the whole world is going to blow up soon, so they won't bother."

The ski town shrinks in the cracked side-view mirror, and I feel the weight of reality, like a backpack so heavy it's going to topple me over backward. Maddie is in the hospital and may very well die before Tre and I can even get to Xintra.

We pass a billboard that advertises locations for the free vaccines. My stomach twists inside out and the bubble wrap in my chest pops.

Tre glances at me as if he can read my thoughts. "I know."

The car engine hums copper, and Axel crawls onto my lap. I bury my face into his fur and inhale deeply, firing up my rage again. "So where were we before I got pulled over?" I ask.

"Going to war, but with no plan."

"The good news is, I have some ideas." I tell him about Mom's journal and what she wrote and what happened to her. I want to look at *The Book of the Dead* again and those rocks—and Mom's letters to Lodima. Maybe I'll find out what happened once she went inside the vortex.

The green plastic container from Lodima's house sits at my feet. Seeing it gives me goosebumps. I set it on my lap and remove the lid. The two surviving letters to Lodima from Mom sit on top of the rocks, and now that Mom left me with no answers about what happened inside Trinity, I'm dying to read them. The first letter is stiff and dry with big water stains on the edges. With shaky fingers, I read it out loud.

Dear Lo:

I'm sorry it's taken me a long time to tell you what I'm about to write in this letter. First, I want to thank you. You were so sweet to pick me up in Snag. I know it must have been so frustrating that I wouldn't tell you what happened in

Trinity Forest. I've just locked it up for so long, but I know now that I can't keep it in there forever. Especially after seeing more people disappear in these vortexes all over the world.

So here. I'm ready to tell you what happened when I went through that gate.

I stayed at this mansion for a couple weeks, in part because Xin's father was so spectacularly alluring. He had a way of making me feel like my whole body was filled with electric energy. I melted in his presence.

I was so enamored with the adventure of it all that I didn't really let myself dwell on the fact that what was going on there was really bizarre and what had happened in the forest with you and me and Xintra was insane too. They asked me to paint, providing all the supplies, asked me to show them the future, to find lost souls they could rescue. I didn't really know what they meant, but the energy there was so compelling, the drawings and paintings, the faces of people in various places, just started pouring out of me.

While I was painting, Xintra spent more and more time out by these ancient limestone ruins that looked like nine-foot-tall slabs of rock. They were next to a number of caves and what she said was an old mining tunnel. There, she would sit and pore over old books—kind of like the ones we saw in the store that day.

One afternoon, I overheard Xintra and her father arguing in the living room, saying the craziest things. Something about bringing back an ancient civilization that had faced persecution for centuries—and they mentioned a secret society and having finally unlocked the tunnels to Trinity Forest. Lo, I think they used me and you to rewrite the energy grids and magnetic fields of the planet, boosting the power of

Trinity. I still don't understand it completely. But I found out they were going to use that energy to power some ancient witchcraft.

The night of their argument, I woke up to someone singing a haunting song. I looked out my bedroom window and saw Xin, standing in the meadow below, wearing a long billowing white dress. She was alone and a flock of birds flew around her, swooping in formation. Her voice rose up and floated on the tips of the trees, and that weird fog floated low around her. I swear I saw ghosts, faces in that fog, dissolving in her fingertips and mouth.

Terrified, I ran down the stairs and yelled her name when I got outside. As I approached her in the meadow, I could see her hands moving together and away from each other like she was playing an invisible accordion. When I got close enough to see, I was floored. She pulled blue-green lines of electricity between her hands, like string woven between her fingers, back and forth. She turned around to face me, and her eyes were different. They were like green pools so clear, and she spoke differently too. Like she was possessed. I'll never forget what she said.

"You will be rebirthed and find the light inside you."

I told her we needed to go home, that I was scared, but she told me that my destiny was there with her, with her powering me like a battery. I couldn't help but wonder if somehow she had allowed some dark force to take over her body.

I ran, searching unsuccessfully for the gate in the dark, before stumbling upon something buried in the ground. It was a tin of crystals and some sort of old, confusing map with Egyptian symbols on it. I grabbed a handful of the stones and the map and then buried the half-full tin back in the dirt—so

Xintra wouldn't get suspicious. I headed straight for the mining tunnel they had showed me when I first arrived, thinking that was my best bet to get out.

Ultimately, the tunnel did lead me out—though it was horrible, excruciating — and I landed in another confusing place with tall cliffs and a tundra. The air had an electric feel to it, and I saw weird lights and heard distant voices. After a day of wandering, I found some carvings on stone walls and used the map to place the crystals above them. The wall opened up to a cave that went into another hole until finally, I woke up in Snag, where you found me.

I was so shellshocked, I just couldn't talk about it to anyone. I hope you understand.

All these years later, I feel guilty for leaving Xintra there and also afraid of her power. I lost the map in the cave, but I tried to write down what I remembered about the carvings and crystals I found. I still look over my shoulder, worried that either she or her father will show up, ready to murder me, the kids, or Steve because I left. Every time something awful happens in the world, every time someone disappears, I think maybe it's all my fault. The guilt is my own punishment.

Love,

Despina

Your Venus Friday friend

I glance down to find that my fingernails have dented my skin on my palm, next to the scar I got from Zoe. Patches of green and light purple bruises still color my forearm.

Reminders of what I went through are everywhere. I shake my fingers out to try to make myself relax.

"Where's Snag?" I ask.

"I don't know," Tre says.

Maddie's phone sits on the console, so I open Google and do a quick search. "Okay. So it's in the Yukon. Alaska, population five. There's a story here that tells about how in the 1950s, all these planes just vanished. It's apparently negative eighty-five degrees during the winter, so my mom must have been there in the summer, otherwise she wouldn't have survived."

"I bet it's the northern-most vortex," Tre says. "What does the other letter say?"

I nod and open up another letter. This one is shorter.

Lodima:

I found Alessandra's mother, who moved back to Leadville. I can hardly believe what she told me: That whole time, Alessandra's family was protecting Trinity from Xintra and her family. Their job had been passed down for generations, to secure Trinity, keep Xintra's people from tapping it to get enormous power. It's an energy vortex. A time trap.

This is the part that haunts me every day. Remember the party when Xintra spat on Alessandra? Remember how cruel we were to her? It was just the start. Xintra set fire to Alessandra's house a few nights after the cops broke up our party. Alessandra died. I don't know how this wasn't in the news or how we never found out.

Apparently, Xintra and her father discovered Alessandra's hidden coins to enter Trinity and unlock the vortex and then they boosted the magnetism.

Xintra was not who we thought she was. At all. And I contributed to the horror of it all.

My heart breaks and I cannot stop crying.

All my love,
   Your Venus Friday friend
   Dezi

My mouth feels so dry, and a heaviness fills me. "Xintra killed her." I look at Tre.

"Whoa," he says, glancing at me at a stoplight.

Mom should have known. She should have seen the fact that her friend was not a good person. She should have stood up for Alessandra. But that's the thing with hindsight, isn't it? When you're in the situation, you can be so blind to it all. You make such stupid choices.

The radio plays a yellow song—it looks like bouncing lemons in my vision, and it's a huge contrast to the scene in front of us. Dark sky. A torrential rainstorm. Windshield wipers thumping. The end of the world.

We pass a familiar house with a detached garage in the little town of Minturn. "Stop here," I say.

"Why?" Tre pulls over on the side of the road and puts the grumbling truck into park.

"That's my old cross-country coach's house. She used to do welding projects with Gram. Maddie said she was one of the people who died after the outbreak." A heaviness falls on me with that reality. "She wouldn't care if we borrowed some stuff." *Like a blowtorch.*

46

NISHA

The dark BMW is unmistakable. I follow the car, hanging about two hundred yards back, driving slowly, and taking the next turn long after he does.

I roll to a stop, kill the engine, and wait, as does Caius. After a few minutes, he slowly opens his door, and then slinks across the street, moving swiftly past the chain-link fence and slipping between the house and a lopsided evergreen tree. He would be invisible, wearing all black, except for the bleach white hair.

I tiptoe behind him, pulling my knife from its leather sheath, moving through the tall grass as swiftly and lightly as a cat. Ahead, Caius sits hunched against the side of a maroon pickup truck.

The wooden screen door to the house opens with a squeak, and Ember emerges into the drizzly air. Her hair is a mixture of white and dark and she looks to be mumbling to herself. The screen slams shut with a bang behind her, and she walks to the one-car garage, reaches down to release the manual garage door. It clicks and groans as it rises.

Caius rocks back and forth, probably deciding if now is the time to pounce. Inside the dim light of the garage, Ember stands with her back to us, her hands on her hips. She takes a couple steps toward a workbench in the back, touches her lips with a finger, and then slowly runs her hands over various lawn tools and heavy equipment. Swiftly, she snatches up a blowtorch and a can of lighter fluid, then turns on her heel and puts them in a pile on the dirt floor.

She trots back to the garage, touching her head in thought before moving to the gun case. She tries the steel door but it's locked. She shakes it, then kicks it before howling in pain and grabbing her toe.

Then she takes something off a shelf nearby. A black plastic bottle of something. She tosses it into the truck, before heading back into the garage and standing close to the workbench. From the corner of my eye, I see Caius is gone from his squatting position behind the car. Adrenaline surges through me.

My eyes dart back to Ember, and then, he's on her. His knife against her throat, his mangled face is close to her cheek. My heart races, and I run. I want to be the one to do the honors here.

I charge at them as fast as I can, my stride long, my body bent forward, determination flowing through every vein in my body.

Before I can get there, Caius cries out, letting go of Ember. His knife drops to the ground and slides out of his reach.

"You bit me, you bitch!" he says.

Ember sees me just a few feet away from Caius, and she crouches low, hands spread, ready to fight. She pants loudly amid the dusty air. "Get away from me!" she screams. Her voice is so loud it goes hoarse.

Caius notices me and his nostrils flare. "What the hell are you doing here, Zoe?"

"Checking on you," I say.

Ember's eyes are wild, but it's not just fear: it's anger written across her face. Good. That girl has fire and she needs to bring it in order for us to finish this thing.

Caius extends his left foot to scoot his knife back toward him, and slowly he bends down to pick it up. He stands upright, cockier now. "Payback time."

Ember's eyes dart from me to him, uncertain which of us is the greater threat.

"You're not doing anything to that girl," I say, gritting my teeth. I lunge for Caius, hoisting my knife up in the air. He moves and I miss.

I belly flop onto the concrete, pain cutting into my ribs. My heartbeat thumps loudly in my head as my knife spins and slides beneath the workbench. *Shit.*

I crawl on hands and knees and reach out to retrieve it. Behind me, there's a struggle: the sound of feet sliding, skin and bodies and fabric colliding, grunting, followed by a deep, swift sound. *Whap.* Ember shrieks and then there's a crash of metal and glass and tools and objects flying off a table. I can't get to the knife.

Then, he's on me. Caius's arm wraps around my waist and tugs me up to stand. The cool, sharp blade hugs my throat. I grunt and squirm, but the more I move, the deeper the knife tears at my skin. Something warm drips down my throat. Blood.

I strain my eyes to see Ember in my peripheral vision and I can make out small movements in the corner of the garage.

"So you thought you could beat Xintra," Caius says, "thought you could leave her and survive? After all this time..."

Ember has risen now, and I can see her zombie-walking toward us. Our eyes meet. She drags her gaze slowly to the two steel pipes lying on the workbench. A signal. She runs and picks one of them up, holds it like a bat, bends her knees.

"How are you going to take on two of us at once?" she asks from behind Caius.

Caius flips his head to look at her and releases his grip just enough that I can lean forward, stretch my fingertips, and grab the other pipe. In one swift movement, Ember and I simultaneously swing at him. My blow nails his kneecap with a crack, and Ember hits the backside of his head with a nauseating crunch. Caius falls to the floor in one heap.

Ember stands, arms at her side, panting. She drops the pipe. "Is he dead?"

47

EMBER

I look up at Zoe, the lead pipe dangling in her hand. The guy's white-blond hair is matted with blood and his mouth gapes open. His leg folds unnaturally. I did that. I totally did that. *She* did that.

I look up again at Zoe again, disbelief washing over me. She stands different, more like a warrior than a super-model. All spice and sass—and, of course, that same towering confidence. She still looks beautiful like she always did. The golden eyes and skin. Her hair a little more wild. Tall, lean. But she's different.

"You're awake," I say.

She nods, her chest heaving with each breath. Up until a few minutes ago, Zoe was my enemy, the evil witch sucking up our lives and spitting us out as murderers.

"You saved me?" I say. It's supposed to be a sentence but my shock makes it a question. My whole body tingles, from scalp and cheeks to kneecaps and toes. Adrenaline detonates inside me, and my heart pounds so fast, I can't catch my breath.

She drops the pipe onto the concrete floor, and it makes a loud silver clanging noise. "Looks like you saved yourself," she says.

"I don't get it. You *rebirthed* me. You helped Xintra. You're...you're her...person."

"*Was* her person," she says, kicking the guy with her foot so he rolls over onto his back.

I squat down, place two fingers over his neck before looking up at her. "He's alive. Let's call 9-1-1 and get him help."

Zoe frowns and puts her hand on her hip. "So he can get patched up and come after you again?"

"He's just like we were," I say. "Brainwashed by Xintra. He's probably not a bad person."

"Yeah, but who's to say that whack on the head even did anything? It doesn't mean he'll wake up to his old self."

I stand up. "Well, when I'm done with Xintra he will." I walk past her out of the garage and up the three concrete steps to my coach's back door. My body still trembles. "I'll call for help after we leave."

"Where're you going?" She swings open the screen door and follows me inside.

"Tre and I are going back to Trinity to stop Xintra."

Inside the kitchen, Tre slides large kitchen knives into a backpack. He looks up and sees the two of us. "Nisha. What are you doing back?"

"Nisha?" I ask.

"My real name," she says. "Don't call me Zoe. Unless you want me to call you Oshun."

I nod. "What do you mean *back*? When were you here before?"

"She dropped me off here at your house," Tre says.

"I had a feeling Caius was on your trail... so I hung around. You didn't hear all that action going on out there?" She and I look at each other in disbelief.

"No, what happened?"

"Caius. He tried to cut up Ember, and we both slammed him with lead pipes."

Tre clenches his jaw, seething. "Where is he?"

"He's in the garage," I tell him. "Knocked out, but alive. We'll call for help once we leave."

Tre strides to the screen door, looking ready to kill someone with his bare hands. "No way in hell does he do that to you–"

I reach out and grab his shoulder to stop him.

"Tre—"

"He tried to kill you," he says and shakes my hand off him. He takes two swift strides to the door and punches the screen open with a fist before charging outside. I follow.

"Tre, stop," I shout. "He's asleep, rebirthed, just like we all were. Xintra's the one we need to stop."

He stands over Caius, seething, his fists clenched by his side.

Zoe calls to him from the doorway. "Uh, you *do* know that *you* were the one who sent Caius to kill Ember."

Caius did try to murder me three times, but here I am begging Tre not to finish him off. "Xintra's the problem," I say quietly, taking Tre's arm and pulling him toward the house. "Let it go."

Tre grunts and kicks Caius in the back, hard. The strike sounds heavy. The color of sand.

"Is anyone else after us?" Tre asks, looking around the dark driveway.

"Don't think so," Nisha says.

I get Tre back inside, and Nisha makes herself at home in this vacant house, opening and shutting cupboards in the kitchen until she finds the water glasses. She takes one, fills it up at the sink, and chugs the water. She wipes her mouth with the back of her hand. Those mannerisms are so unfamiliar. So un-Zoe. She leans back against the counter—more like she used to do in Trinity.

"Ember says you're going back to Trinity. But there's no way you're getting back inside," Nisha says.

"We figured that," Tre says.

"We're not going to the gate," I say.

"How else will you get in?" Nisha asks.

"I read my mom's journal and she talked about a mining tunnel. I think it's a back way in."

She crosses her arms. "You guys really think you can stop Xintra? Just the two of you?"

I nod, stand up straighter. Tre puts his arm around my shoulder. He's still trembling. Simmering rage. "Unless you want to come, too. You're kind of a kick-ass fighter." Though I wonder if I can trust her.

"It'd take an army. Xintra has some crazy-ass power."

"An army? Who else would even believe us, let alone risk their lives to stop her?" I ask.

"Rebirthers who woke up," she says.

"Who else has woken up?" I take a step toward her. The prospect is so encouraging, I almost don't want to believe it. I imagine everyone—politicians, actors, police officers, nurses—all dropping their agendas and walking out on Xintra.

She shrugs. "When I left, I started making house calls to rebirthers. Started a chain letter of sorts with people reaching out to each other."

"How many did you reach?" Tre asks.

"If my plan worked, maybe 150. I don't have a clear memory of everyone else and their rebirthed lives." She turns around and fills her glass again. "I didn't expect it to work, but I think the stone from your necklace—that big gold-looking rock?" She turns around and looks at me. "It might be disrupting the magnetic power between Xintra and the rebirthers."

I remember the necklace, but once I used the crystals to open the caves in Trinity, I lost it. "You mean that big gold-colored rock on the necklace... when I was Oshun?"

She nods. "That's the one."

"Wow, so *that's* what the rock did. I knew it did *something* but I didn't know what. Do you still have it?"

"A piece of it, but I went and bought a boatload of the same kind of rock at a gem store and I've been handing them out to rebirthers who are waking up. You know, to protect them from Xintra's eyes."

"So where are all these people?" Tre asks.

"All over the country, but most were told to flee the coasts."

I press my lips together, stare at a bubble in the linoleum floor, trying to remember details from Mom's journal. Hidden details.

"An army," I say. "My mom did talk about how Xintra used the energy of lots of people in Trinity—by holding a party there—to boost the magnetic power of the place.

Maybe we need a lot of people to undo it all? We need to bring those awakened rebirthers here. To fight."

I take a step toward her.

"Nisha, you need to get a message to them. They could be the army we need."

Nisha nods and inhales deeply. "Either that, or we're going to lead a hundred fifty people to their deaths."

48

LILLY

The driver glances at me in the rearview mirror, waiting for me to get out of the car. I twist my hair and look at the MeToo feed in my field of vision.

A message from Xintra: *The tsunami will hit in eight hours. Rebirthers need to take cover in the vortex.*

A door slams and two people climb out of their cars and walk into the brick house. All of us rebirthers are getting the same message and the ones in California are headed into the basement tunnel. My heart pounds. I don't want to go back to Trinity. Because now I know I'm not Tonia Davies, the actress who slips poison to powerful dignitaries. I'm not the girl who inspires race riots and numbs people's sensitivity to murder and violence through my movies.

I'm Lilly.

If I stay here, I'll die from the tsunami or the virus. But if I walk through the vortex, Xintra might know it's really me again, that I woke up, and she'll for sure kill me. My ears ring. I twist my hair tighter around my finger.

"Miss Davies do you need help exiting the vehicle?" The driver's gray eyes and bald forehead rise in the rearview mirror.

"No," I say, scooting over to open the car door. The sun is so bright, you'd never expect the disaster that's coming.

I pull my rounded sunglasses over my eyes and fall in line with four other people entering the house. A woman with a long nose I recognize as a Hollywood agent. Another stranger in a dark suit. Maybe a pro wrestler? A male TV anchor eating a ham sandwich as he walks. He's interviewed me before. I walk up the stairs to the house and file in through the front door.

Without a word, we move through the ugly kitchen, past a dusty plastic table I'm careful to not touch. We slip through the hallway and down the back stairs. It stinks in here, like mold maybe. I vaguely remember this entrance. As a rebirther I went through it regularly. It's almost like I'm driving on autopilot, like I'm stepping back into a dream I've been having every night for years.

Downstairs, it's dark and smells wet and musty. I stand in line next to an old tractor wheel, lifting my fingers to avoid touching anything. My heart pounds so loudly in my head that I can't hear the sound of the vortex door opening. I'm going to be hiding from the storms with a cluster of murderers. Mind-controlled murderers. My muscles tense, and I consider running back up the stairs.

Instead, I freeze, standing there, unmoving until it's my turn to enter the stone vortex doorway. My exhale sounds shaky as I lift my ring finger to the nondescript door. My silver ring, the one with the silver-colored pyramid with an eye on it, is my key. I wait for something to happen. What's supposed to happen? The memories of our ritual hang on the edge of my mind, a pattern you can't really remember.

I wave my finger to the vortex door again, this time more frantically. It won't unlock! My body trembles, and I spin around to look at the others behind me. "Can I go in with you?" I ask. My voice has a really high pitch to it.

"No." The anchor pushes me aside and puts his ring up to the door. It opens, and I dart to try to squeeze in behind him. But the door slides shut too fast with a thunderous rock-on-rock *thud*, catching the front of my blouse in the door. I yelp, pulling back, trying to remove it, but it's stuck too tight between the door and the stone wall.

"Can you please help?" I ask, turning to the woman— the talent agent—behind me. She stares at me, cold, for a long second. With one firm yank, she rips my silk blouse. A patch of skin on my belly shows through the jagged tear, and it feels like I've been stripped naked.

"Looks like you'll be swimming in that tsunami in a few hours," she says. Her smile is weird, with bared teeth.

Panicked, I shake my head. I can't just stay here in Los Angeles and drown. I need to get to a safe spot. Maybe I can fly somewhere. But the rain, the fires—no place is entirely safe.

"Best go run along now," she says, putting a hand on my shoulder. Her touch is like a dose of Valium, and my legs go weak.

Everything...

...looks...

...swirly.

I collapse to the tile floor, high-heels sliding out from beneath me.

"Maybe catch a bus to Texas," another person says. His voice thunders above me, and in the flickering florescent light hanging from the ceiling, the faces of the rebirthers look like they're coming apart, like the zombies in my movies. Footsteps ring down the stairs. More rebirthers arriving. I'm surrounded, trapped.

My heart pounds in my head and I slide my shoe to stand up. The talent agent takes a step closer to me, and my knees wobble and my mind feels kind of thick. Is this what I did to everyone else? Is this what it feels like to be surrounded by brain-eating zombies? They're everywhere, and I half expect them to come crawling and staggering through the windows.

Panting now, I stumble backward and run up the stairs, slipping on the uneven treads. I want to scream out loud like I do on set. But this time, it's real, and I feel as though their energy alone is tearing off my skin.

When I get outside, I totter on the buckling sidewalk, my heels catching in the pits and holes in the concrete. Someone approaches me from a car across the street—a woman with red hair. I pick up the pace, look straight ahead in case she's rebirthed—or maybe she's one of my whackjob fans.

"Lilly," she says. I stop. My kneecaps bounce from nerves. Someone knows I'm Lilly. That I'm awake. That's not good. I slowly turn to look at her.

"My name is Valerie, and I'm awake too. We're all going to Colorado where we'll be safe."

49

EMBER

The motor of the truck hums and the muffler groans and spits those burnt-orange swirls in my Color Crayon Brain. We swing around the winding road in the dark, the rain hammering the windshield. The wipers don't do a very good job of getting rid of the water, and I squint to see the road.

"Damn, your grandma's truck's loud," Nisha—I still can't get used to calling her that—says. "It's like we'll be announcing to the whole world where we're headed."

"It's, like, thirty years old, and the muffler has a big hole in it from when she high-centered on a big rock." I think she was hauling junk for the second-hand store at the time.

Axel jumps on Nisha's lap, and she frowns. "Why you gotta bring this cat?"

"Cats suck up negative energy," I say. I don't tell her it's because the color of his mewing is the same as Lodima's and Mom's voices combined. That he represents hope.

We're almost there, and I press the brakes as I veer around tight corners. The rain settles into puddles on the road, and for a moment, we glide, hydroplaning on the water. I hold my breath; this is near where Mom and Dad and I slid off the road so many years ago.

The wheels grab the road again and I exhale, gripping the steering wheel. "So you're sure they'll be there?" I ask. "It's such short notice."

"They've got resources—personal planes, cash, power," Tre says. "The MeToo implants are great for alerting the Annunaki, and the storms will make them want to duck for cover here for sure—even if they're awake."

A few minutes later, we come upon a series of black sports cars and sleek SUVs lining the sides of the twisting highway, as if someone is throwing a party in the middle of the woods.

"Looks like your message got through," I say, slowing the truck.

When we get to the front of the line, I pull over to the edge of the winding pass and put the truck in park. I climb out of the cab, and the blood drains from my face. There they stand: a hundred of them at least. Rebirthers—all colors, ages, and shapes—standing in front of a tall chain-link gate leading down to the edge of a massive cliff.

I hold onto the open door to keep steady. The sheer number of the people is amazing. And the way they stand, unmoving in the dark along the road is a little unnerving.

At the front of the pack stands Lilly, her white-blonde hair wet and sticking to her shoulders. She wears torn, skin-tight jeans with a peasant top. She scowls at us. Chris, dressed in a wet suit and tie with his hair neatly trimmed, stands somewhere near the edge of the pack with his hands on his hips. I scan the faces of the others, past so many beautiful, perfect-looking specimens— it's like Hollywood just scooped up the most gorgeous people in the world and plopped them right here. There's a guy dressed in black with his head shaved, and immediately, I do a double take. Pete. Sneering, he barely looks like himself—more like a hardened criminal with the scar that stretches down the side of his cheek.

The girl with the rose-petal lips from Hawaii, who I knew from my notebook: Laurie Parker, wearing a coat with its white fur matted by moisture. Phil Sei, taller than the rest, in a black beret. Valerie Monsette, a statue of red lips and slicked red hair. I remember her from the rooftop party in LA.

"Are they all awake?" I whisper.

"Let's hope so," Tre says. He slams the door with a tinny thud and walks around the truck to stand by me. He takes my hand. "If they are awake, we've got a kick-ass army. If they aren't, we've just scheduled our own massacre."

Tre and I walk hand in hand across the street, ready to meet our fellow warriors. My backpack feels heavy and my body is wired. Nerves bounce around inside me, but I'm anxious to kick some butt.

"Hey, guys, glad you got the message," I say. "We know you woke up—"

"Ember?" Pete asks, squinting, hesitant. He smiles, then suddenly, the expression drops off his face, landing hard on the wet pavement. The others recoil as well.

I'm instantly confused. Did they just fall back into their old rebirther identities? But the flickering expression on

Lilly's face is not the hardened look of a rebirther—it's shock. And it's also panic.

A rousting murmur of confusion trickles through the crowd. The sound rises in tan ripples in my Crayon Brain. "It's a trap!" yells one man. His voice is lime green.

I hear a flurry of words in the crowd. *"Storms." "Cover." "Not our fault." "Where are we?"*

Chris's familiar twang rises above the others. "Xintra sent them to eliminate us!"

"What? No...no, no, no." I shake my head and take another few steps toward them, hands up. The response from the group is that of a defensive shield. They stiffen, and a couple move forward with fingers spread and shoulders forward, ready to fight.

"Get them!" Phil Sei yells, and several people take off running toward us. I freeze.

"Wait!" Nisha moves out from behind me, holding Axel. She has the stance of a fearless, hardened woman.

I realize *this* is why they thought they'd been trapped. The sight of Zoe. She's always been Xintra's ally. To them, she's a beautiful, magical demon. A trap. A taker of lives.

"Zoe woke up, too!" I yell, panicked, waving my arms. "She's one of us!"

"Her name is Nisha," Tre calls.

"But what about the cliffs there?" Chris shouts. He points to the chain link fence and the dramatic six-hundred-foot cliff overlooking the Eagle River beyond it. "Why the hell are we here? This is no man's land!"

"Because you're no longer part of the Annunaki," I tell them. "You're awake. And now, you know the evil of it. You know what's about to happen to the world. You know that you were pawns. Xintra's pawns! And now, we're asking you to help us fight the Annunaki. Shut down Trinity and stop this terror!"

Tre squeezes my hand, and my insides burn bright from our partnership and the strength rising from me.

"We're going to stop Xintra. Reclaim our lives. Save the world," he says.

A number of the people shake their heads and mumble to one another. "I'm just getting my life back," Valerie yells. Her voice is sunflower yellow. "We're not enough to stop her."

We walk toward them and I raise my voice even louder to be heard. "What choice do we have? If we do nothing, the world will be wiped out from the storms. At least if we fight, we have a chance. We can't just stand by and watch Xintra do this!" Raindrops run down my forehead, and my T-shirt is soaked. My voice is stronger and more powerful than I ever knew it could be.

Tre comes behind me, and with two hands on my waist lifts me up onto a large boulder so I can address the crowd. *Thump. Thump. Thump.* My heart pounds heavy in my chest—not from nerves but from confidence. Determination.

"We can't just stand by and watch innocent people die. We have to stop her!"

A deep orange-colored voice calls from the back, "How?"

"We go back there, united, with a plan. Ready to fight, ready to bring our energy to undo all this. I believe in my heart that my plan will work."

50

LILLY

Ember looks like a drowned rat up there trying to rally us. "We have to stop this," she says. My ass we do. This is not what I got on that plane for. I got on that plane because Valerie told me we would be safe here. I didn't know it was a call for a goddamn rebellion.

I jiggle my leg. It's so dirty and wet here. The mud is ruining my Jimmy Choos. Look at Tre, standing right there next to her. Of course he is. He just flies from broken girl to broken girl. I look up at the sky. Dark clouds move swiftly across it, and the rain is picking up. I've got to get out of here.

But I feel suddenly shaky. What am I even doing here? Where will I go if I don't have Xintra's power?

I spot Pete a few people over, and I squeeze between bodies to reach him. "Pete!" I squeal. He hugs me tight. His skin is tan and a scar makes his face look kind of tough. I like it.

"You're alive," he says. "Can you believe we're out of Trinity?" He smiles but it's a flash. Hesitant.

I lean in to whisper, conspiratorially. "Okay, so are you totally freaking out that we woke up? And we had, like, power." I swallow, wondering if he's as disappointed as I am.

"I found myself in the wreckage from a bomb I set off."

I frown and jiggle my leg and cross my arms. "What do you think?" I nod my head over to Ember and Tre and crinkle my nose. "Of their plan? Do you want to fight?"

He shakes his head and rubs away the rain dripping into his eyes. "Yeah, I'm kinda scared." He laughs. "I liked the idea of Trinity way better when we just played in lakes."

"Me too," I say, smiling. I take his hand and peer into his face. He's not Tre, but he'll do. "It's good to see you again."

"Yeah," he says. "You look good." He pulls away to scan my body. I suck in my stomach and throw back my shoulders.

"So what're you gonna do?" I ask. "Maybe we should just bail." Maybe he'll drive away with me, tell Tre and Ember to stick it. Screw those people who die in the hurricanes and from the virus. I liked being rich.

"There's a big monsoon that's supposed to wash out a lot of the mountains here with mudslides. Fires from the downed power lines. An earthquake, I think... it's all happening somewhere around here. Could be ugly."

I nod. The devastation is going to be total. Maybe there won't even be movies anymore. And if Xintra's in charge, maybe I won't be famous or rich. Or alive.

"I'm going to head back to Trinity with Tre and Ember.

It's our best bet," he says, pausing, holding my hand, before gazing for a few seconds at the black pavement. He looks up and raindrops drip from his eyelashes. "I killed a lot of people. A lot of innocent people. It isn't right what Xintra's doing."

I nod. "Yeah, we should do what they say." I gaze at the line of black cars, longing to run away with him. I stand on tiptoes and whisper, "But Xintra could kill us."

He shrugs and nods.

Ember's scratchy voice rises above the crowd's conversation. "Okay guys, follow me. We're headed into a back entrance to the vortex!"

51

EMBER

We climb the tall chain-link fence, one by one, and hike down to the bottom of the chasm toward the ghost town of Gilman. A cluster of dilapidated white wooden houses sits empty. The government shut off all public access to the mining town in the 1980s, saying the toxicity levels here were too high. When I was growing up, kids used to tell stories of people who went to Gilman and came out weirdly deformed.

We pass behind the buildings to a narrow path along the far edge of the town. One misstep, and any one of us could slip down into the vast canyon below. My stomach rolls with the sight of the drop.

Nisha walks behind me, holding Axel under her arm like a purse. "So your mom really mentioned Gilman in her journal?"

"Yeah. Xintra's dad apparently bought it and shut down the mine, and all the residents left. A bunch of them disappeared."

"He took them to the vortex," she says.

"Oh," I say, surprised I hadn't considered this. "I figured this had to be the way into the vortex system. I think Mom got out through this tunnel too."

"I'm beginning to remember. You know, after James brought me on the inside of their system and rebirthed me," Nisha says, "he wanted private access to the tunnels because they cross the ley lines for the vortexes. I wasn't allowed inside. Good thing, though, because apparently it's horrible in there—more traumatizing than the other routes he discovered later."

"What do you mean *traumatizing*?" A stress laugh ripples out of me, and then I take a long inhale and focus on my feet. The path along the ridge is narrow, slick, and muddy. My shoes slip, and I hold my hands out for balance.

I glance over my shoulder, and Nisha shrugs.

Just down the path sits a wooden door. Not a door to a house or a building, but a door that takes you inside the cliff. I always noticed it when we drove past here a thousand times as a kid. It's weirdly out of place—like spotting a refrigerator sitting on someone's roof.

Somehow, I always felt it was important in some way. In fact, no matter what music played or who was talking in the car, I always saw lavender dots pulsing over the top of it. I knew it was weird what I saw, so I never told anyone.

Standing here now, the lavender dots reappear. I assume it's my Crayon Brain conjuring up colors from the mixture of sounds around here: the breeze whistling through the canyons, the rain hitting the ground.

Besides the sounds of nature, there are voices and the rustling feet of the awakened rebirthers. Having a hundred people follow me feels intense, like an invisible weight of expectation. We're going up against an enormous power—and I've promised them hope. The anticipation and the pressure are about as heavy as wearing a coat made of lead.

I approach the door and find it has a rusted padlock bolting it shut. Not that I thought it would be easy, but my heart deflates nonetheless.

"Here," Tre says, stepping in front of me. He raises a leg and kicks, but he cries out in pain when the door doesn't budge. "Shit. That's about as thick as the doors in the Trinity basement."

"And it has a *lock*." I open my backpack. "My turn," I say, finding a lighter and a blowtorch inside. I pull my coach's welding helmet over my head. "Look away, guys."

I flick on the lighter, turn on the propane and easily ignite the blowtorch. The blue flame rises and hisses. I drop the lighter onto the ground and raise the torch with two hands up to the metal lock. It takes some time, but the metal on the lock begins to bubble and dent, and then finally it pops. The lock opens.

"It worked!" I shout and the tension among our soldiers releases. Voices chatter.

I push the door with my foot, and it creaks open to reveal a dark tunnel. The wind picks up on the cliff behind me, screaming hazy peach colors through my Crayon Brain. The rain pelts our faces. Without any hesitation, I step inside the dark cavern.

52

NISHA

Xintra's father, James, told me about this entrance—I'm almost certain. It's one of the tunnels leading to the other vortex entrances, but traveling through it was so difficult that he set out to find and uncover the other routes used by the ancient people.

Everything about James feels vague now. I can't really even remember what he looked like, exactly. Red hair. Handsome. But he's mostly just an outline of a person in my mind's eye.

I follow Ember and Tre inside the tunnel, Axel's fur against my skin a soothing contrast to the damp darkness around me. The walls leak. *Ooze* might be the better word. The wet drops echo when they hit the puddles on the ground. We move through muddy, oily water, traveling down a slope that takes us far beneath the earth's surface. The tunnel feels cramped, and Tre is so tall he must duck his head.

Ember and Tre talk in low tones in the dark, but I can't

see them. I only see the small light from her bouncing flashlight. Walking in the dark beneath the ground doesn't scare me. It's the others behind me I worry about. They're so newly awakened, they're unpredictable. And they didn't come here for a fight. They came here to hide out from the storms like a bunch of yellow dogs.

Armed yellow dogs—thanks to whatever we found in that lady's garage and kitchen. Gunpowder and matches. Knives. Rocks. Lead pipes. Shovels. Just behind me, Chris swings an ax. With all the money and power these people once had, someone should have brought some goddamn guns. Who goes to war without a gun?

We walk for a good mile in single file through the dank-smelling tunnel, guided only by the small glow of Ember's flashlight. Again, every single one of us should have flashlights. Instead, I shuffle in the dark, holding a kitchen knife out in front of me.

Someone screams and it sends a shiver down my spine. Ember spins around and shines the light on the crowd of people, zeroing in on Lilly, squealing and bouncing on her toes, her white hair covering her face.

Ember shines the flashlight to track a cluster of fat gray rodents the size of sub sandwiches scurrying across the tunnel.

"Just some rats," I say.

"Just rats?" she screams. "Get me out of here!"

Pete calms her down. "Hey, it's okay, it's okay."

"Get over it," I say. "Just kick them out of the way. Let's go, Ember!" I wave my arm and we shuffle forward.

We continue our march into the abyss. Our shoes thwack and slosh. The tunnel takes a deeper incline, and the muddy floor becomes more slippery. Soon, the inky black burrow we've been inside for a half hour transforms to a creamy gray. I can make out the rough stone edges of the walls and the chocolate-colored puddles dotting the ground.

I pass two stalagmites on the walls. They look a little fluorescent green. A swishing sound echoes in the tunnel. It's faint but it sounds like it's coming from ahead. I hold my breath, knowing the vortex is coming.

Ember stops and shines the flashlight on me and the rest of the crowd.

"You ready for this?" she asks.

53

EMBER

The ground shakes thunderously, and wind swirls inside the tunnel. It howls, moving from a deep roar to a high-pitched scream and back again. The gold and green colors of the sound rattle my bones.

I grasp tight to the wet tunnel wall with two hands to avoid being blown away, and Tre, immediately behind me, does the same. After a moment, I crouch low to the ground and find relief from the wind.

"Get down, guys," I yell to the others over my shoulder. They drop down with a series of scuffling and thuds.

I crawl through the tunnel on my hands, knees, and stomach. The glow from my flashlight moves low to the ground, sweeping low and jiggling with each movement forward.

The wind still howls and spins in a furious vortex, but it's above us now. The psychedelic colors wash over the tunnel, flickering against the walls in light green, pinks, purples, golds, and silvers. A pulsing, crazy dance club. I have no idea if this is how it really looks or if it's just my Crayon Brain going berserk.

The farther we crawl into the tunnel, another sound begins to emerge. At first it's a low humming, that green-gold swishing noise I heard right before we stepped into the wind. But it grows louder, as if it's moving closer to us, like an oncoming train racing through a mountain pass. Soon it's upon us, roaring and pulsing and low-pitched. The sound becomes bright orange pinwheels, like a live electric wires. It cloaks us, pressing tight. The air feels cool, the pressure squeezes my head, and the smell of sulfur overpowers me. My skin and scalp tingle, and a faint dizziness whips through me.

I shout over the noise. "Keep going!"

After another hundred yards, my flashlight illuminates the spot where the tunnel opens into a small cave. Standing again, I spin around with the light and take in the white and orange stalagmites protruding from the walls. At least eight other tunnels branch off the space, twisting in all directions.

"This must be where the vortexes meet," Tre says, climbing to his feet beside me. The cave is the size of a small bedroom, so there's not enough space for all hundred-plus of us.

"Which way should we go?" I ask.

I shine my light on Nisha and she blinks and raises a hand to shield her eyes. "Do you mind?" she asks.

I train the light on the floor instead, making her delicate features look more ghostly. "This is the hard part," she says. "If you pick the wrong tunnel, you're screwed. I'm talking the middle of Antarctica. Egypt. Maybe even middle of the ocean in the Bermuda Triangle."

The bubble wrap in my chest grows, popping a little as it expands. "So which one?"

She shakes her head slowly.

I look at Tre and he runs his hand through his damp hair. "I gotta say, I don't know either, Ember."

People continue to file into the tiny space from the tunnel, until we're sandwiched together as if we're standing in a crowded elevator. The pressure to make a decision mounts.

"Hey! What are we doing?" a golden voice calls.

"Stay back in the tunnel, guys," Tre shouts, pushing and waving people back into the windy passageway. He's greeted with muffled chatter and shouts of frustration, a smattering of gray and pink ripples.

The crowd moves backward and then forward like a single organism, which eventually tosses Tre into the wall of the cave. So many people pack so tightly into the room that the beam of my flashlight, pointed at the floor, is smothered. Everyone's voices, muted back in the tunnel, grow louder, a mixture of rainbow colors.

"Hey! Where the hell are we?" Chris asks. I recognize his twangy voice.

"We're at the center—where we could go through any number of vortexes," Nisha says, though I can't see her anymore.

"What happens in those tunnels?" It's Lilly—her voice is the color of raindrops.

People shove, swaying in a wave back and forth. Next to me, Valerie gets pushed into a cluster of stalagmites and cries out. This is going to be chaos if we don't pick a path quickly.

"Calm down, everyone! Don't worry—I'll lead us the

right way!" I say.

"Who made you queen?" an unfamiliar voice rises. The color of banana yellow.

I inhale deeply to give him an answer, but Nisha speaks up. "She's no queen," she yells. "But she's the reason you fools are awake. She beat Xintra's system. The first one in history to wake up. So you best be saying thank you and back your sorry asses up into the tunnel so we have room to figure things out!"

There is shuffling of feet, moving, adjusting, grumbling and cursing among the crowd. But the space in the cave clears. I've got to hurry. How much air is there for all of us down here anyway?

I duck my head into one tunnel and listen carefully, trying to block out the sound of the crowd. The noise in this narrow tunnel is neon green stars. I know this. I see it.

Quickly, I listen at the entrance of another tunnel. Pearl-colored swirls. I go to each of the openings, listen for their colors. The colors of the sounds become confusing at times, often crashing together, whooshing and whistling, screaming and pulsing. Then, one emerges from a tunnel to the left. It's high-pitched, but it's the deep blue and black color of it that draws me closer. In my Color Crayon Brain, it looks like an ocean in the midst of a hurricane, out of control, treacherous. Raging. The sound of Xintra.

"This way," I yell, waving everyone to follow as I step inside the dark tunnel. The walls reach at least seven feet high, and the tunnel's width stretches just as far. Tre and Nisha catch up to me, and together, the three of us lead the crowd over wet, marshy ground. In the distance, a silvery net of whirling cobwebs looms like a pale haze, and I drag my fingers over the wet bumps protruding from the wall.

The walls begin to glow purple and pink, twisting like saltwater taffy being stretched and pulled on a candy machine. The smell of sulfur comes again and a wave of nausea strikes me. I double over, trying to keep everything from rising up and pouring out of me. My head pounds and it feels like my stomach is being tied into a knot.

It must not be just me, because Nisha moans and Tre dry-heaves. The cat hisses and there's a deep retching sound behind us. Someone behind us is puking; the acrid scent wafts through the tunnel. I cover my nose with my hand. A number of other barfing sounds follow, and I hear squeals and shouts of "Ahhh, man!" and "Don't step in it!"

My stomach curdles, and I pick up the pace, trotting deeper into the tunnel. My head pounds and I can't see straight. The walls feel like they're waving, breathing in and out.

Xintra's black and blue hurricane sound grows louder and the colors are almost too much, as if the sea itself is rushing over me. The ground rumbles like a volcano and a deep pressure squeezes my head. "Do you feel that?" I shout, touching my temple.

"It's like we just sank to the bottom of a deep swimming pool!" Tre shouts.

After at least half a mile, the tunnel comes to a dead end and there's a small dark cave that opens up in the wall. Remembering the holes I climbed through last time to escape Trinity, I shake my head, take a deep breath, and crawl inside.

My flashlight flickers and then shuts off. All sound disappears. All light. It's as if I'm being buried alive, and it takes everything inside me to not scream.

54

PETE

This place is too crowded, and the dude wearing the knit cap leans into me, his shoulder pressing against mine. I fall into the fat guy on the other side of me. Irritated, I elbow the knit cap guy and glare at him. He looks familiar and if I were a girl, I'd say he was good looking. Maybe he's famous.

Yeah, I think he's some sort of TV guy. He pushes me again, and I hold my elbow firm, so he gets it in his side with the next push. When his skin touches mine, though, my knees get real rickety, and I feel kind of like I did when I was around Zoe in Trinity.

The feeling makes me turn to look up at the guy, really take inventory of him, and I feel like I'm seriously gonna puke. There's that ash-colored aura above his head. It moves around like a big thundercloud, disappearing for just a second and then reforming in some sort of weird shape.

I feel kind of like when you wake up from a dream

where you're falling and your body jerks, breathless. It's that kind of *holy shit* moment, seeing that black fog, because what I'm seeing tells me that he's not fully awake. He's still a rebirther right here among us. That means he's on Xintra's side, controlled by Xintra— and he'll fuck us up for sure.

I breathe heavy through my nostrils and stare straight ahead like I didn't just notice this fact. Like I'm not pretty damn scared. After a second, I glance at the knit cap guy again. He's tall, middle-aged and has a blond beard. The black fog pulsates and then scatters for a millisecond before reemerging. I can barely see it, but I think that's because I'm newly awake.

He's gonna know that I know he's a rebirther. He will. We all had that sixth sense. We all had that way of just seeing stuff. Shit.

I continue to stare straight ahead, inhaling the scent of minty shampoo from the girl in front of me, knowing I've got to do something. I want to spread the word, just so everyone is ready for him. But if I say something out loud, all hell will break loose.

Shit. Inside my chest, it's like a hockey game is underway, with guys being slammed up against the boards.

The crowd staggers forward, all of us taking small lumbering steps, and from what I can see over all the bodies and heads, it looks like everyone is slipping into one of those tunnels ahead. I've got to make sure he doesn't get into the tunnel with us.

Of all the people here, I'm the guy. I've built up skills I didn't even know I had as a sab. Fighting. Murdering. A hardened shell still stays with me, a bitterness that leaves me feeling angry inside, like all this killing has shrunk my heart. In many ways, I feel worse about myself now than I did in Trinity. Seriously, all I wanted was a vacation from my life, which, looking back now, was a pretty fucking good one. Stuff happened to me, some bad stuff, but I could have dealt with it.

I look at my hands. Thicker with calluses now, hardened skin from life on the run. From the blood of thousands of innocent people.

The memory of that red shoe buried in the wreckage comes barreling back to me, and it feels kind of like being on one of those elevator drop rides.

I decide I'd rather die being a hero than a coward. I lean into the crowd, cutting off the rebirther in the knit cap, slowing my pace as we move into the cave and letting the others pass. I feel his energy from just inches away. For a half a second, my fingers go limp and I nearly drop the gardening shears in my hand.

Eventually, everyone has gone through the tunnel. Everyone but me and the rebirther behind me. The guy pushes me with two fingers. "Hurry up, man."

I turn around, hold up my weapon and block the tunnel. "You're not going anywhere," I say.

55

EMBER

I touch a stone wall ahead of me. This can't be a dead end. It can't.

Slivers of light shine in through the edges of what looks like a stone doorway. I push hard with my hands, tucking my feet up against the sides of the passageway as leverage. With two pushes, I knock the stone out of its hole like popping off a bottle cap and stick my head out into murky daylight.

Relief comes with giant exhale, and I scramble the rest of the way out of the opening in the limestone cliff wall, then hop down to stand on the ground.

The sky is gray, and a barren, muddy landscape opens up before me. Trees loom like crooked black claws. Ominous gray clouds hang low, like a charcoal drawing of puffy swirls. A low fog and dark shadows obscure the terrain, and the cliffs stand like jagged giants watching us, waiting to swallow us whole.

I shiver. It's as if a bomb went off in this place. Tre climbs out next, gaping at the scene. "Whoa," he whispers.

I can only assume that ahead of us is the same gorgeous flowered meadow that I saw when I stepped into Trinity so long ago. But as I spin around to take in the horrific view, a trickle of regret runs through me. Was it a mistake to come back here?

The others climb out of the tunnel one by one, and their reactions are similar. "What the—" Phil says.

I move aside, giving the others space to clamber out. Each person who makes it through the tunnel, one after another, looks at the scene before us, shocked. It's amazing how many people we woke up, how many of them agreed to come back to Trinity to fight.

Lilly emerges, wiping off her wet jeans and blouse. She looks up, mouth gaping. "I don't know about this…"

"Oh come on you guys," Nisha says loudly. She holds Axel under her arm. "It's all different when you're not lost. This is what Xintra's energy really looks like. She can make this nasty place look as pretty as you want—if you're susceptible. She can bend light and reality here."

"You brought a cat through this?" Chris asks.

"Yeah, cats suck up negative energy. Don't you know that?" She winks at me.

"Shake it off, guys. We have a job to do," I say, walking briskly toward an open area of dead grass and charred ground.

Maddie. I have to stop this for Maddie. For Mom. For all these people. For all the people I helped Xintra murder. For all the people who are about to die at her hands in the storms and from the virus. Xintra's reign has to end.

Something burns in my core. I will take this place down if it's the last thing I do.

Lilly's blonde hair swings wildly in front of me. She's swiveling, looking for something. "Where's Pete?"

I search the crowd. "I don't know."

"He's still in there," Tre says, taking a few steps back to the wall. "Maybe I should go back and see if he's okay."

"It's a one-way street, boy. You can only use that tunnel to come in," Nisha says. "Xintra's dad closed it up after Dezi left."

"Do you know that for sure?" Lilly asks. She releases a loud sob. "Oh, Petey..."

Nisha crosses her arms. "Yeah, Xintra's father found the other tunnels. They're not as painful—no puke—and they let you go in *and* out."

I bite my lip and grab Tre's arm, pulling him back to me. "Afterward," I say. "We'll go back and find Pete afterward. From the other side."

"He could still make it out," Tre tells Lilly, resting a hand on her shoulder. "We need your help, Lil. We don't have much time. The storms are coming."

56

PETE

This dude's energy is so strong, it reverberates through my quads and biceps and makes it tough to stay coherent. I don't get how we didn't spot him in the crowd earlier. We should have *felt* him.

I hold the gardening shears out in front of me and crouch. The guy with the beard sneers and slowly stands upright. Then he laughs. *He laughs.* More of a chuckle, really, all high-pitched and staccato, and it sounds really loud inside this cave. After a few seconds, I realize he's mimicking me. That's *my* laugh when I get stoned.

"Dude...that's—" I start.

"You," he interrupts, straightening.

It looks like he's chewing his cud like a cow. What an arrogant prick.

"Yeah, you *sound* like an idiot because you *are* an idiot," he says.

I shake my head. He's trying to play the Zoe card, where she'd just scratch at you, playing on all your insecurities. I'm not buying it this time. I know who I am now, who I can be—and it makes me feel strong. "Go home, man, or you're gonna regret it."

"You think you can beat Xintra? You? A loser stoner?" he asks. "The only time you were powerful was when you had *her* power. The rebirther power. Before that, you were just a skate rat who couldn't hold a job."

That's it.

I launch myself at him, extending the gardening blades out in front of me. I fly headfirst into the other side of the cave, crashing my shoulder into one of those slimy bumps on the wall. Pain shoots through my neck, and I wince.

The guy's quick. Like, cat-quick. I turn around just in time to see him walking into the tunnel with the creepy sound, heading after the others. I raise my shears and with one gigantic freaking thrust, stab the back of his leg. *"Yeeeeeaaah, boy!"* I sing.

He cries out in pain, before reaching around and, with one hand, yanks the blade out of his hamstring. I grab him by the waist, pull him out of the tunnel and toss him into the wall of the cave. He lands with a pretty big thud, and I seriously hope I've knocked him out, because for real, I cannot take another murder.

He stands up slowly, holding my gardening shears in his hand. He's calm and icy. Crap. This dude is an expert. He must be a sab. The one good thing about being under Xintra's control is the lack of fear. I didn't have it then, but now that I'm awake, I sure as hell feel it now.

My heart pounds, and I run at the guy, head down like a rusher on a football team. I grit my teeth and grunt. My shoulder slams hard into his ribcage, sending him flying back into the wall. But his energy is tough, almost electrifying, and I'm pretty sure it shocks me, because my muscles freeze for a good two seconds.

The cave starts to look darker now, like someone just dimmed the lights. Without meaning to, I let go of him and drop to my knees. Something pinches. Why does my back feel so funny?

I feel something wet, liquid trickling down my back. It leaks into the waistband of my pants. It's gotta be blood. I look up at the guy, feeling dizzy, and his face begins to blur. I grasp his bloody leg to stay upright but it's like my hands don't have any strength in them. My fingers won't work, and they slide down his legs.

He watches me. Smiling. Yeah, I think he's smiling.

Then, I feel nothing at all.

57

EMBER

Nisha holds Axel close to her chest, and the cat's mewing shows up sage green with that hint of muddied amber again. The colors hover and float in my vision, and after a moment, I notice they're clustered mostly at the center of the burnt meadow, like a pulsing dot on a GPS map.

A map! My Color Crayon Brain, the thing that made me weird to the rest of the world, has become my super power! I followed the color at Lodima's house to find the book. I followed the colors at the Gilman Mine to discover the door. I followed the colors down the vortex tunnel to get to Trinity. I've got to hope that the sounds and colors of this place will lead me to undoing Trinity for good.

Right now, the sound of the cat should show me what to do next.

"Can I hold him please?"

Nisha frowns and I reach out to take the cat from her, then run with him to the middle of the meadow. Tre follows. "We need to put the rocks here," I say, pointing to the ground.

We pull the plastic bins from my backpack and pile the stones on the blackened ground. Small and large. Pitted and flat. Shiny black and round. Hints of green and orange flecks. Rough pink and smooth silvery sheens.

I remove the shimmery red crystal from the pile on the ground. Goldstone, according to Google. I hand it to Tre. He frowns and studies it.

"Put it in your pocket" I say. "I think it represents the light that can always be found in the darkness. It deflects unwanted energies and is considered protective."

"What?"

I shrug—I'm more like Mom than I thought, I guess— and Tre slips it into his pocket. Quickly, I scrounge for the other crystal. "Give this one to Nisha. It's azurite. My mom said it's called the Stone of the Heavens. It wakens psychic abilities and helps you with spiritual guidance."

Nisha approaches us, holding up her own reddish crystal. "You keep it. Got my own. It's a piece of agate."

Perfect. *Agate gives warriors strength in battle. It means good luck,* I remember.

I slip the azurite into my pocket.

"Now what?" Tre asks.

I feel our soldiers moving behind me, like aliens placed on a foreign planet. Lost and confused, afraid, uncertain of their mission. They hold their weapons at their sides, still taking in the ghastly terrain.

"We need to start a fire! Grab all the branches and kindling you can!" I yell, cupping my hands around my mouth. Then, I dart off to the edge of the meadow, toward a throng of broken and blackened trees.

As I approach, something moves in the shrubs about fifty yards away to my right—maybe a marmot or a raccoon.

But it's not.

It's a tall man with a blond beard and a knit cap, late to come out of the tunnel. His body is streaked with blood, and I stiffen, my heart sinking like an anchor. Is he hurt?

The man sneaks up behind Valerie, who is bent over and gathering branches. He raises an arm, his knife pointed down. Information computes in my brain. This guy is a rebirther who isn't completely awake, and I'm betting he just killed Pete. Now he's going to strike Valerie. Yet it takes a moment before I react.

"Valerie!" I yell. She spins around with just enough time to push the man, causing him to stumble backward. A handful of others jump on him, pounding him to the ground. They wrestle him—a cluster of bodies seen in bursts through gnarled pinion trees and black bushes. Somewhere in the scrimmage, someone raises a shovel in the air.

"How nice of you all to come back to join me." The familiar oceanic voice of Xintra.

I turn around to find her standing just ten yards away, wearing a black coat and pants, her arms crossed. A chill slithers across my skin and my heart lurches to my throat. I freeze with my hand on a branch.

"And you brought your friends!" She motions to the others, who are busy gathering branches at the edge of the meadow. Some men are still wrestling the bearded rebirther. Everyone else is oblivious to Xintra's arrival. "Looks like we'll have a party for the start of the new world order."

A low hum rattles in the air. It's forest green in my Crayon Brain, but it's not exactly clear where the noise is coming from.

I follow Xintra's gaze to the hillside, and I see them. An army of rebirthers. Thousands of them march down from the Trinity House and emerge from all corners of the meadow and forest. They walk with a purpose and determination that my newly awakened army does not have. The sight of these people all under Xintra's control, the sheer number of them, takes my breath away. The branch drops from my limp fingers.

Then that fire blazes in my gut. My army has something hers does not. Real human emotion. Pain. Resentment. Fury. "She's here!" I scream.

Xintra laughs and then points at Tre. "You know, I always told myself that my baby brother—once I found him—would fall short of all my expectations. Sadly enough, I was right."

An earsplitting crack pierces the air, and Tre's body convulses in a twisted dance, moved by a glowing blue line that extends from Xintra's pointed finger to his chest. He screams a blood-red sound. Terror seizes me and I cry out, sprinting toward him.

I leap in front of him, holding my hand out to block the blue bolt of electricity, and the most excruciating pain courses through my body, sizzling, zapping, cramping, and tearing. I fall to my knees, and a surging, hot energy sweeps through my veins. The sky and ground and crowds of people become indistinct. My eardrums ring, and then, like the snap of a finger, the sound stops.

As quickly as it came, the pain lessens, though my legs

and torso spasm and my skin feels like it's on fire. After a moment, I lift my head to look up.

Five of our awakened soldiers—men and women— scream with deep-seated rage, the color of fall leaves. They've knocked Xintra down, saving me, saving Tre, and they're thrashing about to fight her. *Oh my God, thank you.*

Tre staggers over to me and kneels down to touch my face. I try to speak, but my body jerks in random fits and my skin still burns. A tingling pain lingers in my muscles. He leans into me, placing his cheek on mine, and I feel his stubble and his hot breath. "You okay?" he asks.

My body stills and I exhale loudly before nodding. "Uh-huh. You?"

He winces. "Yeah."

We climb to our feet, as we watch Chris and the others —all thrashing bodies and torsos, heads and arms, lead pipe, shovels, and axes—doing battle with Xintra. I'm inflated by their bravery.

But then one by one, their bodies freeze, then jolt, and sparks fly from their clothes. Xintra rises from beneath them, moving from a crouch to a standing position, discarding the people, dropping each body to the ground like she's shaking dead leaves off her coat.

Smoke ripples from an unconscious man in a dark suit. There's a gouging hole in his chest where his heart should be. He lies limp on the ground, eyes open wide. Dead.

I stop moving, stop breathing, terror lacing up my chest. It's Chris.

No.

"You can never stop this!" Xintra's voice booms and she sneers at the crowd of fearful onlookers. "Today is the

Dark Day. The start of a new world. Traitors will be punished."

Her hurricane voice strikes me like a physical blow and I gaze at her, stunned by her supernatural power. Like a conductor, she whisks her hands in the air, delicately commanding the wind with her fingertips. The air stills and then a breeze sweeps across my skin, giving me goose-bumps. Heavy thunderclouds roll in above us. Wind kicks up, whipping Xintra's red hair and blowing dust about her feet. And that fog, the creepy ghostly fog, begins to ripple into the meadow, twirling and twisting as it crawls.

Xintra moves through the grass, taking large, regal steps, pointing her finger every now and then, zapping people with her twisted electrical power. Our soldiers scream and run while her mass of rebirther troops descends with a thunder of footsteps.

In the midst of the confusion, I see a color. It floats around my head like the tiny stars you might see when you lose oxygen. I focus on the color and realize where I've seen it before—it's the silvery call of the red-winged black-bird. The color of angels' wings. I turn to search for the bird, which always reminded me of Mom when I was here in Trinity, but all I see is the color of its call. It pulses over *The Book of the Dead*, which has spilled out of my backpack and onto the ground.

Something pounds in my heart, like the drumbeat at a concert. I look up. The first of the rebirthers have arrived in the meadow. The rest march behind them like a mind-less army of zombies. They swarm our small number of soldiers, raising their own weapons—not garden tools, but real weapons. Swords. Hatchets. Guns.

My heart stops.

I reach for the book and turn page after page, my fingers trembling and throat sticky, and follow the silvery colors on the paper. The color of the bird's call dances and pulses over the words and drawings. Finally, I turn to page 264 and the sparkling color becomes a large orb.

"What is it?" Tre asks, pointing to the book.

"A spell. I knew we needed a spell, but my intuition says it's this one."

The only way to beat Xintra is with the same kind of power that she used to build Trinity. Witchcraft.

Her voice booms across the canyon, sending a crawling, sticky feeling across my skin and roaring ocean waves through my Crayon vision.

"With each lost soul, I reap more of the earth's power, I reap more from my ancestors, who wait patiently to serve me, to have their second chance. You can *never* stop this." She spits the last words and then punctuates the sentence with a toss of her head and a wicked guffaw that leaves my ears ringing and nearly blots out my vision entirely with inky black stains.

I cannot believe that *this* is the girl who was once my mom's friend. She must have been rebirthed herself, alone in that meadow, singing that song and using the birds' energy. She must have transformed herself into a monster, feeding on her own desires for power, instead of feeding on insecurities the way she did with us. Because there is no way in hell this woman is human.

The clashes begin, metal on metal. The thud of bodies falling to the ground. The sickening sound of slicing and stabbing and slick blood. A firecracker *pop-pop-pop* rings through the air, and I scream.

A blur passes in my peripheral vision. Lilly's white hair,

fluttering, as she runs in bare feet directly at Xintra. I'm surprised by her bravery—but I'm afraid that she, too, will be crushed by Xintra's power.

Lilly drops to her knees, cupping Xintra's hand with her own and placing her forehead on her arm. "Please!" she screams. "I didn't want to wake up. I didn't choose that. I want to go back to my old life as Tonia Davies. Please. I'll do anything!"

Tre and I exchange shocked glances. She's choosing her own fame and fortune over the pain of others, selling her soul. Just like her red-lipped momster.

Xintra looks down at her. "Of course," she says before looking out at the melee around her. "The traitors will be punished."

Lilly smiles and then begins to rise to her feet but stops midway. Suddenly, she drops to her knees. Her body quakes and at first, I think perhaps she's crying, or maybe even laughing.

Xintra looks down at Lilly again. "You were a bad girl."

Lilly collapses onto her side, lifeless.

Xintra must not see me and Tre, because she turns and walks in the opposite direction of us, and we slink down behind a few others dashing for the fire pit. I glance back over my shoulder, and Xintra tilts her head down and then swiftly extends one arm to the sky.

It's as if this redheaded girl controls a switch to the electricity in this crazy place, because a lightning bolt flies from a charred thundercloud above. A deafening crack rings out, followed by an explosion of light and electricity. A thousand suns burst. I shield my eyes with my arm, and when I look up, a rounded lady with eyebrows that look like dark commas lies crumpled on the ground, struck by lightning.

Xintra stands still with her legs spread, arms dangling at her side, as the crowd flees away from her.

Icy determination ignites inside me even more now as I look at the dead woman with the plump, round cheeks and the perfectly arched brows. This has to stop.

Tre and I hold hands, running on wobbly tingly legs again to the center of the meadow, squeezing through the crowd of people—awakened rebirthers now terrified. They scream and run for cover.

In glimpses, between shoulders and heads and bodies, I spot the pile of branches we gathered. Tre yells something to me and I lean in to hear, but his voice is overwhelmed by a deafening crack of thunder and breaking trees and rumbling rocks that tumble down the hillside. Turquoise blotches streak my vision like a watercolor painting.

The earth cracks open at the east end of the meadow and a jagged line races across the ground, cutting and swerving and heading right for us, leaving gaping holes in its wake. People shriek and run in all directions. A man falls into the mouth of the earth right in front of me.

An earthquake. This is a freaking earthquake.

58

NISHA

What in God's name is that girl trying to do? The ground lurches and shifts, and Ember stumbles and falls and then rolls farther away from all those damn branches she wanted put in the middle of the field.

Someone bumps me from behind. It's Phil Sei with the beret—I'm surprised that thing is still even on his head with all this turmoil. A young woman—Vladimira, who was rebirthed as homeland security director— shouts and runs directly at me, and, quickly, I jump out of the way to avoid her. It's a good thing because a pine tree crashes down right where I was standing. The sight of it, wider than me and broken in two, takes my breath away.

This is pandemonium, and I can't find enough saliva to swallow. Something brushes my feet. It's Axel. I pick him up, shielding him from the cracking thunder, the flashing lighting and the swirling wind.

I run to follow Ember and Tre, both determined to get

to those magnetic rocks, when another damn fissure races toward them, an earthquake stretching and gaping.

Oh no.

Foot by foot it screams toward them like a runaway train. Ember's so close to the rocks and branches, just fifteen feet away, when another crack in the earth swims swiftly across the meadow and opens up the earth, cutting her off from her goal. I taste blood in my mouth and realize I'm biting my lip so hard it's bleeding.

My heart pounds as I run to her and Tre, swerving to dodge a swinging ax, cringing as Ember dives across the crack, just as it widens into a gaping hole. She lands flat on her stomach, clinging to the muddy edge of the earth with two hands. *Hang on, Ember.* She claws the dirt with her fingernails and manages to scramble to her feet.

I catch up to Tre, breathing hard. Someone bumps me again, and the ground tilts. "We have to get out of here!" I shout to him, clinging to the cat.

Tre nods, but then in a single stride, off he goes after that girl, following Ember, leaping across the six-foot crack and landing on his two feet with his fingertips on the ground.

I look around for Xintra. Her red hair flashes in the crowd. People who come into contact with her drop like flies. "Hurry. Hurry," I whisper. My heart pounds and I cling to Axel. Why is this damn cat not sucking up all of Xintra's negative energy? He's not doing his job!

Xintra makes her way closer to us, and at least ten people lie on the ground, convulsing, in her wake. Even more drop to their knees before the rebirther army she brought with her.

Together, Tre and Ember race across the lopsided

ground until they reach the branches and rocks. That pile is at least seven feet tall.

Ember unlatches her backpack and hands something to Tre. Lighter fluid? I'm shoved, and then someone grabs me from behind. Two strong hands pull me off my feet and back to the ground. The cat slips out of my hands.

I feel the hatred in my attacker's skin, feel it in his hot breath on my neck as I squirm and struggle, clawing at his arms. My pulse races, fueling my bones to fight. One of his hands wrenches my chest and the other jerks back on my hair. Lying toppled on him, I kick and swing my feet wildly in the air, but his rebirther energy makes me feel weak and dizzy. Then suddenly he lets go, screaming in anguish. I scramble to my feet and look back at him on the ground. His long black hair is falling out of its ponytail, and his chiseled jaw is twisted in pain. He yells out in anguish and covers his eyes, blood trickling from beneath his hand. With his free hand, he reaches for Axel, who hisses and dances around him. Well, I'll be damned if that cat didn't just save my life, scratching that guy's eyes out.

I kick the rebirther in the nuts, hard, and run away on the tilting ground with Axel in my arms. I've got to get to Tre and Ember.

Across the chasm, Tre squirts the lighter fluid onto the dead, twisted branches; Ember opens that tub of gunpowder I packed for her and she dumps it onto the pile. She reaches in her bag, and I know she's looking for that lighter we packed.

Shit. I'm pretty sure I saw her set the lighter down after she lit the blowtorch to pop the padlock back in Gilman.

I back up, sprint as fast as I can, and take a giant leap over the gaping crack in the earth.

59

EMBER

Something hits the ground hard next to me. It's Nisha, crouching behind us with cat in hand.

"I can't find the lighter!" I scream, digging my hands into the empty backpack. "It's not here!"

"Rebirthers are notorious smokers, don't you know?" Nisha reaches into her jeans pocket and pulls out a cigarette lighter. She flicks the switch and lights a branch on the pile, and we both dive away from the explosive whoosh of the fire.

I throw my arms around her neck. "Zoe!"

"Nisha," she snaps with a quick pat on my back.

I don't care what her name is. This girl saved my ass. I squeeze her tight as the flames stretch high into the sky and the heat scorches my skin even from several feet away. The blaze roars.

Maddie said these rocks lose their magnetic properties when heated 170 degrees—it's got to reverse the power of this place. It must. But Xintra boosted the magnetic power by saying a spell and using the fire.

I reach into the backpack, pull out *The Book of the Dead*, and drop to my knees. I scan the pages: *Ancient cultures believed in pole shifts that could occur with mathematical combinations with the constellations. The pyramids served as one giant tet or master magnet.*

Trinity, I think, must have been triggered to become an even larger magnetic receiver. I read the rest of the paragraph.

Reversing magnetism involves reversing the poles. The earth will start turning in the opposite direction.

WTF? None of this makes sense.

Tre and Nisha crouch down next to me, hovering as my shaky fingers drag along the page until I find the spell listed immediately below the last one we read. On the opposite page, I scan a section that talks about the power of three. The triad is universal. I read the words quickly.

The number three equals completion. Beginning, middle, and end. Earth, water, heavens. Past, present, future. Harmony, wisdom, understanding. Body, soul, and spirit.

Three.

I point to two corners around the fire and instruct Tre and Nisha to stand there so we create a triangle. "Go over there! It takes three of us!" I have to yell as loud as possible to be heard above the wind, the screaming, and the thunder.

I remember how, in the ceremony with Mom and Lodima, Xintra drew a serpent, which if I remember correctly from Mom's Crazy Woman Notebook was a symbol of divine authority and the symbol of the goddess Wadjet.

"Get into a triangle around the fire and draw lines connecting us in the dirt!" I yell before dragging my foot near Tre. I use my foot to create the shape of an ankh cross, the symbol of life and peace.

"Hurry, Ember!" Tre shouts.

The earth tips and I fall to the ground. On my knees, I remove the ankh cross pendant from my back pocket and hang it around my neck. Then I clasp the azurite stone in my palm and read straight from *The Book of the Dead*. This spell has to work. It must.

Shaken, I read the chant on page 264 aloud. "Whisper softly to the wind, transform from sleep to wake. Night to light. The flame of life. Let the dead go free and be at peace. *Alta pax. Solve fasciculos magnetismus.*"

After a moment, Tre joins in. So does Nisha. She screams the chant, her voice rising over the storm.

I catch a glimpse of Xintra on the other side of the crevasse, standing above the fray on a large boulder just two hundred yards away. Her voice carries across the canyon. "*Novus ordo mundi.* Hail Ki. Hail Tuatha Dé Danaan. I call on earthly powers. Connect us now and in all energies. Connected we shall be!"

I shut my eyes and say our words, our spell, with more force. This will be a battle of wills. "Whisper softly to the wind, transform from sleep to wake. Night to light. The flame of life. Let the dead go free and be at peace. *Alta pax. Solve fasciculos magnetismus.*"

Over and over, we chant. With my eyes shut, I see nothing but darkness and streamers of color. Pinwheels of blue. Bursts of silver angel wings. Red triangles and shiny black splotches. Lavender and moss green. Muddied amber.

I block out the rumbling thunder, firm up my legs amid the shifting earth, and drown my fear that Xintra will point her electric blue finger at us.

Soon, the screaming quiets. And the fighting slows and after a few seconds, the rebirthers still. I open my eyes, mumbling the chant, watching as black charcoal ash rises from the heads of the rebirther army. It rises from their fingertips in haunting, stretched shapes, bending and wrapping around trees, the faces of dark spirits spinning like cyclones, swirling up into the sky, melding with the black clouds above us. Tre, Nisha, and I watch with gaping mouths as the mass of people begins to wake up.

Oh my God. *It's working.*

"Whisper softly to the wind, transform from sleep to wake. Night to light. The flame of life. Let the dead go free and be at peace. *Alta pax. Solve fasciculos magnetismus.*"

The rebirthers drop their weapons one by one. *Clink. Thud. Thud. Thud.* The man with the beard who tried to kill Valerie blinks his eyes and looks around the canyon as if he just woke up from sleeping. He gazes down at his hands, bloodied, and all expression slides off his face.

"Whisper softly to the wind, transform from sleep to wake. Night to light. The flame of life. Let the dead go free and be at peace. *Alta pax. Solve fasciculos magnetismus.*"

Electricity vibrates between me, Tre, and Nisha—our triangle, pulsing and fading, as if it's something you can physically touch. It's just like what Mom described in her journal, except instead of expanding, it feels like it's shrinking, moving away from us.

A blue bubble of electricity rises from the ground along our triangular dirt lines, vibrating and climbing before being sucked into the middle of the fire like a circular water fountain on rewind.

The ground grows still, the cracks stop moving, the trees stop swaying. Smoke from the fire rises into the black night air, and I look up. The clouds begin to clear and the night sky is finally visible. A single star shines brighter than the rest.

Venus. Mom and Lodima's bright light in the sky. *Our* planet.

I stop chanting, but I can still hear the chorus ringing through the canyon, asking for peace. Across the crevasses, a couple of girls hold hands, repeating the same thing in unison. "Whisper softly to the wind, transform from sleep to wake. Night to light. The flame of life. Let the dead go free and be at peace. *Alta pax. Solve fasciculos magnetismus.*"

At the edge of another crevasse, even more people stand together, looking at the sky and saying the words. Laurie Parker. Phil Sei. Samantha, Jeff, and G who were in Trinity with Tre. At least forty-five others I don't know. The power of all these people, the magnetic force, the fire, the rocks, the wish for peace. It did something.

A deafening crash reverberates through the canyon, and I lift my gaze to the hillside, to the Trinity House. The top floor of the house, including the window of my old bedroom, tumbles down like a slow-motion Jenga tower. The rest of the house follows, crumbling piece by piece. Lilly's room. The living room. The kitchen. The deck. The game room. All of it lands in an enormous mushroom cloud, a plume of rubble and dust.

Suddenly, I feel incredibly hot.

The whooshing sound of fire is bronze, and it grows

louder as flames spread from our nest of branches and ignite the dead grass in the meadow.

"Everything's catching fire," Tre yells. "We've gotta get out of here!"

He reaches for me and Nisha. Together, without a second thought, we all three make a tense leap over the crack. We run, following the flood of surviving rebirthers —all awake now—who dash and shout and stumble in panic, tripping over dead bodies, leaping over enormous cracks in the ground.

We don't know where we're running. Just away. Following the crowd to what looks like an opening in the woods—the spot where the gate once stood.

I scan the chaotic terrain for Xintra but see no sign of her.

She's gone.

60

NISHA

We book it out of the forest, covered in soot and sweat. The walking dead. Hundreds of us, maybe more. One girl with long black hair has a burn in her blouse and she's shoeless. Some other guy, who I swear I rebirthed, actually still has his briefcase. I lead Ember and Tre through the mess of pine trees and shrubs, over downed logs and around boulders.

"It's like you have haunted forest GPS," Ember says.

I shrug. Trinity was part of me for so long. It's like it's permanently mapped on my brain.

When we get to the dirt road, the barbed-wire fence with the *No Trespassing* sign, a throng of reporters and police and fire officials greet us. A couple of EMTs rush to wrap blankets around the shoulders of two trembling young people. A female reporter waves her cameraman to follow her and poses questions to a young girl with dark hair, a heart-shaped face, and perfect plump lips.

Ember smiles. "Laurie Parker! She's alive."

"I can't believe *any* of us are alive," Tre says.

Pete. Lilly. Chris. They're all gone. Sadness wells within me. I took them, and now they're gone.

We weave through the crowd, ducking the cameras, and Tre puts his arm around Ember's shoulder. They stop and kiss. Tre puts his hands to the sides of her face, and she leans into his chest.

They *are* kind of sweet. I can only imagine what they'll tell people when asked how they met.

For a long while, we walk on the road in silence. I clutch Axel. We led this whole showdown, and I've got to say, I still don't really get how everything happened, how it all unfolded. But somehow, a shit ton of us are walking out of this forest right now. My legs and arms still quiver, and I wonder if the electricity from that place will circulate in my veins forever. I suppose in a way, it might.

About twenty minutes later, I pull up alongside the brick hospital in Vail and put the car in park, but don't turn off the ignition.

"Aren't you coming in?" Ember asks, pausing with her hand on the car door.

I shake my head. I feel like an empty closet. Lonely, nothing to give, but I guess there's room there for more inside that space. Lots of potential, I suppose.

"Where will you go?" Tre asks.

"I don't know." Part of me wants to go home to Chicago. Another part of me wants to head someplace entirely different. Maybe Brazil or Greece. "But I'll figure it out."

I climb out of the car and Ember hugs me tight, smelling like smoke. "Thank you, Nisha."

It feels nice hearing my name—and hugging someone. I haven't felt someone's kindness like that in years. Decades.

"Yeah, thanks," Tre says, embracing me next.

"*Thanks?* You *do* know I got your sorry butts into this mess. I rebirthed you." I go for lightness, but the heaviness, the guilt of all the death I contributed to will always be with me. This, I know.

"You were a true hero," Tre says.

Ember agrees with him and gives me one last smile. Once they walk off into that hospital, I honestly don't know what's going to happen. But at least I'll drive away as Nisha. Screwed up, maybe, but *me*.

Ember shuts the door, and Axel climbs onto my lap. I roll down the window, yelling to her as she walks into the building. "We all deserve second chances, right?"

61

EMBER

Maddie's face has returned to its pink color, but every few minutes she launches into major coughing fits.

"See, I told you the vaccine would help," her mom says, leaning over the hospital bed, pressing her lips to Maddie's forehead.

Maddie looks at me and rolls her eyes.

"I didn't think the vaccine was...a good idea," I say.

"No, this new one they've put out makes it so she's not contagious, and it should increase her odds of making it through this unscathed." Her mom ruffles Maddie's hair like she's a little girl. "I think she's doing pretty darn good!"

"Better than Emby and Tre. They pretty much look like crap," Maddie says. "No offense."

"Thanks." It's a relief to see Maddie back to her snark. A good sign.

I lean my head into Tre's shoulder, and he presses his lips against my temple. He smells like forest fire—but also like Tre. I drink in the feel of him, his hand on my waist. He's solid. He's real. He's alive.

"What a crazy day," says Maddie's dad. He stands close to the TV, gazing up at the screen. "The meteorologists are saying that today was the strangest day in weather history. That forest fire just petered out. The tornado, too. And that hurricane brewing in the Bahamas. All of it, all at once. Isn't that weird?"

"Must have been the constellations," Tre says, winking at me. "Venus is the planet of good luck, you know."

We grin at each other. His smiling eyes look like the sky outlined in black lashes. *We did it.* We stopped Xintra.

Maddie's mom leans back into her husband's arms. He's a light post of a man, holding up a woman twice his size. He wears a beard now and his hair is gray. He looks so much older than the last time I saw him three years ago. I know they're thinking I look different too. In fact, I keep catching them staring at me every once in awhile. My nose. My bad dye job. My enormous chest.

Her dad claps his hands together. "Since you're feeling better, I'm going to get us some dinner." He pats Maddie's foot beneath the white blanket and then points at Jared, still camped by her bedside. "You probably haven't eaten in forever, either."

Her mom points to Mads. "And I'm going to find *you* some ice cream for dessert."

Her parents leave the room and the rest of us, exhausted and shaken, take a virtual exhale.

"Dude, I want all the details," Jared says. He holds Maddie's hand.

I gaze up at Tre, wondering what will happen next. I

squeeze his waist. I'm not letting go again. Of myself, or of him, or Jared, or Maddie—or life.

"You wouldn't believe—" I start, but the TV silences me.

On-screen, a news reporter stands at the entrance to Trinity Forest while people pour out of the woods behind him. It's the scene we successfully snuck by when we exited.

"Officials say they've never seen anything like this before, Kim." The reporter nods, his square jaw serious. "Thousands of people are emerging from the woods of this local forest, escaping a deadly fire and earthquake—all isolated in a hundred-mile area."

I still don't really know if the fire made Trinity lose its magnetic properties for good. If it will close the vortex forever. The destruction there might have just been the power of white light and darkness crashing together, a world split in two.

I think about Nisha telling me about Xintra's ability of illusion, how she could make Trinity look however she wanted. Did the Trinity House really crumble? Or did she just make us *think* it crumbled?

Behind the reporter, a crowd of people mill about. Ambulance workers care for people on gurneys. People huddle with blankets on the ground. Police lights flash, and emergency personnel attend to a bloody young man on a gurney. I think of Lilly, Pete, Chris. I see their faces, their smiles, in my mind, and then I think of all the anonymous people who died in the meadow, and my stomach twists.

Then, I see her on the TV.

I hardly recognize her at first. Maybe because I'm

expecting Xintra to look the way I've always seen her: the flash of flaming red hair, the snow-white skin, the piercing eyes that see into your mind. You know, like Mom said: *Full of demons and splendor and dangerous propositions.*

But she isn't any of these things. Her skin is washed out. Her red hair dull. Her lips pale. She fades into the crowd, another ordinary girl—which for Xintra, was always worse than death.

I think about that word: *ordinary*. I spent most of my life taking ordinary for granted. Our little trailer, two parents who actually loved each other. Stress over school. Friends. And after my parents died, once ordinary was gone, I wanted to be gone, too. And in a way, Xintra had given me my wish. She made Ember disappear—for a while, anyway. But she also did something unintentional: she lit a fire in me. She made me see how much I wanted my life back. And for that, I could almost thank her.

ACKNOWLEDGMENTS

I am so grateful for my husband, Kevin, and both my boys, Jake and Brendan, who doled out the encouragement and patience while I wrote this involved trilogy. You three know this world as well as I do, and without you, the Trinity Forest story would not exist. I love you!

A huge thanks to Kate Angelella, who was right there with me throughout this series, coming up with smart ideas, guiding me and helping me to develop these characters and this story. You are my extra brain and so talented. This book series was both of ours.

I am also indebted to Corey Ann Haydu, author of the *Careful Undressing of Love,* who, as the teacher of my online fiction class, got me started, and then hung on to coach me through all three books. Thank you!

To Caroline Teagle Johnson: for months you helped me with the book covers, the branding, the technical issues. You are an angel, and so good at what you do. A huge thanks to the keen eyes of copyeditor Jessica Gardner, who has a knack for spotting all things big and small that could undo a novel. I owe you! A special thanks to Jesikah Sundin (author of the *Biodome Chronicles*), Nina Silfverberg, Bella O'Donnell, John Stewart and Michelle Alm for your eyes and insights.

I am so lucky to have so many friends and family members who have supported me and cheered me on and contributed to this story in big and small ways— whether it was by asking questions, offering feedback, reading early drafts, sharing my work with your friends or listening to me talk incessantly about Ember's journey. Mwah!

WANT MORE?

I'll give you exclusive digital content related to the Trinity Forest series, including videos showing inside Trinity, clips of Oshun singing, psychic quizzes and a look at the Crazy Woman notebook. Plus get alerts on new releases by author Jennifer Alsever and other great YA finds.

Tell me where to send your free stuff!
www.trinityforestseries.com/sign-up-now-alsever
trinityforestseries@gmail.com

Made in the USA
San Bernardino, CA
23 February 2018